MY VINEYARD

Mine own vineyard have I not kept

My Vineyard

BY

DOROTHY HOYER SCHARLEMANN

Saint Louis

CONCORDIA PUBLISHING HOUSE

1946

DEDICATED TO

MARTIN

in the hope that this book may,

in its small way, contribute to the work

to which he has dedicated his life

Contents

Contents

MY VINEYARD

CHAPTER I

The Glory of Israel

Mᴵᴿᴵᴬᴹ loved the Temple. She stood now in the little back street, her hand clutching the silver coin her mother had given her to deliver to Neariah the Pharisee. She dug her brown sandaled toe into a crack between the cobblestones of the pavement, trying to decide whether to go first to the Temple, whose snow-white marble terraces and golden spiked roof towered so dazzlingly a few blocks away, or whether to do as her mother had told her and deliver the money without delay.

After all, she argued, the Temple was closer, and she might even meet Neariah there and save herself a long walk through the hot, dusty streets. She was tired already, and if she stopped a few minutes in the Temple, she could rest a little. And because her mother loved the Temple, too, Miriam knew she would not mind. Indeed, this might be the Day, the very Day of which her mother so often spoke, the Day when the Messiah should reveal Himself to His people.

Rachel, her mother, had already seen the Messiah, though she had not known that it was He till much later. But now she was sure of it. Miriam never tired of hearing her mother's low, sweet voice tell the story.

1

It had happened when Rachel herself was a young girl —
about Dismas' age now. She had come with her parents to the
Temple, for, living as they did at Bethphage, scarcely more
than a Sabbath's journey from the city walls, they felt themselves privileged to make offerings to the Lord even at times
when the Law did not require it.

So it was that, one cold, wintry day, Rachel awaited her
parents near the Beautiful Gate. She had found her favorite
place, a little bench under one of the great stone pillars of the
colonnade, where she could watch the people. Here she remained, warm and sheltered from the wind, while her parents
moved on into the open court beyond, with the clear cold sky
above.

There were not many people in the Temple that day. Those
that were, brought their sacrifices rather hurriedly to the curtained door of the sanctuary, where the white-robed priests
received them. The wind blew in sharp little gusts along the
pavement, and no one lingered. But Rachel sat a long time in
her quiet corner, thinking there was no lovelier place in all
Jerusalem than the Temple of the Most High. She was about
to rise to her feet to see whether her parents were returning,
when her attention was attracted to an approaching couple
with a tiny Baby.

They had almost reached the bench where Rachel sat when
an old man stopped them. Rachel knew him. She had seen
him often in the Temple — almost every time she had been
there, in fact. He was rather poorly dressed — not like many
others who were often there — the scribes, for instance, who
had offices in the Temple and who taught the people. But she
loved this old man, with his long white beard and kindly face.
Nearly everyone in the Temple seemed to know him. His

name was Simeon, and whenever he saw her, he never failed to speak to Rachel and to lay his wrinkled old hand on her dark, curly head. She stood up now to greet him, but this time he did not see her. He was looking at the little Baby in the young woman's arms. His faded old eyes were bright and shining, and Rachel thought she had never seen him look so happy. Without a word he took the Child from the astonished mother's arms. Then he raised his eyes to where the gold and marble of the Most Holy Place shone beyond the pillars of the portico and said in a trembling voice:

"Lord, now lettest Thou Thy servant depart in peace, according to Thy word, for mine eyes have seen Thy salvation, which Thou hast prepared before the face of all people, a Light to lighten the Gentiles, and the Glory of Thy people Israel." He smiled then at the parents, and, as he returned the Baby to His mother, he said earnestly to her: "Behold, this Child is set for the fall and rising again of many in Israel and for a sign which shall be spoken against — yea, a sword shall pierce through thy own soul also — that the thoughts of many hearts may be revealed."

"The Glory of Israel," repeated a voice behind Simeon, and Rachel turned to see an old woman standing near by. It was Anna the Prophetess. She was so old and bent that she was hardly any taller than Rachel. Yet she was always in the Temple. She, too, took the Baby in her arms and thanked God and blessed Him. Yet Rachel, try hard as she would, could find nothing unusual about this Baby. He was not nearly so richly dressed as many babies she had seen brought to the Temple. And His face was just as soft and puckered as every other baby's. But Simeon and the old woman made much of Him and talked earnestly together as the young couple and the Baby left the Temple.

Almost Simeon did not notice the little girl standing near, and Rachel was just turning away in disappointment when he saw her and laid his hand on her dark hair. "The Lord bless you, my child!" he said with a smile, but Rachel felt as though he did not actually see her, but was looking at the Baby all over again.

Her parents came then, and Rachel turned to them eagerly with a question: "What is the Glory of Israel?"

Her father laughed. "Here stands the child in the Temple, which is the envy of the pagan world, worshiping in the house of the Most High, and yet she would know wherein lies the Glory of Israel!"

Rachel returned his smile a bit uncertainly, but her mother shook her head sadly.

"Nay, child, but it is not in these days as of old, for the glory is now departed from Israel. Yet it will come again, when the Messiah shall gather His people unto Himself and Judah shall reign again."

Rachel was not satisfied. "Nay, but why should old Simeon speak so of a mere Babe?"

But by this time they had descended the terrace steps and were threading their way through the noisy Court of the Gentiles, and Rachel's question went unanswered. Yet she did not forget it, and resolved to ask Simeon himself about this Babe when next she saw Him in the Temple.

But the next time she could not find old Simeon. It was the first time she had been at the Temple and missed him. She looked for him a long time and was just about to give up when she saw the old woman, the Prophetess Anna, who had also blessed the little Babe, coming down the colonnaded walk. Rachel, not knowing her as well as she knew Simeon, approached her timidly.

"If it please you," she began in a small voice, "can you tell me where Simeon is today?"

"He has seen the Lord's salvation," answered Anna, peering down at the little girl, "and last week departed in peace, according to the word which the Lord had spoken to him."

Rachel was disappointed. It saddened her that she would no longer see Simeon here in his beloved Temple. Yet, remembering the joy that shone on his face and the brightness of his eyes when he had held the Babe in his arms and had asked the Lord to let him depart in peace, she could not but feel happy for him. Only she wished she had found out what he meant by the "Glory of Israel."

Not till many years later, when Rachel sat in the cool of the evening on the roof of her husband Jacob's home in Bethphage, with baby Miriam on her lap and little Dismas standing before her, proudly reciting the lessons he had learned that day in the synagog, did old Simeon's words take on meaning.

" 'Unto us a Child is born, unto us a Son is given,' " recited Dismas in his clear, high-pitched voice. " 'And the government'— Mother, will the Messiah really be a Child — a babe like Miriam?"

"So the Scripture says, Dismas," answered Rachel gently.

"But He will live in the Temple, will He not?"

Rachel was a bit taken aback.

"Indeed, I know not, Dismas. But surely it will be in the Lord's Temple that He will reveal Himself to His people."

"A Babe in the Temple," mused Dismas. "It would be lovely to live in the Temple, Mother!"

"That Babe in the Temple!" repeated Rachel, and at the sudden change in her voice Jacob looked up from his sharp-

ening of the pruning hook in wonder. "Now I know indeed
what old Simeon meant. This Babe that was the 'Glory of
Israel'—'tis the Messiah Himself I saw that day!"

Pruning hook and lessons were all forgotten as the little
family gathered closer to hear. Even baby Miriam seemed to
understand, for, when the story was finished, she waved her
chubby little hands and crowed till Dismas gave her a big
kiss right on her little pug nose for very joy and love.

*   *   *

So it was now that Miriam, standing in the crowded Jerusalem street, did not hesitate long. Her mother went but seldom to the Temple these days, for, since Jacob had died and
they had moved to the city, she was far too busy. From the
gray-lit dawn till flaming sunset she toiled the hot hours
through in wealthy palaces, then trudged wearily home to see
that her own two children were fed and properly clothed for
the morrow. So, though her soul yearned for the tabernacles
of the Lord as her body did for the peace and contentment
Jacob's love and care had once brought them, it was only on
the Sabbath and on feast days that she could attend the
Temple services. But she never ceased to admonish her children to be constant and faithful in attendance, so that when
the Messiah should reveal Himself, they might be among the
first of His followers.

Miriam held her coin a little closer as she removed her
dusty little sandals, tucked them into the pocket of her bright
red girdle, and made her way across the Court of the Gentiles. It was noisy and confusing where the animals for sacrifice were bought and sold, but up the steps and beyond the
terrace, near the Beautiful Gate, it was quiet and calm. She
found the little bench where her mother had sat that eventful

day so long ago and scanned the worshipers with eyes that would eagerly have proclaimed the Messiah in every young man that passed by.

The hum of the voices about her, the warm and sultry air, and her own tired body, leaning against the cool pillar, wrapped a welcome drowsiness about her, till she realized with a start that she had almost fallen asleep. Her slack fingers closed spasmodically about the coin in her hand, and she was relieved to feel its hard edges press against her palm. It would be a sad thing indeed to lose that coin. It represented many days of hard labor on Rachel's part. Moreover, if it were not paid to Neariah this day, something exceedingly dreadful would happen. Miriam was not quite sure what. There was a mortgage on their little home in Bethphage, and this little coin kept it from taking their house and vineyard away from them entirely. To be sure, they did not live there now. Neariah was taking care of it for them. And they had to pay him for keeping the mortgage away. It was good of him to do it, Rachel always said. So now the coin must be delivered, and without further delay.

Miriam sighed as she stepped out into the busy street again. She had stayed longer in the Temple than she should have, and now she still had the long hot walk before her to the edge of town where Neariah lived.

She had gone but a short distance and was turning into one of the narrow, shop-lined side streets when a terrific racket arose at the other end. Down the street, his huge bulk almost touching the walls on either side, lumbered a camel, his ugly head bobbing about as if in fright, his ungainly legs knocking down the jars and lamps and other merchandise set out before the shops. Out of each doorway, as he passed, ran an irate shopkeeper, shouting and gesticulating, and some even throwing things at the bewildered beast. Terrified, Miriam shrank back against the wall, trying to make herself as small as possible. Then she heard a man's comforting voice beside her.

"In here, little maid!" it said, and a strong brown hand drew her into a little alcove in the wall. The man laughed as the camel ran by in a flurry of dust and loud cries and curses.

"Verily," he said, his speech sounding strangely in Miriam's ears, "the wilds of Galilee and the storms of Gennesaret are but child's play to the perils of your great city."

"You are from Galilee?" asked a voice behind them. An old man sat there in the alcove, bent almost double over the rug he was weaving, his eyes peering up at them in the light of the little flickering oil lamp that tried bravely to illumine the dark corner.

"Yea!" laughed the young man again, his white teeth gleaming against the tan of his face. "Simon, son of Jonas, a fisherman of Galilee, come to see what there is to see." He turned to Miriam. "Where dwell you, little maid with the great dark eyes?" he asked.

"Beyond the Temple, in the fifth street," answered Miriam, smiling shyly. She liked this gay young man.

"Come, then," he said. "The danger is past, and our raging beast has by this time no doubt been captured and confined. Let us go, and I shall see you safely home."

But Miriam drew her small hand from his.

"Nay, I thank you," she said, "but I have an errand, and truly I must hurry, for it grows late. You have been very kind." And before the man could stop her, she was hurrying down the street.

As she turned the corner, she was startled by a great shouting down the street. A short, fat man was running toward her, his dirty brown robes flapping like enormous wings as he waved his arms in excitement.

"My beast! My camel!" he shouted. "Dogs of the streets!" He suddenly stopped before a group of three or four boys who stood idly watching him and laughing. "Where is the animal? Was it you who loosed him? Name of thunder!" He stopped for sheer lack of breath, and the boys suddenly sobered as he grasped one of them by the arm.

"Nay, nay, sir!" cried the fair-haired lad he had caught. "We know naught of your beast! Nay, indeed, sir, and if your camel is gone, the devil himself, or the evil spirits must have taken him for your sins. Of a surety," his voice took on a slyness overmature for his years, "*had* you a camel, or has merchant Abel's wine confused your wits?"

The man looked into the guileless blue eyes and the fair face which, in spite of its dirt, seemed as innocent as that of a two-year-old, uncertain whether to give the boy a blow for his impudence or to believe him. Then, with a groan, he released him and ran on down the street, followed by the unrestrained merriment of the boys.

"He went that way!" shrieked Miriam after him. She felt a bit sorry for him, yet she could not help laughing at his comical figure and flapping robes.

"Ho, Miriam!" cried one of the boys suddenly. "What do you here?"

"Yea," the blond boy frowned at her. "Why not let the fat fool look for his own beast? Had his ears not been stopped by drink, he would have heard the racket and found his camel long ago. Saw you ever such a sight?" And the whole group went off into another gale of laughter.

"Nay, Zabad," said the first boy. "She knew not it was a project of yours."

"Dismas!" reproved Miriam. "Did you chase his camel off? That was unkind!"

"Unkind, but funny!" giggled one of the boys, to renewed laughter.

"Who is this little girl, Dismas?" asked Zabad, for Miriam had sidled up to Dismas and was regarding Zabad with wide, apprehensive dark eyes. She had heard of Zabad. His mother had been a heathen slave and his father a criminal, but he was an orphan now, living on the streets of Jerusalem, where he was already becoming known for his trickery and thievish ways.

"My little sister," answered Dismas, taking her hand. "What do you here, Miriam?"

"I go to Neariah's house, to pay the money", answered Miriam shyly. "I — I thought you were in school, Dismas."

"School's out," said Dismas. "It is late. You will never get to Neariah's and back before dark. Did you loiter?"

"I — I stopped in the Temple," confessed Miriam. "I had hoped today might be the Day. . . ." She stopped in confusion, for Zabad was smiling sardonically at her.

"And, like most women," he said smoothly, "you were undoubtedly so interested in worship that you forgot the cares of this world and lost the money?"

"That I did not!" retorted Miriam indignantly, holding out her small hand in which lay the silver coin. But she drew it back almost instantly, for there was a speculative look in Zabad's eye.

"Look you," he said persuasively. "Why not give the coin to Dismas and let him take it? He has but to stretch his legs a little and can be there and back before ever you reach home. It is a long hot walk to that part of town."

"Yea," agreed Dismas. "Give it to me, Miriam. I will go in your stead."

But Miriam only clutched the coin tighter. She did not trust Zabad.

"Could we not go together, you and I?" she asked Dismas. "I can walk fast, and I do not fear the dark if you are with me."

"And so the little boy and the little girl will go walking hand in hand down the street to Neariah's house," jeered Zabad, his face suddenly unpleasant. "How tender a picture! Dismas, why do you not tell her who is master? Or do you let a girl lead you?"

Dismas dropped Miriam's hand as though it had suddenly become hot.

"Give me the coin," he said roughly, "and cease your prattle. I will go, and do you go home to mother. You have tarried long enough."

Without another word Miriam handed him the coin. She hated to anger her brother, for he was not one to forget his anger quickly. She turned away at once, for she would not let them see the tears starting to her eyes.

"Now, be not a talebearer and tell mother!" called Dismas after her. "I shall return in time for supper."

CHAPTER II

Judgment

ISMAS did not return in time for supper. As
Miriam helped her mother set out the flat
loaves and warm the savory stew on the
little clay stove, she sought to distract her attention by re-
lating her day's adventures. In answer to her mother's question concerning the coin she replied simply that it had been
safely delivered. Of her encounter with Dismas and Zabad
she said nothing, for she knew it would only worry Rachel.
Rachel's chief concern in the two years since they had left
Bethphage had been that her children should keep themselves away from evil companions. With the four families who
shared the dark building with them here in Jerusalem, Rachel
would have nothing to do. Indeed, for a time, after she had
come upon two of the women grinding meal on the Sabbath,
she sent Miriam to the neighborhood cistern to draw water
much earlier than was the custom that she might return before the others set out. Should she discover that Dismas was
roaming the streets with Zabad, she would surely not sleep
this night, nor many a night to come.

"Dismas is late again." There was a worried frown on
Rachel's forehead. Observing it, Miriam opened her mouth to

take the blame upon herself, but, remembering Dismas' warning concerning talebearing, she closed it again with a little snap.

"I must speak to him," Rachel went on. "The boy is too young to be on the streets. He should come directly home after school. It is seeking trouble to loiter these evil days."

"Mayhap, mother,"— Miriam hesitated, but with the memory of Zabad's leering face before her, she gathered courage and went on. "Mayhap, if you would let him work as he wishes. . . . He has no love for school and no desire to be a scribe. If he could help you pay the mortgage. . . ."

"Nonsense, child! You speak of what you know naught. Had we our own vine and fig tree he should indeed be helping with their care. But I will not have him twisted in mind and body as are so many children who work with the men of the city. When he has finished his schooling and the mortgage is paid, then we will live in the village again in contentment, as we once did. . . ." With the thought the burden of anxiety in her eyes lifted for a moment.

In silence they finally began to eat and had almost finished their meal when Dismas returned.

"You have tarried long, Dismas," said Rachel, her frown returning. "Where were you?"

Dismas shot a quick glance at Miriam, but she was busy thrusting a few more twigs into the fire beneath the clay pot in which Dismas' stew was warming.

"You should not loiter in the streets," went on Rachel. "It can only lead to harm. What did you after school?"

"Indeed, I was running errands for the scribes," he answered a bit sullenly.

Miriam, ladling out the hot stew for her brother, almost

dropped her bowl in consternation.

"Nay, Dismas!" she exclaimed.

"What ails you, girl?" interrupted Dismas sharply. "Can you, then, not even hold a dish properly?" and the angry look he gave her set her to trembling so that she could hardly place the dish on the mat before him.

"There is no need to speak so sharply, Dismas," Rachel reproved him. "But I was in error. I rejoice that you labor for your teachers. They are good men, and the Lord is well pleased with such service."

Miriam was puzzled and distressed. How often before had Dismas given such false excuses? She felt a little sick. She started again to say something, but Dismas nervously kept on talking as he toyed with his meal. He did not seem to be very hungry.

"It was hot today," he said. "Even the synagog rooms offered little comfort. And the Temple was no better."

"Nay, but it is ever lovely there," said Rachel, sighing a little. "The Lord, I think, makes his sun to shine more gently in His Tabernacle. Did you attend there today, my daughter?"

"Aye." Miriam could bring out no more than that one word.

They sat in silence then, while Dismas finished his meal. Miriam was troubled at his downcast face and eyes that would not meet hers, but she said nothing. And Rachel, exhausted by the day's labor, noted nothing amiss.

Later, when the bowls had been washed and set away, the sleeping mats spread out upon the floor, the tiny lamp lighted and set into the alcove in the wall, and Rachel's steady breathing betokened her deep sleep, Miriam could no longer keep silence.

"Dismas!" she whispered, nudging him. "Dismas!"

"Nay, then," grumbled Dismas. "What now?"

"Did Zabad go with you to the house of Neariah?"

"He did not," answered Dismas shortly, lowering his voice. "I had thought he would take the money from you. Did you, of a surety, give it to Neariah himself?"

"Think you I am a thief?" Dismas' whisper was furious. "Cease your prattle and go to sleep, lest you wake Mother!"

"Nay," said Miriam, not to be so easily distracted. "I know you for no thief. But Zabad *is* a thief. All men know of his cunning and trickery. Therefore Mother bade us beware of him and avoid him. Yet you make common cause with him. Did he try to steal the money from you?"

"It was not stealing," protested Dismas before he thought. "It was a fair game."

"Dismas!" cried Miriam, sitting up in blank dismay. "Truly, did you play for the money? Verily, then, Zabad has it and not Neariah!"

"Hush!" whispered Dismas desperately. "Speak not so loudly. Would you wake Mother? And fret not yourself. Tomorrow is yet another day, and I shall win it again."

"Nay, nay, Dismas!" Miriam's whisper was terror-stricken. "You will but lose more. And if Neariah has not the money, he will come himself tomorrow to tell Mother. Then what shall I do?" She began to cry softly.

Dismas sat up quickly and took his little sister into his arms to quiet her sobs.

"Nay, nay, little Miriam, hush, hush! You will wake Mother surely. Look you, Neariah will not come ere evening, for he knows Mother will not be here till then. By then I shall have redeemed the money. Weep not!"

"How will you redeem it?" asked Miriam, drying her tears.

"Today I did not understand the game Zabad played," explained Dismas. "But now I know, and tomorrow I shall surely beat him at it."

"Nay, Dismas, have nothing more to do with Zabad," pleaded Miriam. "He is evil and will only lead you to harm. We will tell Mother, and she will forgive us, and we will work for the money to repay her."

"Assuredly not!" Dismas released her angrily. "You are ever the preacher! Say nothing of this to Mother!"

"I shall tell her," said Miriam, suddenly brave, "unless you promise to see no more of Zabad."

"Nay," answered Dismas. "You have no right to choose my companions. I shall see as much of Zabad as I wish."

"Then Mother shall be told!"

"You must not!"

"Then promise me!"

Dismas rolled over on his own mat and turned his back to her.

"Promise, Dismas!"

"Very well. After tomorrow, I promise. And now sleep! A man cannot work without sleep."

So Miriam lay down again. But she lay awake far into the sultry night, and she knew from the way Dismas tossed on his mat that he, too, could not sleep.

                           *   *   *

Miriam's days were never idle enough to seem long, yet she thought that the next day would never end. Even her morning chores seemed endless, for everywhere there was delay. There were others at the cistern before her, and she had to wait to draw water. The goatherd was late, and, moreover, when he did arrive, his beast had already been milked nearly dry, so that she got but half her container full of the warm sweet milk. By the time she had prepared the round, flat loaves of bread, and, together with the dish of peas and lentils, had brought them in her basket to the public baker, it was already high morning. There she met yet further delay, for the fire had been slow to draw, and the baker had not yet drawn his first batch from the oven, while it seemed to Miriam's impatience that there were sufficient people there before her to keep her waiting till noon.

But the morning finally passed, and the noontide hour for rest. An hour more she spent in the synagog, where she and other girls of the community learned to read and to write and to recite the words of the Law. But after that there was nothing to do but wait. And the waiting was the hardest of all, for with every hour her fears mounted that Neariah should arrive before Dismas and she should stand before him with no word to say.

And so, indeed, it happened. With painfully beating heart Miriam, from her bench in the courtyard, watched Neariah and his son Rodanim approaching down the narrow-walled street. The neighborhood children stood in little clusters and pointed, while from doorways and high narrow windows their elders stared in unashamed curiosity, for it was seldom that a Pharisee ventured his fringed robes into the dirt and squalor of this part of the city. Indeed, Neariah, as he passed the not too respectful watchers in the doorways, drew his robes a bit more closely about his angular body. Rodanim was obviously not so concerned about himself, although his robes were as fine and the phylactery upon his forehead almost as broad and well wrought as that of his father. He did not stare about him, as became a well-bred lad, but in his grey eyes was a look of pained incredulity which told plainly of a life whose sheltered ease had never before included scenes such as this.

Strangely enough, Miriam found Rodanim's presence there almost as frightening as Neariah's. Before this she had known Rodanim only as a happy companion in the little village of Bethphage, for the house and vineyard of Rodanim's mother's family, which had fallen to Neariah at her death, adjoined Rachel's. That, incidentally, made it quite convenient now for Neariah to cultivate Rachel's vineyard along with his own.

Rodanim greeted her now politely enough, but, besides his shock at seeing his former neighbors in such circumstances, Miriam sensed in him a new and somewhat forced dignity, as though he felt that on this visit he must maintain as stern and uncompromising a countenance as that of his father.

Neariah had no difficulties on that score. His heavy black brows that met in a straight line above his hawklike nose, his piercing black eyes, the angular lines of his face beneath his full black beard seemed never to have known a kindly moment. Certainly there was no kindliness now in his look as he bade Miriam lead them to her mother.

Trembling, Miriam led them through the dark passageway to the two little rooms where they lived. As the flimsy door opened, Rachel came forward to greet them, and the look of surprise on her pale face was followed by instant apprehension. Neariah did not visit his poor tenants out of pure benevolence.

"Peace be with you!" Rachel's voice was uncertain, but she would allow no fears of hers to hinder her hospitality. "And may peace be multiplied upon you!" answered Neariah, stooping to enter the low door and casting a disapproving eye about the room.

"Will it please you to sit?" Rachel pushed forward the one low stool they possessed, while Rodanim, perforce, had to sit on the floor with the women. "Miriam, haste and fetch water and fruit, that our guests may partake of such hospitality as we have to offer."

Miriam was only too glad to leave and busy herself about the small back room. But Neariah evidently wasted no time in stating his business. She had hardly filled the small gourd with water from the stone jar in the corner when, through the curtain which separated the two rooms, she heard her mother calling. Frightened and trembling, she left the water and returned to the company. Rachel's face was sorrowful and apprehensive.

"Miriam, Neariah has not received the money you were sent to bring him yesterday. Where is it?"

"I — I know not," stammered Miriam, miserably.

"Lost you the coin, child?" Rachel asked. "Truly, it was careless of you, and evil, for many a day's work must I do before I can earn its equal. But you should have told me, and we would have sent word to Neariah."

"It was not lost," said Neariah harshly, his piercing black eyes looking keenly into Miriam's face. "The child has a guilty look. Stole you it?"

"Nay, nay, I did not steal it, Mother!" protested Miriam, almost in tears and longing to run to her mother's protecting arms.

"Then where is it, Miriam?" Rachel's sad, stern eyes kept her little daughter at a distance.

Helplessly she looked from one face to the other, biting her

lips to stop their trembling. She dared not betray Dismas, yet
she knew of no other way out. Tears welled up into her eyes,
and she held her breath to keep back the choking sobs. In a
moment she would break down before those sternly accusing
eyes and sob out her story at her mother's feet. And Dismas
would hate her from that time forth, and Rodanim would
despise her, though, indeed, he looked now almost as unhappy as Miriam herself.

Yet the sob, when it came, was one of utter relief, for there
in the doorway across the room stood Dismas. He shot one
glance at Miriam's distressed face, then went directly to
Neariah and held out his hand.

"Rabbi, here is the money," he said.

Rachel and Neariah both turned startled eyes on him.

"Where got you this?" demanded Neariah, looking like a
hawk whose prey had suddenly escaped.

"Miriam gave it me yesterday to deliver to you, but I had
work for the scribes and was prevented from coming. Only
now I walked to your house, to find that you had come here.
I am sorry I was so late." He kept his eyes carefully averted
from Miriam, but her relief at his coming was so great that
she felt she would not have minded a hundred lies just then.

"Would that you had told me this yesterday, Dismas," said
Rachel, her eyes clearing. "I fear your thoughtlessness has
caused Miriam a great deal of pain. So, then, haste now and
wash, and Miriam, child, get the fruit, that our guests may
not deem us lacking in hospitality."

"O Dismas!" whispered Miriam, as they worked together
in the little back room. "I feared you would not come, and I
knew not what to say. But I did not betray you! Was Zabad
angry when you won it from him again?"

"I did not win it," answered Dismas gruffly. He seemed no more anxious to talk about the matter than he had been the day before. "We did not play for it."

"Zabad gave it you again?" cried Miriam, so loudly that Dismas sternly hushed her. "I had not thought it of him," she went on in a whisper. "Perchance he is not all evil at heart."

"Of a truth he is not. Why else think you I choose him for a companion? Now cease your prattle over this matter, lest Mother overhear us."

❖   ❖   ❖

The next day, as Miriam returned from the vegetable market, in her basket a few lentils and a bit of onion she had bought for supper, she happened to pause before the open door of the synagog in which Dismas attended school. One of the merchants, moved by her large, wistful eyes, had given her a few golden-brown dates, some of the first of the season. He had felt himself amply rewarded by the light that illumined her thin face and by the smile of gratitude she gave him. Now she felt she would share the gift with Dismas, for it was near the time for his dismissal. He would be tired and hungry and would welcome the sweet, meaty fruit while they walked home together.

Up the broad stairs and into the long passageway Miriam went, stopping just outside her brother's classroom. Loud and angry voices came through the thinly curtained doorway.

"Hear the words of the Law," a voice rose sternly above the rest. " 'Thou shalt not steal.' 'For when Achan, the son of Zerah, stole of the accursed thing, Joshua and all Israel with him took Achan, and the silver, and the garment, and the wedge of gold, and his sons, and his daughters, and his oxen, and his asses, and his sheep, and his tent, and all that he had;

and they brought them unto the valley of Achor. And Joshua said, Why hast thou troubled us? The Lord shall trouble thee this day. And all Israel stoned him with stones and burned them with fire after they had stoned them with stones. And they raised over him a great heap of stones unto this day. So the Lord turned from the fierceness of his anger.' " The voice paused, then went on: "Why have you troubled us, Dismas? The Lord shall trouble you this day."

A silence so heavy fell on the room that Miriam was afraid they might hear her breathing through the curtain. What did the scribe mean?

"Dismas," said another man's voice. "It has been found and proved that you have stolen from the Lord's treasury one piece of silver. Have you aught else to say than you have said?"

"Naught, Rabbi!" Dismas' voice came faintly.

"Then hear your judgment. Since it is not expedient for others here in our care to mingle with thieves, you are prohibited from entering this classroom again. The Law says a thief shall be punished. But because you promise to restore what you have stolen and because you have expressed yourself as truly repentant, we shall leave your punishment to the Lord Himself, stipulating only that the matter be reported to Neariah the Pharisee, who has so often shown himself your guardian, counselor, and friend, and that your future conduct be left in his care. Go now, and the Lord preserve you from further evil."

The curtain was swept aside, and Dismas came out, his face white and dazed, his eyes unseeing, for he did not notice Miriam till she followed him down the steps and called to him.

"Dismas!"

Dismas started. "Now, girl!" he said angrily, "must you spy on me?"

"Nay, Dismas, I was not spying! I came but to bring you fruit, and then I thought I would wait for you and we would go home together. I — I did not mean to overhear, but — O Dismas, what shall we do now?" Her voice rose in a little wail.

"I know not," said Dismas miserably, all his anger gone. "Zabad would not play, seeing I had no money. So I — I took some from the Temple, thinking I could return it on the morrow. I did not think I had been seen."

In troubled silence they walked through the narrow stone-paved streets.

"We must tell Mother at once," said Miriam at last.

"Nay," protested Dismas. "It will but grieve her."

"It will grieve her more if we say naught and let Neariah tell her," insisted Miriam.

"You are right," said Dismas dejectedly. "O Miriam, how came it that I should do such a thing?"

"It was Zabad's fault," answered Miriam, almost crying herself. "But from now on you will have no more to do with him, will you, Dismas? And all will be well again, will it not? If only Neariah. . . ."

She did not finish her sentence, but Dismas knew what she was thinking. Neariah would be a stern judge. He was a Pharisee, a righteous man, and it would not matter greatly to him that Dismas was repentant and resolved to do better. Dismas groaned, but he said: "Whatever Neariah says I must do, that will I do, for I truly deserve punishment — though not at his hands," he added under his breath.

As the children had foreseen, Rachel was both grieved and
shocked. Yet Dismas was so truly repentant and miserable
that she could not rebuke him. Indeed, the way she sat quietly and looked at him, with white face and sorrowful, hurt
eyes, filled him with greater remorse than any spoken rebuke
she might have uttered. Little Miriam kept saying over and
over again that it was all her fault, till her mother bade her be
quiet. For, bitter as the knowledge was, Rachel realized that
the trouble lay deeper than the stealing of the coin.

The evil that hung like a poisonous vapor in the streets
around them was beginning to infect her children, and she
was powerless to stop it. By her love and her admonitions she
had for a while been able to fan the dreadful mists from
about them and keep them in a purer, cleaner air. But that
time was past. Dismas was growing too old to be guided
solely by a gentle mother's warnings. The temptations about
him were too great, and his growing desire for manhood's independence led him rashly to follow those whom his still boyish spirit could not recognize as evil.

For the first time Rachel doubted the wisdom of her insistence upon Dismas' studies. Had he been engaged in some
profitable trade, he would not only have had less leisure to
become embroiled with companions such as Zabad, but his
feeling of responsibility in helping to support the family
would have kept him from such trifling with money.

Now the decision had been taken out of her hands; Dismas
could not return to school. It remained now to hear Neariah's
judgment upon the matter. If he could and would find a suit-
able place for Dismas, then, indeed, she would owe to him
the salvation of her son. She owed him so much already.

Neariah came that evening. Miriam was glad that he came

alone. It would have been an added bitterness in Dismas' cup of humiliation had his former playmate sat there beside his father as judge.

Neariah talked endlessly. It seemed to Miriam that he must have searched the Scriptures and the traditions for hours to find therein so many thieves and how they had been punished. And it was almost more than she could bear that with every harsh sentence he seemed to imply that of all these sinners Dismas was by far the worst.

But Neariah announced himself as being very generous to the boy. He would furnish him employment among his own laborers in his vineyards at Bethphage. He himself would restore the stolen money to the Temple, and Dismas should work without pay until the sum was redeemed.

If Neariah felt any pleasure at Rachel's gratitude, he did not show it. Nor did his stern face relax one instant when Dismas squared his shoulders and said:

"Rabbi, your judgment is more lenient than I deserve. I will truly do my best to redeem the evil I have done."

CHAPTER III

A Pharisee's Righteousness

RACHEL and Miriam had not expected to see so little of Dismas thereafter. Indeed, Rachel had taken it as self-evident that every Sabbath should find her son worshiping with them in the Temple and seated with them at mealtime. But it was not so. Neariah must indeed have had much work for his laborers that they could not be released in time to make even the short journey from Bethphage to Jerusalem before the Sabbath began. Yet, as week after week passed by and Dismas did not come, Rachel grew uneasy, and, in spite of the pressing need for the money she might earn, decided for one day to take Miriam with her to Bethphage to see for herself how her son fared.

They started early, while the shadow of Olivet still lay over the rousing city, before the sun should lift the cool mists from the valley of Kidron and turn the dusty white roads on the mountain side to paths of twisting heat. Miriam would have liked to linger where the brook, now a mere trickle in the summer heat, wound among the rocks in the green shadow of the ever faithful oleanders. She stopped to wave at old Laban at the olive orchard of Gethsemane, where they had formerly brought the olives from their own trees to be pressed. Rachel nodded and smiled, but did not pause for talk, for her anxious heart was already high up on the hill where her son would welcome them.

By the time their own little village came into view around the last bend of the road, the sun was already full upon them. The shimmering silver green of the olive trees and vineyards surrounding the town looked cool and inviting. Their own little plot of land lay close to the clustered houses, and among the terraced vines they saw a stooping figure which they knew at once to be Dismas. So they made their way down the little footpath to the low stone wall, where Miriam stood and screamed her brother's name, while Rachel fumbled with the fastenings of the gate. It was no sooner opened than Miriam sped through it like an arrow from its bow. But the ground was rough, and, just as she reached Dismas, she stumbled and would have fallen had he not caught her.

"Nay, girl!" he cried, laughing. "Look to your feet, and be not overhasty! Mother, I rejoice to see you!"

"But, Dismas," cried Rachel as she embraced him. "You have grown! Soon you will be a man, and I shall no longer have a little boy to care for!"

Dismas laughed again. "Oh, aye," he said. "It will not be long ere I am as tall as Father was!" He drew himself up straight and tall, but a shadow came into his eyes as he spoke. He looked about him at the vines heavy with the ripening clusters he had been propping up on stout sticks. A frown settled on his face that Rachel did not like to see.

"Come," she said. "Let us go to the village and rest. There we can speak to our heart's content ere we must return to the city."

But Dismas' frown only grew deeper.

"Nay, Mother, our home is no longer ours, it would seem. Rodanim's teacher dwells there of late, and Rodanim himself comes there daily for his instructions. They would not welcome us."

"Nay, then!" Miriam cried out in quick dismay. "With his great house in the city, and his little house here in Bethphage, does he not yet have room for his son that he must needs take our home? It *is* our home still, Mother, is it not?" Almost in tears she turned to her mother, uncertain whether to cry or burst out in furious anger.

"Hush, child, hush!" Rachel laid a calming arm about her daughter's agitated shoulders. "We are not now using our home, and surely, it were a sin to let it stand empty when others have need of it. But, Dismas — I had thought that you would dwell there as of old."

"Aye, at night I sleep there — not, indeed, in the little back room as Neariah thinks, but on the roof where the stars are cool." He picked up a small stone and sent it scudding along the row to where a magpie, perched among the vines, pecked experimentally at a ripening cluster of grapes.

Rachel's frown grew almost as deep as Dismas' as she laid her other arm about his stalwart shoulders and led both her children down the terraced rows of burdened vines. She nodded in friendly fashion to the other laborers as they made their way past the gnarled olive trees that stood there like dwarfish old men. Miriam ran ahead to where the vineyard came to an abrupt end against the rock bone of the mount suddenly upthrust through the fertile soil. There stood the large-leafed fig tree Jacob had planted many years ago, and in whose shade they had been wont to sit in the harvest time

when eating their noon meal in the fields. And here there
came a sound of a steady chip-chipping that brought her to
a puzzled halt. Beyond a big boulder she caught sight of a
bowed white head and broad, square-built shoulders. With
a little inward chuckle she slipped around the rock to where
old Ephraim, her friend from long ago, was sitting with his
back toward her, carefully shaping a stone. Miriam came up
softly behind him and, when she was quite close, suddenly
threw her arms around him in a hug that nearly knocked
him off his perch.

"Now may the fathers preserve us!" he exclaimed in a
tremendous growl as he dropped his stone and clasped the
little hands at his throat. "What means this levity?" But his
eyes, as he turned to Miriam, twinkled like blue stars above
the silvery beard.

"O Ephraim!" exclaimed Miriam. "Truly it is good to see
you! But what do you? What are you building? — See,
Mother, here is Ephraim!" she cried as Rachel and Dismas
came up.

Rachel's astonishment very nearly robbed her of speech.
She greeted Ephraim, then looked about at the hewn rock
and the shaped stones, and, as her eyes again met Ephraim's,
his kindly face was full of consternation.

"Nay, then, did you not know?" His voice was troubled.
"It is by Neariah's orders, but he gave me to understand it
was your wish. What manner of tricks is the old goat up
to now?"

"Hush, Ephraim, friend!" warned Rachel, with a quick
glance at Miriam, who was busily piling up rocks near by.
Dismas chuckled. "I am sure Neariah has only good in mind.
But — what is it that you make?"

"Nay, it is a wine press, and one of the best ever seen hereabouts, hewn as it will be from the living rock. But truly, I know not whether to go forward with the work or no, since it was not you ordered it."

Rachel was silent, and Dismas looked at her out of the corner of his eye.

"I know your thoughts, Mother," he said bluntly, seating himself upon a rock. "A wine press is a good thing indeed to have in one's vineyard, but whence got Neariah the authority to build on our land — as though it were already his?"

"But," Rachel's words came uncertainly. "We have ever pressed our grapes at Samuel's press in his vineyard. Why, then, should Neariah build another? We have no need of it, and 'twould only take Samuel's business from him. And on our land — indeed, it is not neighborly of him."

"Neighborly!" Ephraim spat vigorously on the ground, and his blue eyes held sharp edges. "Where Neariah can lay his grasping hands upon a few shekels, there is no thought of neighborliness!"

"Nay, Ephraim!" Rachel's voice held sharp rebuke. "I will not have him spoken of in such wise. All this I do not understand, but I do know that Neariah has helped us greatly in these years since we were left alone, and I will not believe evil of him!"

But Ephraim was not so easily silenced. "Neariah has helped you? Then why are you and your children not dwelling here in your rightful home? Why do you labor there in the homes of the rich till your soul is nigh torn from your body with weariness? I tell you, Rachel — Jacob was as a son to me, as the son God withheld from me. I helped his father build your home here in Bethphage — and I helped Neariah build a great and rich house in Jerusalem. Yet not since the time that Jacob refused to sell his inheritance has Neariah ceased to envy you this vineyard — nor will he leave you in peace till it has come at last within his grasp."

Dismas leaned forward, a speculative look in his eye. Rachel shook her head firmly.

"It is evil to speak evil of others," she said. "Neariah is a righteous man and a Pharisee — there is no evil in him. Enough of such talk. Let us sit here in the pleasant shade, and do you, Dismas, tell us how you fare."

But before Dismas could answer, Ephraim turned abruptly from them.

"My old bones are in need of rest," he said shortly, "and my throat is parched. Do you stop here and visit as you will; I go to the village."

"Farewell, Ephraim!" called Miriam as she saw him begin to limp away. "When you return, I shall have your wine press finished, see?" and she pointed to where her pile of stones leaned lopsidedly against the rock.

"Then, indeed, it would be seven years and more till I should return," laughed Ephraim, his good humor restored. "But look that you fall not and break your little bones. You are no mountain goat, that you may clamber where you will."

"Nay, but I am sure of foot, see?" and to prove it, Miriam stepped high upon a loose flat rock, that teetered precariously as she balanced there, waving good-by to Ephraim.

"Now, Dismas," began Rachel, seating herself on the grassy plot beneath the fig tree. But a muffled shriek from Miriam stopped her. The rock had not proved so well balanced, after all, and in a flurry of dust and skirts and dark brown curls she fell to the ground amid the rocks she had so

carefully piled up. With a laugh, Dismas ran to pick her up.
He set her on her feet again, and she stood quite still while
he began brushing the dust from her skirts, undecided
whether to laugh or cry at her sudden humiliation.

"Come, child, you are not hurt!" Rachel smiled and held
out her hand invitingly. Very much subdued, Miriam came
to her and sat down meekly by her side. Dismas, with a teasing little grin, sat down beside her; but when Rachel again
asked how it was with him, he frowned.

"I fare well enough," he said, a bit sullenly. "I work a
long day, I eat with the other laborers, I sleep by the grace
of Rodanim's teacher on the roof of our own home. I have
long since paid off the silver coin, but silver or copper for my
own labor have I received naught, for Neariah says it is not
fitting that a thief receive money to tempt him further."

"That is not right," she exclaimed, her eyes flashing. "The
Scripture says, 'The laborer is worthy of his hire.' Neariah
dare not keep you without wages. I shall speak to him."

"Nay," said Dismas hopelessly. "It will avail nothing. He
will but say my wages go to pay the mortgage. Mother, how
long will it be before that mortgage is fully paid?"

"Still, it is not right," insisted Rachel, ignoring his question.
"The money I pay to Neariah is sufficient to meet the payments, as he told me. That which you earn should be yours."

"But, Mother," asked Dismas again. "How long will it be?
Two years now have you been paying Neariah almost all
that you earn. Surely it cannot be long before the farm is
ours again. How long do the papers say?"

"I — I know not."

"You do not know? Nay, then, Mother, Neariah can keep
us paying forever. We shall never live here again."

"Nay, Dismas," protested Rachel. "Neariah is a righteous man. He will not charge us above that which we should pay. He told me the price every month, but the total he did not say. But he is a righteous man. A Pharisee dare not do wrong."

"That I do not believe," answered Dismas bluntly. "Neariah would do many an unjust thing if it meant money in his pouch. Did you yourself ever see the mortgage paper, Mother?"

"Yea, Dismas, and with your father's signature."

"Did Father ever speak to you of it before he died?"

"Nay, he did not. For that reason it — it hurt me sore to leave this place, for I knew naught of the matter beforehand. But of what think you, Dismas?"

"That Father did not truly sign those papers; that they might have been forged."

Miriam, who understood but half of what was being said, turned wondering eyes on Dismas at this, but Rachel's face was stern.

"Enough of such talk, Dismas. It is wrong to think evil of others, and you must not let Ephraim put such thoughts into your head. Neariah has been most kind to us, and we must not repay him with wicked accusations."

"Look you, Mother!" Dismas' voice took on a patient air, as though he were explaining something to a child. "For these long years we have been listening to your praises of Neariah's goodness to us, yet I have noticed that whenever Neariah does us the favor of intruding in our affairs, it results in hardship for us and advantage for him. Why, think you, is he so interested in us, if not because we are so easily duped that he may expect more and more from us as the years go by?"

"That I can answer you clearly and well," replied Rachel firmly. "It is for the sake of Rodanim's mother — Neariah's wife, Leah, who in her girlhood was as a sister to me, even as our names were those of sisters of long ago. And because she loved me and because, as she lay dying, she called for me and I came to her and laid her infant son in her arms ere she passed away, for that reason Neariah has been watching over us and done what he can to aid us."

" 'Tis indeed a strange way to show his good will in that I slave for naught and you turn your wages over to him as fast as ever you earn them."

"Is it, then, Neariah's fault that in our folly we do that which brings upon ourselves disaster?"

Dismas flushed darkly, for he knew that the pain in her voice was brought there as much by his small thievery as by Jacob's mortgage.

"Look you, my son," Rachel went on more quietly. "Well I know that Neariah is a stern man and harsh in his judgments. But when he seems to you hard and mayhap even cruel, I would have you remember that he is not a happy man. He loved his wife dearly, and if the pain he felt at her loss has turned his love to such bitterness that he can scarce abide even his son near him, then we must bear with him. It is not ours to judge. I shall speak to him of your wages, but beyond that he has dealt honorably with us, and we must trust him. He is a good man."

* * *

Because Rachel could ill afford to lose another day's wages, she and Miriam went that same afternoon to see Neariah. It was the first time Miriam had been in Neariah's great house, and she gazed about her in astonishment at the painted walls, the windows of fixed lattice work, the candlesticks as tall as her mother, the low tables inlaid with mother-of-pearl, the floors of smoothly polished flags. She could have sat contentedly there an hour or more looking at the rich draperies and furnishings, but when Neariah came, he sent her at once to the garden with a maidservant.

Miriam stood still for a few minutes after the maidservant had left her on the terrace. Never in all her life had she seen so beautiful a place as Neariah's garden. It was surrounded by a colonnaded walk beyond which were other apartments of the great house. Each delicate pillar had its tracery of graceful vines or climbing roses. At her feet spread a brilliant carpet of every conceivable variety of flower. Some of these she recognized — the anemones of royal red and purple, the gracefully curved spikes of gladioli, the fragrant rose of Sharon. Others were there that she could not name. And in the center of this blanket of loveliness splashed a little fountain, cool in the shade of a pomegranate tree.

Breathing in the perfumed air with little sighs that remembered the disagreeable odors of her own poor dwelling, Miriam descended the low steps, preparing to explore the sanded path that wound among the flowers. Then she saw that under the pomegranate tree stood a little marble bench on which lounged a familiar figure.

"Ho, Rodanim!" she called with a pleased little laugh. "I had thought you were in the village."

"I returned but an hour ago," answered Rodanim, putting aside the scroll he had been reading and smiling at her as he rose, "for tomorrow is the Sabbath."

"Truly," said Miriam, flushing a little in embarrassment.

"I had forgotten."

"It matters not," said the boy loftily. "Little girls are apt to forget. But we Pharisees never forget the Lord's day." His face grew so solemn that Miriam laughed again.

"Are you a Pharisee, too?"

"Of a surety. As my father is, so am I."

"How wonderful it must be to be a Pharisee," sighed Miriam. "To be rich and have such a lovely house and garden and fine clothes."

"The Lord blesses us because we are good," said Rodanim simply. "My father goes every day to the Temple to pray, and he gives tithes of all he has. If your mother did that, mayhap the Lord would bless you, too."

"She can't," said Miriam practically. "She must work and pay the mortgage. What is a mortgage, Rodanim, and why must Mother pay so much for it?"

"It is a debt."

"But Mother has not borrowed from your father," protested Miriam. "She has often told us never to borrow, and would not do it herself."

"True," said Rodanim. "But your father did. It is all written on paper. I have seen it. My father keeps it in his cabinet in our home in the village. There I study, and a few business records he keeps there that I may know how 'tis done. I know all about my father's affairs," he bragged.

"Dismas says —" began Miriam, then stopped.

"What has Dismas to say?" inquired Rodanim.

"Naught that matters," she answered, flushing a little, remembering how her mother had scolded Dismas for his thoughts.

"Nay," said Rodanim, angered because she would not tell

him. "Naught that Dismas has to say could be of any importance. My father says he is a thief."

"He is not!" protested Miriam hotly. "He is not a thief, and it is wicked of your father to speak of him in that way!"

"My father could do nothing wicked," said Rodanim loftily. "He is a Pharisee. And you are but a poor widow's daughter whose father could not even make provision for his family after he died. You should have naught to say concerning my father or me."

Miriam did not answer, but her eyes grew larger and darker as the tears welled up, and she turned her head to hide them.

"Nay, Miriam!" cried Rodanim in quick dismay. "Weep not! I meant not to be rude! Come, I will say no more, and we will feed the little fish in the pool."

Only a little sob answered him.

"Look you, Miriam!" he said desperately. "I — I will give you something — a pomegranate or a flower — you shall have anything you desire — come, take your choice!"

Under her lashes Miriam made a quick survey of the fragrant colors before her. But it was not hard to choose. Beside the bench grew a small rosebush, evidently not long planted, for it was small and bore but a single dark-red blossom. As he followed her gaze, Rodanim's brows bent into a little frown.

"It is my father's latest planting," he said hesitatingly, "and long has he awaited its blossoming."

"You said I might have any I chose," said Miriam petulantly.

"Aye, and therefore you shall have it."

But Miriam caught his arm as he reached out to break the blossom.

"Nay, Rodanim, do not pluck it," she cried. "See, I will choose another."

"Nay, I have promised!" said Rodanim stoutly and broke the stem with a little snap. Then he carefully removed the tiny thorns and gave it into her hand.

She brushed the velvety soft petals with her fingers, then held it to her face and drew a deep breath. Over the flower she looked at him with eyes merry through her tears.

"Will your father be angry?"

" 'Twill not be the first time — nor yet the last," answered Rodanim, his smile ending in a sigh.

"I am truly sorry, Rodanim," Miriam's eyes were repentant. "I should have chosen another. Is — is your father often angry?"

"Not without cause, I suppose. Tell me, Miriam," his voice was curious, "was your father so, too, that you could neither work nor study nor play in his presence, but you must anger him in some wise?"

"Nay," said Miriam soberly. "Father was ever laughing and kind, though, indeed, he could punish when there was need. And Mother, too, though now she works and has no time for laughter."

"I would my mother — were here now. I remember nothing of her, but she would have loved me, I know — and she was beautiful."

"Mayhap, Rodanim," said Miriam softly, tears blurring her sight of the rose, "mayhap if she had lived she would be poor and ever working — like my mother."

"I think not. But," he turned abruptly, "let us sit here by the pool. There are two new fish, one with a tail like black gossamer — you must see them."

The fish were indeed fascinating, and Miriam could have watched them all afternoon. But Rodanim's aunt Martha came to call her back into the house, for Rachel was ready to leave. Martha was Neariah's sister, and, while she had a thin forbidding face much like his, she always seemed to Miriam to be frightened half to death. She walked about on tiptoe and seemed always to be peering around corners before she herself ventured to turn into a passageway. She kept house for Neariah and saw to it that Rodanim was kept well fed and clothed. She was not a lovable person, and, remembering Rodanim's words about his mother, Miriam's heart ached for him.

As Martha turned back to the house, Miriam bade Rodanim farewell, then tried uncertainly to hide the rose in her palm without crushing it, but her hand was too small.

"Never mind," smiled Rodanim. "Father will scarcely notice you, and assuredly not the flower. But look not so guilty, or he will verily have you searched for stolen jewels!"

Miriam laughed and left him. Her mother was waiting for her alone, her eyes bright and angry, her mouth shut in a tight thin line. But she said nothing till they had passed through the tiny vestibule and out the narrow doorway to the stone-paved street.

"It is not right!" Miriam heard her say then.

"Will he not give Dismas his wages?" she asked timidly.

"Nay," answered Rachel. "He says the payments must be larger now because he is making improvements on our land. It is not right. He did not ask me. Our vineyard was good as it was and needed none of his improvements, and surely not a wine press. It is not right, but what can I do to right it?"

"He is a wicked, mean old man!" burst out Miriam, and for once her mother did not reprove her.

"For the first time," she said, as if talking to herself, "I mistrust him. He has been good to us, but this — it is not good. And I can do nothing."

Miriam did not know what to answer; so she just held her mother's hand a little tighter as they hurried homeward.

CHAPTER IV

The Document

THE day after the Sabbath Rachel waked Miriam early. "Come, child," she said, "you must go to Dismas today. I cannot go — I must work and work evermore — but Dismas must be told, and you know the way. If you do not loiter but go directly to do my bidding, the Lord will watch over you, though you are young. Tell Dismas all that I have told you, but bid him be of a cheerful heart, for the Lord does not forsake those that call upon Him. One hour may you stay with Dismas; then you must hasten home again, lest it grow late ere you reach home."

So, shortly after dawn, Miriam passed through the big city gate. It was a long, long walk, and she would have dearly loved to stop and rest in the shade of some friendly tamarisk or oleander. But, determined this time that no harm should be done through any loitering of hers, she trudged steadily on till she reached the village, high up on the hill. There she found Dismas again in the vineyard, tying up the laden vines.

He only nodded his head a bit somberly at what she had to say, as though it were after all a matter of little consequence. Then he found a small cluster of early ripened grapes for her and bade her rest in the shade of the olive trees while he finished the row upon which he worked.

Ephraim was not working at the wine press today, and, as she ate of the sweet cool fruit, Miriam wondered whether he had simply stopped working in defiance of Neariah or whether some other task had taken him elsewhere.

Dismas came then and sat heavily down on the ground beside her, pushing back the turban from his hot forehead and sighing deeply.

"Look you, Miriam," he said at last. "I have had speech with Ephraim. He will not say all that he thinks, but he has told me that Father never would make a debt while he lived, and he does not understand how it is that he should have made out a mortgage to Neariah so shortly before he died. If there were but something we could do — I would I might see that paper."

"He keeps it in the cabinet in our house," said Miriam.

Dismas sat up suddenly, as though a thorn had pricked him. "How do you know that?"

"Rodanim told me. He knows all about his father's affairs," she answered, mimicking Rodanim's bragging.

Dismas viciously dug his knife into the ground, then stood up in sudden resolution.

"Let us go to the village," he said, "and find that paper."

"But Dismas," protested Miriam, "Rodanim may be there, and his teacher."

"They come not till later, as the usual thing," answered Dismas. "And should they find us there, we will say only that you desired to see the house once more. Rodanim likes you, and they will suspect nothing."

"I fear we should not," hesitated Miriam, but Dismas took her by the hand and led her away.

It was not far to the village, for their vineyard lay close to its outskirts. They followed the little footpath past three or four of the village houses. Their own home stood near the center of the village, across from the synagog and but one house from the fork where the road from Bethany joined the eastern caravan route from Jericho to Jerusalem. It was Samuel's house that stood there by the crossroads, and many a time in former years had the two children run to their good neighbor's roof to watch from there the stately camel trains with their jingling bells and exciting bundles piled high on their humpy backs.

Samuel and Leah were not at home that morning, nor, indeed, were many of the other villagers; for it was near the harvest time, and all hands were busy in the fields. Their own house was as deserted, for up on the roof, where the sweeping branches of the scyamine tree and the carefully trellised vines formed a shady bower, there was no one to be seen. The gray and white doves in the courtyard came forward with little cooing sounds and heads nodding as if in greeting. Miriam clapped her hands sharply and then gave a pleased little laugh as they rose with a whir of wings that sent them high above the housetop. But Dismas' quick frown stopped her short.

"Now, you are indeed of great help!" he exclaimed in exasperation. "Letting all the mount know that someone is lurking about Rachel's courtyard!"

Very much subdued, Miriam followed Dismas through the door and into the strangely unfamiliar rooms. The one window was so heavily draped that the room was almost in darkness. All of Rachel's bright draperies and cheerful pottery that had once made their home so attractive had been replaced by others of richer texture but somber hue. It gave the place so gloomy and forbidding an air that Miriam hesitated in the doorway.

"Nay, Dismas — where are all our furnishings?" she asked in dismay.

"In the back room," answered Dismas shortly. He went directly to the small cabinet in the corner, but there he stopped, dismayed.

"It is locked," he said. "Truly, I should have known. He would not leave it where others might find it."

"Then let us go at once," begged Miriam, but Dismas was not ready to give up so easily. He knelt by the cabinet and examined the lock carefully.

"Verily," he said exultantly, "it is the same lock Father used. Once he showed me how to unloose it — if I can but remember...." His voice faded into a murmur as he turned the lock this way and that.

"Thus it should go, I am sure," he said finally. "Miriam, do you stand by the door and watch carefully lest Rodanim come upon us unawares."

Obediently Miriam hastened to the door and opened it to peer out upon the road. One or two fruit vendors on their patient burros were returning from the markets in Jerusalem, but otherwise the road was deserted.

It seemed to Miriam an agonizingly long time before Dismas exclaimed: "It is done!" and swung open the door of the cabinet. Inside were several rolls of parchment before which he hestitated.

He picked first the smallest one tucked away into a corner

as though it had not been recently examined. Unrolling it carefully, he frowned as he tried to read the complicated legal language.

"Surely, this is the one," he said after a while, "for it has Father's name inscribed thereon beside that of Neariah. Yea, and the scribe who executed it is old Daniel. I know him. He is a good man. But I must have more time to tell what it all means."

He puzzled over it till a gasp from Miriam made him look up. She suddenly shut the door and leaned against it, hardly able to speak, for, coming down the road she had seen the tall erect figure of Neariah himself coming toward the village.

"Neariah!" she choked. "Dismas, he is coming!"

"Quickly, take this!" commanded Dismas, hastily rolling up the parchment. "Hide it in your girdle!"

Obediently Miriam tucked the parchment into the voluminous folds of her bright red sash while Dismas swung around and closed the cabinet door, fumbling with the lock a moment until it snapped shut. Then he snatched Miriam's hand and ran with her to the other end of the room.

"We must pretend to be doing something else," he whispered. "Let us examine these plates and bowls on the shelf."

Hand in hand, with hearts beating wildly, they stood looking at the shelf, all the while waiting for the door behind them to open and to hear Neariah's whiplash voice. But the door did not open. After a while Dismas whispered: "Was it indeed Neariah you saw?"

"Aye," quavered Miriam. "He was coming down the road toward us."

Another long minute they waited. Then Dismas stole quietly to the door and opened it a crack. Cautiously he peered out, then opened it a little further. Suddenly he laughed and flung it wide open.

"There is no one about. You must have been dreaming."

"Nay," said Miriam positively. "I do not dream about Neariah. I saw him. He was walking down the other side of the road."

"Mayhap he went into the synagog," said Dismas thoughtfully, "We are in luck. Come, I will hasten back to the vineyard, and do you return home, and Neariah will never know we have been here."

"But Dismas," protested Miriam. "Will you not first return the paper? Truly it feels as large as a sausage here in my girdle!"

Dismas laughed as he pulled her outside.

"Nay," he said, closing the door carefully behind them. "You must take it home and hide it. Do not let Mother see it. Next Sabbath is a feast day, and I shall come home. Then we shall go to old Daniel to see what can be done about the matter."

His voice was firm and hard, and Miriam dared not protest further. But the stolen paper made her very uncomfortable, and all the long road back to Jerusalem she felt as though all that she met must see that she was hiding something in her girdle. And all that week she slept fitfully, always fearing that she might roll over and crush the paper hidden under the edge of her rug.

* * *

Early the morning after the Sabbath, old Daniel was greatly surprised at the two youthful visitors who were ushered into his presence. He received them kindly, but it took a long time before Daniel could recall to his mind who they were. He was indeed a very old man, thought Miriam, for his hand shook as he stroked his sparse grey beard.

"Aye! aye!" he nodded finally, "you are Jacob's son, who had the vineyard next to Neariah's. I remember it well. He was ever a good man. And you are his son?"

"Aye!" answered Dismas patiently. "And I have a matter that I cannot well understand, therefore came I to you." He spread the parchment out before the old man.

Daniel took the roll and held it up before his fading eyes. His hand shook so that Miriam wondered how he could read at all. He nodded his head over it several times as he read.

"Aye, aye!" he said, "Such a document I did draw up for Neariah — there is my signature and that of Neariah, but. . . ." He frowned as his palsied hand began again to stroke his beard. "Nay, this is not right. Not for your father did I draw up this paper, though it would appear that his signature, too, is here. It was for — nay, Neariah told me for whom it was, but I cannot recall — but it was not for Jacob. Jacob was a careful man, nor would he mortgage his land, though well I know Neariah has envied it him these many years. But I do not know — I cannot recall — I am old." His eyes turned almost pleadingly to Dismas. "Take it away, my son, I am too old to see to these matters, and Neariah is a powerful man. But it was not for your father that I wrote this, of that I am sure. It was not for Jacob."

Once again out in the street the children looked at each other. Miriam smiled a bit doubtfully.

"Does that not mean that the farm is surely ours and not Neariah's? And we should live there, and not Rodanim and his teacher?"

"Aye," answered Dismas shortly, his mouth a thin line.

"That is what it means. But how are we to prove it?"

"But Daniel knows!" answered Miriam. "Surely, he will help us."

"Daniel could not help us if he would. He is old and feeble and cannot even remember for whom Neariah said he wanted this paper. Who would accept his word against Neariah's?"

"But you could tell them. . . ." Miriam's voice was uncertain.

"And who would believe me — one who is still accounted a child and, moreover, branded by Neariah as a thief?" Dismas' words echoed bitterly against the walls of the narrow alley through which they were passing, and Miriam could do no more than tuck her little hand inside her brother's and trudge silently by his side. Finally she ventured another question.

"Shall we tell Mother?" she asked.

"Nay. It will but trouble her. And she will fear lest I get into greater difficulty with Neariah. For I will not let the matter rest so. I will not have Mother working her life away for what she does not owe, nor will I see her cheated of what is rightfully hers."

"What will you do?" asked Miriam, proud of the determination in his voice.

"At the least I can go to Neariah and tell him what I know. I can threaten to tell others, and mayhap it will frighten him into dealing honestly by us, though I have little faith that it will. But a way I will find if it takes me till I die!"

❊　❊　❊

When Dismas returned from Neariah's house that afternoon, his face was white and his eyes angry. Miriam had not accompanied him, for, said Dismas, "I wish to meet him as a man, not as a child." But it was more as a child than as a man that he stumbled down the dark passageway to their rooms, almost crying with anger and humiliation.

"He met me with laughter!" he choked, as Miriam ran to meet him. "He treated me like a child and bade me go home to my mother!"

"But — but did you not show him the parchment?" inquired Miriam.

"Nay, for he would have snatched it from my hands. But I told him I have it, whereupon he threatened to call the guard and have me arrested for — for a second thievery."

"O Dismas!" cried Miriam, frightened.

Dismas smiled faintly at her. "Do not fear. Neariah will do nothing against me, for he is not overly anxious that others should see the document. But I have accomplished nothing; for were I to make this thing public, he would arrest me at once, and what defense have I against such a man as Neariah?"

"But look you, Miriam," he went on after a pause. "Neariah will do all in his power to recover the mortgage paper. Do you therefore keep it, and let no one know you have it. I dare not keep it, for Neariah would have his servants search it out if I had it. You he will not bother; for you are but a little girl, and he will think you know naught thereof. And Mother must not know. Neither will Neariah speak of it to her, for he hopes she knows nothing of it. I must return now to the farm and work for that "righteous man," as Mother calls him. For a while I shall pretend that I have given up all hope of seeking justice. But I shall yet find a way."

"Do not let him hurt you, Dismas," begged Miriam. "Truly, it is better to live as we do, than that Neariah should do you harm."

"No harm will come to me, little sister," answered Dismas, meeting her solicitude with a smile. "Do you but guard the paper and say naught to anyone. That is your part."

But if Miriam's eyes could have followed Dismas farther than the turning of their little street, she would indeed have had cause for worry; for there, a few yards farther on, he encountered Zabad, who walked amiably with him to the city gate.

CHAPTER V

An Errand Undone

Mıriam hardly knew which way to turn when Neariah made his appearance at their home that evening. To Rachel his visit was most confusing, for she could not determine just what his object was, though usually he never left her long in doubt. But Miriam knew, and when he asked whether Dismas had spoken to them of a paper that had been lost at the farm, she was as agitated as Rachel, but for a different reason.

"Nay," said Rachel, her eyes troubled. "He said naught thereof. Surely, you do not suspect him again —" her voice failed in her anxiety.

"Do not trouble yourself, good woman," answered Neariah with a cold smile. "I have no reason to suspect Dismas beyond that he has once before taken that which was not rightfully his."

Miriam could see the relief in his eyes as he spoke. "The old goat," she thought, remembering Ephraim's phrase. "He wants only to see if Mother knows of the paper."

But Neariah was not finished. "The thing is of no consequence," he said. "It was rather another matter about which I came to speak. While I have no specific complaint to make

concerning Dismas' work, yet I feel that all is not well with
him. I fear he has yet too easy a contact with his evil friends
of the city. Now I have a brother in Galilee, who is in need of
help in his fisheries. To him I will send Dismas, for the boy
will be well cared for there and, indeed, better off than here."

"Nay, there I do protest," said Rachel firmly. "Dismas is
still a child, and I will not have him go so far from those who
love him. And, of a surety, you must be mistaken concerning
his companions, for does he not work on the farm every day
and for so long that he cannot even join us for the Sabbath?
Only yesterday was he here in the city, and then we three
were ever together. It cannot be that he keeps evil company."

Neariah's black eyes stared coldly at her. "My good woman," he said, biting off each word precisely. "Is it known to
you that your son Dismas was this day roaming the streets of
Jerusalem rather than working at the farm as you thought?"

Rachel caught her breath. "Nay," she gasped. "Dismas
would not — he is a good boy, he would not deceive me —
surely, you are mistaken!"

"I am never mistaken. With my own eyes I saw him this
day, doubtless awaiting his friends for some mischievous purpose of his own."

This was too much for Miriam. "He was doing no mischief,
Mother!" she cried. "Neariah hates him and would have you
believe evil of him that he may send him away ere he — " she
caught back her words just in time.

Neariah fixed his piercing eyes on her. "What talk is this?"
he asked harshly.

"Miriam!" cried Rachel, aghast. "What are you saying,
child? Forgive her, Rabbi, for she is but overfaithful to her
brother."

But Neariah held Miriam with his black eyes, and the hate within them was like fire beneath ashes.

"That paper of which I spoke must be returned to me within the week, or it shall go hard with Dismas," he said and, rising, left them without another word.

Rachel stared after him, too bewildered even to show him to the door. "What is this?" she asked, as if to herself. "First he says Dismas is not to blame, then he says it will go hard with him. I fear for Dismas. Mayhap the boy *should* be sent far from Jerusalem. Knew you that he remained here today, Miriam?"

"Aye, Mother, I knew. But, believe me, it was not for mischief he remained in town. He—he had important business—I cannot tell you, but. . . ." Miriam stopped, for Rachel was not listening. She sat staring at the bare wall before her, her face pale and troubled. She turned to Miriam with a faint smile.

"My child," she said, "you are indeed a loyal sister. Pray that your brother be worthy of it. But I fear it can only mean evil that he deceives me thus. Even now — I can no longer trust him — I know not whether he be in Bethphage or with evil companions here. . . ."

"Nay, Mother," Miriam protested earnestly, "believe me, I know that Dismas has gone back to the village. He did not willingly deceive you — 'twas for a good work he must do — indeed, Mother. . . ."

Rachel silenced her agitated little daughter by laying a gentle hand across her mouth. Then she kissed her tenderly and bade her prepare for slumber. Miriam could have wept at the pain in her mother's eyes, but she said no more, because she, too, must do her part, as Dismas had said.

It was two days later — troubled days for Miriam, and troubled days for Rachel — that Rodanim came late in the afternoon to bring a message from his father. Rachel had not yet come home, and Miriam received him dubiously, wondering what of good or evil he brought to them this time. And, indeed, he seemed most uneasy and unlike his usual straightforward self, though his message was kindly delivered and joyously received.

"The early grapes are ripe to harvest, and on the morrow we go to pluck the first fruits and carry them to the presses. My father's sister would rejoice to have you accompany us to the vineyard to help in gathering the grapes."

Miriam clapped her hands in unconcealed delight. Of all the times of the year she liked most the joyous vintage season. The whole village, men, women, and children, turned out then to work in the fields. The singing in the vineyards and the happy shouting of the men tramping out the grapes in the presses made labor light and hearts glad in wholesome comradeship.

"I shall rejoice to go," she cried. "Indeed, it is kind of you to ask me, and I am sure Mother will let me go. Shall we leave early?"

"No later than sunrise." Rodanim's smile at her eagerness seemed a bit reluctant. "Asaf and Aunt Martha shall come with the cart for you and bring you to my father's house, where I and others who go thither will join you."

"I shall be awaiting them, Rodanim. Oh, it is wondrous kind of your aunt to take me! 'Twill be a joyous day — and I can also see Dismas and tell him. . . ." She stopped short at remembrance of what it was she had to tell him, and her face suddenly lost its happy animation. Rodanim said nothing, but regarded her with so intent a gaze that she became uneasy.

"Say unto your aunt that I indeed appreciate her kindness and shall be prepared when she calls," she said, rising as if to dismiss him in as formal a manner as she could assume.

But Rodanim seemed to be in no hurry to go, though his strong young fingers plucking at the fringe of his robe betrayed his uneasiness.

"Dismas will rejoice to see you, and — I have a new game to show you, Miriam," he broke off abruptly. "Do you have about the house a piece of paper or parchment, mayhap?"

"We are no scribes here, Rodanim," said Miriam, laughing a little at the ridiculousness of the request. "How, then, should we have paper?"

"My father thought — " Rodanim stopped short.

"What did your father think?" asked Miriam, suddenly cautious.

Rodanim hesitated. Then he rose and faced her squarely. "Look you, Miriam. My father has asked me to come here to see if by stealth I might discover whether you have here a paper from your home in the village which, he says, Dismas has taken. I will do nothing by stealth, but do you tell me if you have it, and, if so, give it to me that I might restore it to my father with no further trouble for Dismas."

Miriam backed away, extremely conscious of the paper tucked away in her girdle.

"It is not your father's paper," she said, trying to keep her voice steady. "None has a better right to it than Dismas."

"If that were true, my father would be the first to give it into his hands," said Rodanim evenly. "Do you, then, give it to me, or tell me where it is that I may find it."

Miriam answered nothing, wondering desperately if he

would actually take it from her should he discover its where-abouts.

"Look you, Miriam!" Rodanim's smile was persuasive. There was no longer any hesitation or uneasiness in him, for he was going about his errand in his own way now. "You know that my father is a righteous man, and just, and that Dismas has ere this been guilty of. . . ."

"Your father is *not* a righteous man," broke in Miriam hotly, her words tumbling over each other in her anger. "He is wicked, and the paper is a forgery; and because your father drew it up falsely, we must live here, and Mother must work, and Dismas must work, and we are all poor. It is a wicked paper, and your father is wicked to have written it, and you are wicked to come here to get it from me!"

"My father is not wicked!" protested Rodanim. "He did no such wrong as you say. He could not! You are entirely wrong!"

"I am not wrong!" retorted Miriam. "The paper is false, and someday Dismas will prove it, and we shall no longer have to pay your father for a mortgage, and the farm will be ours again."

Rodanim's face was white. "I do not believe you," he said quietly. "And I am sorry you are so angry. You will regret your words when you discover how mistaken you have been."

With the hot angry tears welling up in her eyes and chok-ing off her voice, Miriam said no more. Rodanim walked quietly to the door, where he said without turning:

"You need not come with us tomorrow to the vineyards if you do not wish to."

"Indeed, I shall not!" cried Miriam, furious that he should be so calm while she was so angry. "You are no longer our friend, and I wish never to see you again!"

Rodanim closed the door upon her last words and made his way down the dark passage and out into the narrow street. His quiet face and casual bearing gave no indication to the curious street children of the perturbation within him. So now he would have to face his father with his mission uncompleted. Yet even that did not disturb him so greatly as did Miriam's accusations: "The paper is false, and your father is wicked, and you are wicked."

Undoubtedly the paper in question was the mortgage to Rachel's farm. And equally there was no doubt that Miriam was wrong. Dismas had deceived her for his own ends, but what those ends could be Rodanim had no idea. "The paper is false, and someday Dismas will prove it. . . ."

It was utterly ridiculous. Righteous men whom the Lord prospered must always suffer the envy and hatred of those less fortunate. And yet — the memory would no longer be stifled. Only last week he had asked his father concerning the terms of Rachel's mortgage, for he, too, looked forward to the time when Dismas and Miriam would once more share his leisure hours in the friendly village. Diffidently he had asked, expecting the usual gruff answer, but even he was unprepared for his father's sudden burst of anger. But, then, a burst of anger on Neariah's part was all too common an occurrence to attach any significance thereto. Nevertheless he felt distinctly uneasy as he entered his father's house and crossed the garden courtyard to his own rooms.

He had scarcely had time to have the dust of the streets washed from his feet before a servant summoned him to his father. Rodanim was never sure in what mood his father would greet him, but today he had no doubt as to the unpleasant manner in which the interview would proceed.

Yet Neariah was almost affable as he leaned back in his great chair and greeted his son.

"Now, my son," there was almost a smile on his thin lips. "And what of the paper?"

"I have it not," said Rodanim bluntly.

Neariah's face lost its smile. "Does the girl keep it?"

"That I do not know."

"Nay, then!" the angry lines returned to his brow. "Made you no attempt to find the paper? Can I not send you on so slight an errand without your failing to accomplish it? Did you bid her come to the gathering of the vintage?"

"Aye — but. . . ."

"Then all is yet well. The girl will come to the village and will assuredly bring the paper in the hope of seeing Dismas and delivering it to him. Then I shall have it."

"Nay, but — Miriam will not come!" In spite of himself Rodanim's voice shook a little at the knowledge of what was to come.

Neariah turned furiously upon his son. "What manner of son do I have, that he cannot accomplish the simplest errand? Must I in my own family cherish a fool?"

"I regret, Father. . . ."

"Regret! Of what use to me are your regrets? It is the paper I want, and the paper I must have!" His bony fist came down with a crash upon the table before him.

Rodanim retreated a step. "Nay, then, may I not simply ask Rachel for it? Miriam will keep nothing from her mother, of that I am sure."

"Speak not a word of this to Rachel!" Rodanim was startled by the sudden look in his father's eyes. "As you are my son, naught of this matter must be said to any man. Do you understand?"

"Yea, Father," answered Rodanim. With difficulty he choked back the fear in his throat and, in a last desperate effort to convince himself of the falsity of Miriam's accusations, asked: "But how can one recover a paper of which one dare not speak? What is the paper, Father?"

"It is naught to you," answered Neariah shortly. "Leave me now." He began busily to examine the open roll of parchment on the table before him.

But Rodanim did not go. He noticed that his father's hands were trembling and that that surprising look of fear had not left his eyes. To his mind came again Miriam's words: "The paper is false, and your father is wicked, and you are wicked. . . ." Suddenly he knew that he was no longer afraid of his father, for his father was in need of his help.

"Father," he said quietly, stepping nearer, "I know what the paper is. It is the mortgage on Rachel's vineyard. Miriam says it is a forgery, and I — I cannot but believe her. If, then, you have done them some great injury, let me go to them and correct the matter, and it will cease troubling you."

Rodanim saw the shaking hands pause and hover over the table and knew that his father hesitated. But when he turned, all the blackness of his soul seemed to smolder in his fierce eyes.

"Wretched boy!" The deliberate, venomous voice blistered and seared about Rodanim's ears. "Not content with being a fool, you must needs show yourself to be both unpardonably presumptuous and a miserable ingrate. No son will I have who questions his father's honor. From henceforth come not again into my presence, nor ever anger me with the sight of your face."

"But — but Father — " stammered Rodanim, his face as white as the wall against which he had retreated. "Nay, Father, of a surety. . . ."

With a visible effort Neariah checked his murderous anger. He pressed his clenched fist hard against the table. When he turned to the shaken boy again, his eyes were frozen unfathomable blackness.

"For the sake of your mother you will be provided for as before," he said, with an iciness almost worse than his anger, "but in name only are you yet my son, for I will have naught to do with you from henceforth. Now go, lest my righteous wrath descend upon you and I chastise you with my own hands."

A moment Rodanim stood, unbelieving, searching for a sign of mercy in his father's rigid face. Then, unable to withstand that baleful gaze, he turned and ran, choking and half blinded by tears, across the garden court to his room.

He did not see his father's thin, erect figure stand for a full minute as he had left it, then suddenly crumble and slump into a chair, while the haughty face, now grown suddenly slack and old, buried itself in his trembling hands.

CHAPTER VI

Faithfulness in a Friend

TRUDGING up the hot, dusty hillside, Miriam had ample time to repent her hasty words to Rodanim on the day before. She had told her mother of Rodanim's invitation, but before she could devise a way to speak of her refusal without revealing its cause, Rachel had so warmly rejoiced at the opportunity of communicating with Dismas that Miriam had not the heart to refuse to go. Moreover, she felt that Dismas should surely know of Neariah's threat to send him to Galilee and of Rodanim's clumsy efforts to recover the paper. And, just in case Dismas should wish to have it, she tucked the now somewhat battered paper again into her girdle before setting forth.

So it was a hot and tired little girl who finally left the road to enter Samuel's vineyard, where the new wine was already pouring from the press. She went from field to field where the kindly villagers interrupted their songs and their gossip to throw her cheerful greetings as they plucked the rich fruit and packed it into their small baskets. Boys carried the laden baskets down to the press, and girls even younger than Miriam were snipping the heavy fruit from the vine, pausing now and then to slip a particularly plump and delicious grape into their laughing mouths. Miriam longed to join them, but she must first find Dismas.

He was not in Rachel's vineyard, nor yet across the wall in Neariah's. The hired laborers who worked there told her that he had broken his knife and had gone back to the village to fetch another.

"And bid him haste to return," said one who seemed to be the overseer. "A whole hour has already passed since he left, and the fruit does not wait for the gatherers."

So Miriam turned to the village, anxious to accost Dismas before he should return, that they might speak more privately than would be possible in the vineyard.

She went through the house twice before convincing herself that Dismas was not there. She must have missed him on the path, then; he had likely taken another way and gone around to the other side of Neariah's vineyard. She had just decided to return to the vineyards when a shadow crossed the sunlight streaming in at the open door. She looked up to find Rodanim staring at her in astonishment.

"O Rodanim!" she cried, then laughed gaily at his surprise. "Nay, look not so astonished. I did but change my mind. . . . Truly, Rodanim"— she smiled beguilingly up at him —"I am sorry for my anger of yesterday. I spoke in haste, and I beg your forgiveness."

But Rodanim only stood there, frowning at her. "You should not have come," he said shortly.

"Nay, Rodanim," said Miriam, frowning, too. "I have said I am sorry. Come now, let us find Dismas and go with him to help with the harvest."

"I do not go to pluck grapes."

"But — wherefore, Rodanim?"

He shrugged his shoulders. "They are not my grapes," he said curtly.

"Oh — then I had best go alone. . . ." She felt puzzled and hurt by his strange manner.

"Aye, you had best leave at once," he said, moving a little away from the door.

But Miriam could no longer endure her friend's coldness. "O Rodanim!" she wailed. "Truly, truly I am sorry! See, I cannot bear to have you so angry! I beg you, Rodanim."

Rodanim went to her and took her hands, and for the first time he smiled.

"Nay, nay, little Miriam," he chided. "Do not cry. I am not angry with you. But" — his face clouded again — "I have discovered that — that — nay, it matters not what. But if my — if Neariah should find you here with that paper — he may do you hurt. So you must go at once — back to the city."

"But — I have not yet seen Dismas, and I must warn him. Has aught of evil come to him, Rodanim? Where is he?"

"I do not know. The laborers say he has been gone these two hours, but I do not believe that my father has aught to do with his absence. But I shall. . . ." Rodanim stopped, for behind him the door had quietly shut, and now they could hear the latch drop on the outside. He sprang to open it, but the latch held fast.

"Rodanim!" whispered Miriam in fright. "Who is it? Why should we be made prisoners? Is it — Neariah?"

"I — know not," said Rodanim slowly, as he turned from the door, and Miriam could see that his face was white. "He — he knew not that you would be here, unless. . . ." He stepped to the small window and pulled aside the draperies.

"There is no one about, save a fair-haired lad sitting on the wall," he said. "I know him not — he is not of the village."

"Let me see," whispered Miriam, standing on tiptoe beside him and peering out. "Why it is Zabad. Zabad!" She called his name aloud.

She was sorry a moment later, for the cherubic expression on Zabad's face changed to a mocking leer when he saw her.

"By my ears!" he laughed. "See what a pretty bird we have caught in our net! You keep strange company, Maid Miriam, or do you seek to convert the Pharisees?"

Miriam drew back in confusion, but Rodanim only frowned and spoke in tones Miriam did not know he possessed.

"Release us at once! What child's play is this?"

"No child's play, verily, master Pharisee." Zabad spoke easily as he crossed the courtyard toward them. "Nay, indeed, 'tis man's work, this of ours. Besides, you should not find it so unpleasant there with so fair a companion. Indeed, you are more fortunate than I, who must abide without and only look on."

"Unloose the latch at once, and cease your evil prattle!" cried Rodanim in helpless fury.

"Evil prattle? Nay, and who are the Pharisees to talk of evil? Mayhap I should cloak my countenance in righteousness and my tongue in sternness"; and he drew himself up in such a comical imitation of Neariah, that at any other time Miriam, who had returned to the window, would have had to laugh.

"Please, Zabad," she begged. "Let us go. We have done you no hurt."

"Nay, of a surety, little maid," answered Zabad, exaggerated regret in his voice, "it pains me that I cannot release you and enjoy the pleasure of your company. But other hands than mine fastened the latch — one, indeed, who would be greatly astonished did he know what additional prey he had caught. But I am his faithful friend, and I will assuredly not release you until his return."

"If you do not let us go, I shall scream for help that the laborers will hear and aid us," threatened Miriam.

"Then you may indeed scream till you are as hoarse as a Jordan frog, for the village is deserted, as you well know. But trouble not yourself, little maid, for here comes my friend with that for which he left you in my tender care."

As the door was flung open, Miriam's gasp of surprise was echoed from the doorway. For there stood Dismas, a bundle of clothing in his arms, and a look of astonishment on his face that had in it a bit of anger, too.

"Miriam! What do you here?"

"I — I came but to see you, Dismas," she faltered.

"Nay, and a worse time you could assuredly not have chosen!" interrupted Dismas, throwing down his bundle and frowning heavily. "Why is it I must ever have a silly girl tagging after me!"

"Truly, I — I meant but to be helpful, Dismas," stammered Miriam miserably. Zabad had entered behind Dismas, and now he quietly shut the door.

"Brought you the parchment?" asked Dismas.

"I have it," interrupted Rodanim smoothly. Miriam turned to him in astonishment, but before the words were fairly out of his mouth, Zabad was upon him, and in a trice he was lying on his back with Zabad astride him, pinching his shoulders cruelly to the floor.

Miriam tried to scream, but before she could make a

sound, Dismas clapped his hard hand over her lips so tightly she could scarcely breathe.

"Hush, little fool, hush!" he commanded while his other hand gripped her shoulder so painfully that tears started to her eyes.

"Quiet, now, and I will release you!" Dismas took his hand from her mouth, but held it only an inch or two away, ready to clap back on.

"Nay, Dismas," she whispered, choking over a sob, "You are hurting me — and — and Rodanim has not the parchment — I have it — see, here, in my girdle," and she drew the little roll from the folds of her sash.

Dismas snatched it from her fingers and turned in wonderment to Rodanim, who lay glaring up at his captor, while Zabad sat cockily making faces at him.

"What fool's play is this?" demanded Dismas angrily. "Release him, Zabad, but be ready to stifle him in a moment should it be necessary. Now, what meant you by such talk?"

Rodanim sat up and rubbed his shoulders.

"Mayhap," he said, "I was angered by your treatment of a brave and loyal little sister, and, mayhap," his eyes narrowed as he looked Dismas full in the face, "mayhap I wished to discover what game you are playing!"

"That you will know when I wish you to know it. Now it will suffice you that between now and dusk you are to exchange your attire for the humble garb I have brought you" — he indicated the bundle lying at his feet — "and at night-fall you will accompany us back to Jerusalem."

"To fly over the locked gates, no doubt," commented Rodanim dryly.

"Zabad has ways and means. But — Miriam. . . ." He paused.

"Women do always complicate matters, Dismas," nodded Zabad. "Forget it never, and your life will run more smoothly."

"There is nothing to be done, but you must return at once," said Dismas to Miriam.

"But — I have but just come, and I am tired, and — Dismas, what is all this? What will you do?"

"You seek ever to know what you should not!" answered Dismas testily. "Go you now, and cease your chatter."

"I shall *not* go!" retorted Miriam, angered at his manner. "You are planning evil, and I shall stay till you release Rodanim and — and bid Zabad begone!"

Zabad raised his eyebrows in mock despair.

"Indeed, and such is feminine gratitude," he said plaintively. "Here do I risk life and reputation in a maiden's cause, and she bids me harshly begone!"

"Either you go now, or you stay here till morning, alone and bound!" Dismas' voice was furious. "Mayhap you will learn in time that I know what I do and need not be counseled by you!"

Zabad grinned at her delightedly across the room. She turned abruptly to hide the tears gathering in her eyes and groped her way to the door when Rodanim's voice broke the silence.

"Why should we not all go at once?" he said, as easily as though he were doing the planning. "Then we shall reach the gates before sundown and have no difficulty entering the city."

"Meanwhile giving you a chance to escape on the road," commented Zabad dryly.

"I give you my word I shall accompany you without trouble," said Rodanim.

Dismas looked at him a moment, then nodded to Zabad. "Let us go," he said.

Zabad's jaw dropped. "Are you indeed a fool?" he asked.

"He has given his word," said Dismas, a bit irritated.

"The word of a Pharisee!" sneered Zabad, in a tone that made Rodanim's face flush.

"The word of Rodanim!" retorted Dismas. "This much I do know, that he is trustworthy. Let him up now!"

For answer Zabad shrugged his shoulders and stepped back. But he was angry that Dismas should order him about, and he could not keep his tongue still.

"Nay, then," he said, "if the fellow is coward enough to follow us, meekly as a lamb in the daylight, who am I to sneak him in by night as though he had the courage of a — nay, of a dog, at the least, who has wit and bravery enough to run from his master's leash!"

Rodamin flushed as he rose to his feet.

"I seek but to restore Miriam safely to her home," he said with dignity. "It is my fault that she is here. As for me — it matters naught to anyone what becomes of me!"

"Let us hope it matters to one man at least!" said Dismas grimly.

Rodanim looked at him, knowledge dawning in his eyes.

"So, then, I know your game," he said quietly. And Dismas wondered at the bitter laugh that followed his words.

*   *   *

Miriam was glad that clouds obscured the moon. It made the night very dark, but then she herself was not so apt to be seen. It was long past midnight, and apparently the city was

at rest. Yet Miriam felt movement all about her. A sigh, perhaps — the stealthy slither of a sandal on the pavement — the
rustle of a garment — the sudden movement of a darker
shadow in a dark archway — here in this part of the great city
there was no rest. Leering eyes seemed to follow her, curious
ears to listen to her light footsteps, and, at every doorway —
and the doorways were close together indeed in this narrow
alley — Miriam could almost feel grasping hands clutching at
her skirt or tearing at the flowing ends of the turban she had
wound tightly about her head, concealing her long dark hair.
A gaunt, hungry-looking dog sniffed at her heels, and she bit
her lips to keep back a frightened scream. She had all she
could do to keep her feet steadily moving lest they betray her
and carry her in a panic back to the safety of her mother's
home.

But she had almost reached the end of the street where the
great wall of the city formed a more impenetrable blackness
before her. There at the last doorway, almost in the wall itself, she paused, and, with an audible gasp as of one about to
plunge into cold water, she turned into the dark entry and
fumbled for the latch. It gave easily, and just as the moon
suddenly broke from the clouds and shone full down upon
her, she opened the door.

At the creak of the hinges Rodanim looked up from the mat
where he had been lying and saw her there.

"Miriam," he cried, and sprang to his feet.

Miriam shut the door behind her and leaned against it.

"Rodanim!" she gasped weakly. "Truly, I thought I should
never find you!"

"Wait, I will strike a light," he said, fumbling about at a
low table. "What do you here? Truly, you are like a spirit that
haunts me today!"

As the light glimmered and brightened, Miriam's pale face
looked indeed ghostly, and there was a little tremor in her
answering laugh.

"I — I thought to find you bound, and I came to release
you. But — you are free, and the door is unlatched. Why do
you stay in this — this place?"

Rodanim laughed as her voice trailed off, for she was looking around as she spoke, and her eyes were big with wonder.

"Nay," she said slowly. "I had thought 'twould be a vile and
dirty place where Zabad lived, but here — it is lovely! Where
got he such rugs and tables and cushions? All is lovely and
rich — save that cupboard against the wall — 'tis amazing!
How comes he to live so nobly?" Then, catching Rodanim's
eye, she suddenly fell silent, for she, too, guessed how Zabad
came by such riches, and at once the panic she had felt out in
the street tore at her heels again.

"Come, Rodanim, we must go," she said urgently. "Truly,
this is a vile place for all its beauty. Why do you stay here
when you are free?"

"Why do you come here?" countered Rodanim, frowning.
"You do run a great risk. Small girls are not safe in this neighborhood."

"Nay, but I am not a girl tonight!" Miriam laughed. "See, I
have hid my hair and taken off my earrings and my bracelets.
Tonight I am a boy, and so I am safe!"

Rodanim looked down on her delicate face and sweet dark
eyes and smiled.

"A pretty little boy," he said, "that looks like nothing in the
world but a little girl! How knew you I was here?"

"Dismas told me."

"So simple as that? Nay, I do not believe you!"

"Indeed, he did tell me!" retorted Miriam. "To be sure, he — he did not mean to!" Her smile dimpled at the recollection. "I accused him of keeping you in a terrible place where you might fall ill and, to defend himself, he told me before he thought. Am I not clever, Rodanim?" A little laugh gurgled in her throat.

"Clever and brave and sweet to run such danger for my sake. But now you must go, and Heaven send you home as safely as you came!"

"But" — disappointment clouded her face — "will you not come with me? I came but to release you!"

"I would break my word."

"What is a word given to Zabad? And Dismas — Dismas is as bad, for he plans evil, and no promise need be kept to those who mean you harm!"

"Know you their plan, Miriam?"

"Nay — I plied Dismas with questions till he near lost his mind, but I could learn nothing."

"I think they will do me no harm, Miriam. I doubt that their plan will succeed, but Dismas is honorable at heart and God-fearing and will not revenge himself on me. So fear you not, but go now, and be sure that I am indeed grateful for what you would do, even though I must abide here."

"But — but Rodanim — I am afraid — I thought you would return with me — it is so dark, and there are evil men about. . . ." Her dark eyes grew even larger as she thought of all the dangers she must brave.

"It was as dark before, and as many men were about," commented Rodanim dryly, uncertain whether he, too, were being tricked.

"But then your danger gave me courage. Now I have no reason for being abroad. Truly, Rodanim, I do fear — Zabad might find me, and he would not scruple to do me hurt — I know not what to do. . . ." Helpless tears formed in her eyes.

Rodanim took her hand in his and opened the door.

"Come, then," he said, "we will go together."

CHAPTER VII

Success

THE servants had long since gone to bed, and Neariah sat alone by the flickering light in his library. He had before him on the table a scroll which he seemed to be perusing carefully, for now and then he would reach for the long reed pen at his right, and with the utmost care he would make a tiny mark upon the paper. Sometimes it was no more than lengthening a line here or broadening a dot there or curving a character that had come too straight from the pen of the scribe. Neariah prided himself upon the excellence of his library, and it was through such painstaking perusal of every new volume that it had earned its reputation.

But, as the hours passed, the long reed pen dipped less and less frequently into the ink horn, and Neariah's eyes grew more and more troubled as they wandered from the manuscript to rest for minutes at a time upon the door at the end of the vestibule that led to the street.

It was during one such interval that a knock on that very door brought him to his feet. He hesitated a moment, then snatched up the lamp and hurried to open it. As the lamp's feeble rays struggled against the darkness of the night, his heart suddenly leaped for joy. But he checked himself just in time. The boy who stood there was not his son. His figure straightened, and his brows met forbiddingly as he recognized Dismas before him.

"What brings you here?" he asked harshly. "More thievery?"

Dismas winced, and only Zabad's prodding from behind reminded him that he had a part to play.

"I bring news," he said as coolly as his excitement would allow, "of great import to you. But I care not to stand here in the dark night."

For a moment Neariah only stared at them. Then he turned abruptly and led them to his library, where he set the lamp down with steady hands.

"So, then?" he questioned, his black frown never relaxing.

"I bring news of your son — for a price," said Dismas, hoping that the tremor in his heart did not carry to his voice.

"For — a price?" Neariah repeated the words slowly. Then both Zabad and Dismas were astonished by the sudden relief flooding his angular features. "Ah — then he stayed away — not of his own free will. . . ." The words came in a half whisper, as though fearful of being heard. Then he seemed to recollect himself and turned back to Dismas.

"So, then, our young thief has become also a kidnapper and extortioner," he said suavely. "And what hope you to gain thereby?"

"A statement, over your own signature, that the mortgage on my father's property was falsely drawn up and that the cottage and farm are rightfully mine and free from all debt."

But Neariah had fully recovered himself by now, and his answer was a sneer.

"Your hopes are high, indeed. Think you I could walk in the Sanhedrin again with such a document over my signature? Nor am I convinced that my son is in your hands."

"Here is his clothing," said Zabad, insolently flinging a bundle at Neariah's feet. Neariah fixed his stoniest gaze on him, but Zabad only stared back with guileless, wide blue eyes. Slowly, as if the effort were painful, Neariah stooped and examined the bundle.

"He is safe, you say?" he asked, his face hidden.

"Aye, for the present!" answered Zabad, for Dismas hesitated.

"Then go your way, and release him at once, and seek not to act the part of criminals ere your beards be grown." Neariah's figure was contemptuously erect once more, and his bony hand was unmistakably pointing them to the door.

"He does not believe we will hurt his son," thought Dismas, his hopes fading, for in his heart he knew that he could not harm his former playmate. But Zabad was not so easily deterred.

"Nay, then, for an unnatural father give me a Pharisee! And if you bear no love for your son, you doubtless care much for yourself. How say you if your friends of the Sanhedrin and the Temple found your son toiling as a slave to some Alexandrian merchant of their acquaintance?"

"That you would not dare, nor could you accomplish it," sneered Neariah, but his face paled.

"Nay? Know you not of Ishtaf's son who is now a galley slave on the ship of a merchant of Rome?"

"Ishtaf's son was drowned!" said Neariah harshly.

"Aye? Then why does Ishtaf haunt the ports of Joppa and bribe each captain that he might view his slaves and mayhap buy back his son?"

Abruptly Neariah turned to Dismas.

"Give me the mortgage, and I will destroy it."

"Nay, lest there be more trickery!" interrupted Zabad sharply. "You will make a new document, as Dismas demands."

Slowly Neariah turned to look into those blue eyes, now no longer wide and innocent, but hard and cunning. He seated himself at his table and took his pen in hand while Zabad quietly left the room. With his fingers poised over the paper, Neariah turned once more to Dismas.

"Not yet have you won," he said, his voice grating like sand on pavement. "No document is legal except it be witnessed by another—an adult. Doubtless that little detail escaped your attention?"

"That it did not," said Zabad from the doorway. Behind him stood old Ephraim, looking uneasy but determined.

Neariah's black brows went up.

"Ephraim?" his voice dripped cold fury. "Honest Ephraim? Do you then also consort with thieves and kidnappers?"

"Nay," said Ephraim stoutly. "But with honest lads who seek but to right a great wrong."

"Think not this will be lightly forgiven." Neariah fixed him with a baleful glare, but old Ephraim only shrugged disrespectful shoulders.

" 'Tis little harm you can do me. I am old, my land is free, and I have no widow or children from whom you might take it when I am gone."

Speechless, Neariah turned once more to his writing. But he did not write. Dismas, seeing how his hand trembled, had to choke down a sudden pity for this "righteous" man, now being forced to confess a guilt that would forever discredit him in a world where he had always commanded the highest respect. But the Pharisee was not yet beaten.

"I shall write," he said in a high, strained voice, "that the property is free from mortgage or debt of any kind and is to be returned at once to Rachel and her family. More I will not do."

"That will be sufficient," said Dismas after a moment's thought, though Zabad fidgeted and scornfully shook his head at his lenience.

"And my son?"

"He will be released within the hour," said Dismas.

The document was soon written, signed, sealed with Neariah's signet ring, and attested to by Ephraim, who in spite of his bravado claimed he could not sleep for nights afterwards because of the memory of the way the "old goat's" eyes had bored into him as he signed his name.

❊   ❊   ❊

On their way back through the early dawn Dismas found himself clutching so tightly the little piece of paper Neariah had given him that it was almost torn in his grasp. He laughed a little as he relaxed his hold and then sighed mightily. Zabad looked at him out of the corner of his eye and grinned.

"With an old camel one must use a strong whip," he said. "You thought not to return with such a paper, did you?"

"Nay," admitted Dismas. "And but for you I should not have it now." They went on for a while in silence. Dismas stole a furtive look at his companion.

"Of a truth," he said dubiously; "did you verily — sell Ishtaf's son to the Romans?"

Zabad laughed carelessly. "Nay, but I could have, and Neariah knows it. For aught I know, Neariah himself engineered that little matter. At the least, he knows it could be done. Nay, now that I think of it, mayhap we could use Rodanim to yet further advantage, provided, of course, he has been fool enough to stay with no further bonds than the word he gave you."

"Nay, I will not hear of it!" said Dismas emphatically. But he could not put down a rising feeling of uneasiness as Zabad only laughed in reply. So it came almost as a relief to him when they reached Zabad's home and found it empty.

"So the Pharisaical bird has flown!" Zabad shrugged his shoulders. "There, Dismas, you have the word of a Pharisee, neatly packaged and thrown into your face!"

"I can scarce believe it. Nay — some harm has come to him, here in this vile neighborhood. Mayhap you yourself have engineered some evil scheme. . . ." Dismas' alarm was growing.

"Nay, now, turn not on me who has served you so faithfully simply because a Pharisee broke his word to you. 'Twill not be the last time if you continue to have dealings with them."

"I have not broken my word," said a voice from the doorway. "I am here and am sorry to have caused any delay."

"Rodanim!" Dismas' face cleared in relief.

Zabad laughed. "Now if you are not a bigger fool than even I guessed!" he exclaimed. Then his eyes narrowed in suspicion, and his face was suddenly drained of all color. "Or are you? Where have you been? And why did you return?" Crouching a little, he advanced toward Rodanim, his face contorted.

From the step where he still stood, Rodanim surveyed him with level gray eyes.

"That is my concern," he said coolly. "Suffice it that I am here now."

"It suffices, indeed," snarled Zabad, coming ever closer. "And when the guards you have led here to trap us come upon us, it will suffice them to find naught but your dead body!" He spat out the words like deadly things, and then he sprang. Dismas, across the room, caught the gleam of a knife and cried out in horror. But Rodanim had not been caught off guard. A deft twist of his body and a thrust of his arm, and Zabad's knife clattered to the floor, while Zabad, with a groan, clutched at his twisted wrist. But Dismas had the knife now, and quick as a cat, Zabad sprang across the room to the old cupboard where he faced them, his hands working busily behind him as he spoke.

"Fool!" he cried to Dismas. "What good think you that paper will do you now? When your Pharisee friends accuse you before the Romans, how long will you live in your precious cottage? 'Twill be a Roman prison, or the slave market for you! But not Zabad! And think not to follow me. I have had more than enough of your blundering!" The old cupboard behind him suddenly gave way like a door, and springing into the blackness beyond, he closed it in their faces, and they stood amazed, hearing the sliding of a bolt into its place on the other side.

"What does he now?" queried Rodanim, curiosity in his voice. "Burrow under the walls?"

Dismas stood as if in a stupor, still clutching the deadly knife in his hands.

"Did you, indeed — call the guards?" he whispered hoarsely, not turning round.

"Nay, friend Dismas!" Rodanim laid a reassuring hand on

his shoulder. " 'Twas but a coward's evil conscience at work that made him imagine it." He took the knife gently from Dismas' unresisting hands, then shuddered as he threw it into the corner.

"Let us leave this place," he said shortly. "It smells of evil, and 'tis best to be gone."

The narrow streets were still in shadow as they closed the door behind them. But as Dismas felt in his girdle for the crumpled bit of paper that was to mean new life and a new hope, he noticed that the rising sun was gilding the marble terraces of the Temple on the hill with a resplendent glory the like of which he had never before seen.

*   *   *

It was not until they had almost reached Rachel's home that Dismas suddenly realized Rodanim was still with him.

"Where go you?" he demanded, stopping abruptly.

Rodanim shrugged his shoulders.

"I know not," he said with an uncertain little laugh.

"Nay, then, why do you not return home? Indeed, I did promise Neariah you would return within the hour."

"And that is how you received the paper?" asked Rodanim curiously.

"Aye, he was fearful for your welfare when Zabad threatened — nay, Zabad spoke outrageously, but your father did rescind the mortgage, and the property is ours again, and you may return in safety. Glad I am that the matter is done with and Zabad gone, though I thought not that he would prove so craven a friend. But 'tis well — he would have wished you further evil. Go you now, and know that I am grateful, though it was but unwitting help you gave us."

" 'Twas willingly given, what little there was, even against my own father," Rodanim could not keep the bitterness from his voice.

Dismas gave a little embarrassed laugh.

"Always I forget you are Neariah's son," he said. "You are greatly unlike."

"Nor am I longer his son, wherefore it surprised me that he granted your demands for my ransom."

"I — I understand you not," said Dismas, bewildered. "Surely. . . ."

"He has disowned me," said Rodanim, trying to keep his voice steady. "Yesterday he bade me never again enter his presence, though for the sake of my mother he would continue to provide for me. But I care not for such provision and would seek employment elsewhere — perhaps in the fields — I know not. . . ."

"But — he is greatly eager for your return. . . ."

"You are mistaken."

"Nay, that I am not. And now I understand — when we first spoke to him, he seemed relieved that you were our captive rather than that you stayed away of your own will. Moreover, ere he would sign the paper, he made us promise you would return."

"Nonetheless I will not return," said Rodanim stubbornly.

"Then is my word to him broken," said Dismas.

"You have done your part, and I shall see that he knows thereof. But now let me return with you, and we will tell Miriam and Rachel that their evil days are over."

So they went together to Rachel's dark little apartment, arriving there just as she was about to leave for her day's work.

Without a word Dismas put the paper in her hands, and

she read it over and over before the words seemed to have a meaning.

"I — I cannot believe it! Dismas, is it verily true? Where got you this paper?"

"From Neariah," said Dismas laconically. Though he felt elated and a little proud of himself at her joy, he had no desire to tell of his night's adventure.

"But — I do not understand — Neariah is good after all, and I thought him cruel and cold. Mayhap God was testing me through him, and — and I have failed miserably. Out of the kindness of his heart he has done this, and I shall go at once to thank him and beg his pardon for my doubts."

But Dismas stopped her.

"Mother," he said earnestly, "go not to Neariah. I cannot tell you how I came by this paper, nor how I prevailed upon Neariah to sign it, but I do know that should you come to him with thanks, he would cast you out of his house in anger. He is not happy over the matter and does not love us for it. We owe him nothing now, therefore let the matter rest as we start a new life back in our own home."

Something in Dismas' manner made Rachel pause.

"Nay, but — it is not right to let a kindness go unacknowledged — and such a great kindness — nay, Dismas. . . ."

"It is no kindness on Neariah's part," interrupted Dismas. "Verily, Mother, it were best to leave the matter as it is lest further trouble come upon us!"

Rachel's gaze wandered from her son to the paper in her hand and back again to her son, whose steady gaze seemed to be telling her more than he could put into words. The knowledge was gradually borne in on her that this boy with his father's eyes was a boy no longer, but a man, who had suddenly taken from her the weight of all her cares, and, with an immense and complete relief, she relinquished them to him in the smile with which she answered his words.

"Come, then," she said, "and break your fast, both of you, for you seem tired and hungry. Miriam, haste to bring a little oil from the jar and meal. I shall make little cakes — 'tis unbelievable — I need not work for others this day — nor ever again — haste you, Miriam — they shall eat, and we shall then plan what is to be done."

Miriam, who all this while had been dancing about them like a lively and intensely curious little sprite, brought the foodstuffs to her mother; and as she set them on the floor beside the little clay stove, she said solemnly:

"Know you what I shall do? I shall go at once to our home, and tear down all Neariah's dark curtains, and smash all his good pottery, and then I shall. . . ."

"Be thrown in prison for destroying another's property!" interrupted Dismas with a laugh that seemed suddenly to make their good fortune real. "Be not so hasty! A day or two we will give him, and then — Mother, then we are going home!" With another exultant laugh he forgot he was a man and threw himself into his mother's arms. Miriam was not slow to follow, and Rachel, seeing above the two dark heads the wistful eyes of the son of her childhood friend, opened her arms and her heart to include the motherless Rodanim who in all his wealth and all his honor had yet been more unfortunate than her two in their poverty and sorrow.

CHAPTER VIII

The Talebearer

T HE first years on the farm were not easy.
Dismas found there were large gaps in his
knowledge concerning the management of
a vineyard, and Rodanim was a totally inexperienced, though
willing, helper. But the folk of the village were generous both
with advice and with labor. Old Ephraim, especially, seemed
to feel responsible for their success.

"Nay, and do I want the old goat to bleat in my ears that
Jacob's vineyard is wasting away because I helped a young
boy to possess it? Nay, we shall raise fruit thereon such as
Neariah and his laborers can only dream of."

And so, partly, too, because his age and infirmity were
making his carpentry increasingly difficult for him, he became virtual overseer of the little vineyard. Whether he ever
told his neighbors the truth about Neariah's relinquishing the
land, Dismas did not know. He himself said nothing, and
Rachel was ever eager in her praise of Neariah's goodness of
heart. Dismas marveled that her listeners' open skepticism in
no way caused her to doubt. Not even Rodanim's refusal to
return to his father's house caused her any great concern. She
seemed to close her heart and her mind to everything ugly or

evil, determined to be happy by the simple expedient of acknowledging no sorrow. Should any of the neighborhood gossip reach her ears, she would listen with a faraway look and with such a gentle smile that her informer, abashed, would stop before she had half told her story.

Once Miriam had asked her merrily, "What think you, Mother, when you look so saintly?" and Rachel had turned the same vague look and gentle smile toward her daughter and said: "Your father is a happy man, my child!"

The reply almost frightened Miriam. Indeed, it seemed, now that Rachel felt the cares and responsibilities of the family lifted from her shoulders and was once more living in the contentment of her own home, that her heart yearned evermore to join that companion who had shared it with her in the earlier years. As Miriam grew older and took over more and more of the household tasks, Rachel would sit for hours 'neath the bower on her roof or in the sunny courtyard, perhaps interrupting her reveries only to go to the synagog at the hour of worship to hear the reading of the Law.

Dismas and Miriam did not disturb her. To them, with the memory fresh in their minds of the tired and haggard slave their mother had been, it seemed only good that she should now rest in quiet contentment.

It was Zabad who first put a doubt in their minds. Zabad did not come often, and then usually only at night. He would climb the outdoor stairs to the roof and sleep there with Dismas and Rodanim, and often Miriam was not even aware of his presence till he came down with the others in the morning to break his fast. Miriam did not like it, and protested vigorously to her brother, but Dismas only answered that they owed a great debt to Zabad and must at the least offer him hospitality. And, in spite of her protests and arguments, Zabad continued to come at irregular intervals. Rachel, who had once been so plain in her denouncement of Zabad and his companions, said nothing. She only seemed to retire further behind her gentle smile and vague glance, though she never took her eyes off Zabad. Miriam could see that it made him uneasy, and it gave her a bit of malicious pleasure to see him so. He was not easily put out, and they were all unprepared for his sudden outburst one morning as he shared their meal. He had been growing more and more uneasy, and, as Dismas gave him bread and his fumbling fingers dropped it upon the clay floor, he rudely burst out: "Nay, then, old woman, must you stare a man out of countenance like a veritable death's head?"

Dismas and Rodanim sprang to their feet. Miriam ran to her mother with a little cry; Zabad shamefacedly picked up the bit of bread he had dropped — and then they all stopped still as though frozen by the fear in their hearts. For Rachel continued to smile at Zabad, and in her eyes was neither affront nor displeasure. It was evident she had comprehended not a word of what had passed.

❖   ❖   ❖

In spite of their concern over Rachel the days were not unhappy. But not even Miriam guessed how much of her happiness lay in the fact that Rodanim so fully shared their lives. There were times, of course, when Rodanim's previous Pharisaical training brought friction between himself and Dismas. Rodanim was a willing enough pupil in matters of husbandry, but when it came to the practice of the Law or interpretation of the Scriptures, he deemed himself much wiser than Dismas or any of the village folk. It was but natural since his life had been spent in constant study of the Law. But Dismas had studied, too, and it irritated him that Rodanim considered himself superior.

Miriam would never forget the long, heated arguments that the two held when the day's work was done and they sat in the delightful cool of the evening on the roof, watching the first stars appear — particularly so when a new prophet began to preach in the country round about Jordan. Old Ephraim and some other villagers had made the journey all the way to Bethabara beyond Jordan to hear him and had brought back tales of a man dressed in rough camel's hair, a Nazarite, who preached repentance so eloquently that all men — peasants, fishermen, shepherds, merchants, tax collectors, and soldiers, even a few Pharisees and Sadducees — came to receive his Baptism.

"Is this, then, the Messiah?" Ephraim's account had stirred Rachel out of her usual lethargy.

Ephraim shook his head. "Nay, the Messiah he is not, for he himself denied it. But surely he is a man sent from God, for never have I heard a more powerful preacher."

"So, then," Dismas grinned, "old Ephraim will spend the remainder of his days in sackcloth and ashes because a wild man convinced him of his sins!"

"Nay, mock him not!" protested Rodanim. "Does not the Prophet say that one from the wilderness shall come to prepare the way of the Lord? Mayhap the Messiah is nearer than we think!"

"Indeed, indeed!" cried Ephraim eagerly. "John did speak of one who was to come."

But Dismas interrupted. "Nay, then, if the Scriptures are to be fulfilled, the Messiah should long since have come. For did not Jacob bless his sons and say: 'The scepter shall not depart from Judah till Shiloh come?' And Judah's scepter is long since in the hands of the Romans!"

" 'Tis but the more reason to believe the time will soon come. Nay, mayhap, He is already among us, and we know Him not."

"Aye," nodded Rachel softly. "I saw Him when he was a Babe. He should now be grown to man's estate. Soon He will reveal Himself."

Dismas took no notice of her. "Not know Him!" He laughed scornfully. "Nay, 'twould be incredible! Have not our fathers awaited His coming these thousands of years that now we should not know Him? For all your learning, Rodanim, you do sometimes speak the veriest nonsense!"

Rodanim's color rose, and quick retort was on his lips, but Miriam intervened. She hated these arguments, for, though they usually began in a friendly manner and Rodanim forgot them quickly enough, yet they left little rankling scars on Dismas' spirit that Miriam did not like to see.

"Nay, now, you two," she cried merrily. "You do spoil Ephraim's story. Let him finish now, or I shall set you both in the corner with your faces to the wall, as Mother used to do!" The thought of Miriam, who, it seemed, would never grow much beyond child's height, chastising the two tall well-grown young men, so amused Ephraim that he broke into a laugh hearty and infectious enough to cause even Dismas to join him and forget his irritation.

So Miriam often stole the rancor from their arguments. Yet she was not entirely surprised when Rodanim told her that he was leaving. It was a warm, sunny day, and Miriam was grinding meal in the courtyard. The rhythmic turning of the stone, the little grating noise as the dry grain was crushed beneath it, the sleepy cooing of the few doves about her making the most of the opportunity for picking up a little extra corn, the rasping of a locust in the tree beyond, all combined to make the turning of the mill slower and slower as Miriam's thoughts wandered farther and farther from the task at hand.

"You do grow ever more lovely, Miriam," said a voice near her. The slowly turning mill came at last to rest, but she did not look up, because the voice seemed to be but one of her own thoughts come to life. But the voice was saying words she had never heard before, and, laughing a little, she looked up, for she thought Rodanim was teasing her.

But he was not teasing. He smiled at her from the courtyard gate, but there was no smile in his eyes, only something more like pain that startled her.

"What is it, Rodanim?" she asked.

"I — I go away." There was none of the smile left now.

Miriam sprang to her feet. "You and Dismas have quarreled. . . ."

"Nay, nay, nothing of that!" Rodanim's voice was a bit impatient as he entered the courtyard. "I have spoken to Dismas of this long since. There is nothing of anger between us."

"Then — why — I had thought you were happy here."

"Overly happy. But one makes no progress — being only happy."

"Does one — not?"

"Nay, one does not!" He laughed a little at her bewilderment. "Look you, Miriam, even you should see that I cannot forever be Dismas' hireling."

"Not hireling, Rodanim! Nay, but as — as a brother or friend. . . ."

Rodanim shook his head and smiled. " 'Tis kind of you, little Miriam, and goodhearted, but — I must find a place for myself. I desire my own home and. . . ."

"You — go back to Neariah?" Miriam tried to keep her voice expressionless.

"Nay — nay! That has been made forever impossible. Nay, Miriam, but I have just this hour learned of a merchant desiring an assistant. Ephraim had speech with him as he passed through early this morning, and now I go to the city to seek him to find whether or no he will have me."

"Oh!" There seemed to be little left for Miriam to say.

She looked so small and sweet and bewildered standing there before him that Rodanim laughed again, but there was tenderness in the laughter.

"Look not so forlorn, sweet Miriam," he cried, with a gayety he did not feel. "I shall return — in but a few years, mayhap. And then — look you, Miriam." He was all earnestness now. He took her clasped hands and held them tightly, as if afraid that she would escape before he had finished. "I shall not ask you to wait for me, for you are too young for promises. But I would have you know that when I return I — I shall count it my highest joy and pride if you will — come to me as my wife and share with me the home I will provide." Then, laughing a little because she looked so sweet and tragic and because in his heart he knew she would be waiting for him, he kissed her lightly on the forehead.

"Think of me often, dear Miriam," he whispered, "for I shall never forget you!"

One last fervent clasp of her hands, and he turned to go, leaving her with a new pain and a new hope in her eyes as they protestingly watched him make his way down the stony road to Jerusalem.

✿   ✿   ✿

Rodanim experienced little difficulty in finding the merchant of whom Ephraim had told him. He spoke with him in the courtyard of Salim's inn, and the merchant seemed favorably impressed with Rodanim's straightforward manner and clear replies to his questions. But there was one question Rodanim had not foreseen, and he hesitated a moment before replying.

"My father is a retired lawyer, a Pharisee," he said at last. "But it has been several years since I have lived with him."

The merchant, sitting on the long bench against the wall, leaned forward and eyed him narrowly.

"You are Neariah's son?" he asked.

"Aye!" Rodanim was a bit startled.

"Know you that your father is ill?"

"Nay — I — I did not know. I should have been informed. . . ."

The merchant leaned back against the wall and stroked his beard.

"A tradesman learns much when he waits with servants at the back doors of palaces. You were not informed because, although in his troubled sleep Neariah cries out for his son, in his waking hours he will not have your name mentioned nor have you summoned to his bedside. And, indeed, in that great house there is none who cares to brave his master's anger for the sake of saving his life by granting his secret desire."

Rodanim stood, speechless and distracted, not knowing what to say or do.

"I have been favorably impressed by you, and under other circumstances I would indeed be glad to have you work with me, but — " his voice grew rough and harsh as Rodanim still hesitated " — a son unfaithful to his own father will assuredly not prove an apprentice faithful to his master!"

Dazed, Rodanim turned away. "I — I go!" he said under his breath and stumbled out of the innyard toward his father's house.

*   *   *

Something of joy and contentment went out of Miriam's life when Rodanim left. She tried hard not to show her disappointment, and, indeed, it was not a difficult task. Miriam doubted that Rachel was even aware of Rodanim's absence, and Dismas was so completely occupied by the work that pressed upon him, now that his helper had left, that he had no time to notice how his sister's laugh rang out less frequently or how her smile was apt to end in a lonely little sigh. And if he had noticed, he could hardly have attributed it to its proper cause; for, as it became ever more evident that Rachel was in need of skilled medical care and as, in spite of his best efforts, he could provide little more than food and shelter for her and Miriam, he himself grew moody and irritable.

Knowing the pressure of his work and his worry, Miriam would sometimes join him in the vineyard, training the vines with their delicately fragrant blossoms or even helping to cut away the many little branches, that the life of the vine might be driven into a few main stocks.

It was there one morning early that Zabad found them. He greeted them gaily, grinning at the evident displeasure on Miriam's face.

"Nay, lovely maiden," he cried with his most charming

smile. "Look not so frowning upon such a beauteous spring morning! Indeed, then, and you should rejoice to see a face more handsome than that dour visage of your brother's, now that your Pharisee has returned to his fleshpots."

Miriam had frankly and impolitely turned her back upon Zabad's raillery, but at his reference to Rodanim she stopped suddenly at her work as if frozen.

"Speak not so slightingly of Rodanim," said Dismas, with a glance at Miriam's stiffening back. "I blame him not for seeking other occupation, for, indeed, 'tis a dog's own life, this husbandry!" and he dug his knife viciously into the ground beside him.

"Other occupation?" Zabad raised his eyebrows. "Well, mayhap some would call it occupation — I should call it living in idleness and luxury upon the fruits of another's wickedness!"

"Whereas Zabad lives in charity and goodness toward all men!" Miriam turned on him, her eyes flashing. "Talk not of any other's wickedness till you are clean of your own!"

Zabad seemed to enjoy her anger immensely, for he threw back his long blond hair and laughed till Miriam turned from him again with tears of humiliation in her eyes. But Dismas was angry, too.

"Nay, then, tell us what you have to tell us, and leave the preaching to those who know how 'tis done!"

Zabad shrugged his shoulders and threw his mantle about him as if to leave.

" 'Tis of no moment — only that Rodanim and Neariah are once more playing the part of affectionate father and dutiful son, while Rodanim is no doubt being instructed in the subtler forms of knavery so carefully developed by the Pharisees."

"I — it is not so! I do not believe you!" burst out Miriam, but Dismas only looked at him thoughtfully.

"Nay," he said, "I am not greatly surprised. 'Twas ever a wonder to me that he abode here in poverty and hard labor as long as he did. But the fellow could at the least have been honorable in telling us his true plans!"

"My dear Dismas, have I not repeatedly warned you concerning the so-called 'honor' of the Pharisees?"

"I — I yet do not believe it!" said Miriam stoutly. "Not till I see it, will I believe that Rodanim could so deceive us."

Zabad shrugged his shoulders again.

"You have but to go any day to the Temple at the hour of sacrifice, and there you will see the two together in their fine robes. Indeed," Zabad laughed, "I do believe the fringe on Neariah's garment has enlarged itself by a full finger since his son is returned. As for Rodanim — 'tis incredible that a few short weeks ago such a dainty man of fashion could have been here grubbing in the dirt — though indeed, I thought his skin a bit too tanned to be strictly in the mode!" and Zabad rubbed his own fair cheeks and beard with a look of satisfaction. Then, catching sight of Miriam's disdainful face, he laughed again.

"Nay, nay, Miriam, look not so distressed! Truly, there are others fully as handsome as your Pharisee, and, indeed, quite as well dressed. Now, observe this new mantle of mine — Neariah himself could scarcely be better robed!" and, lifting his tawny arms, he swept it dramatically across his shoulders.

"Aye, 'tis colorful as a snake's skin — and covers a heart as black and cold as ever cowered in body of reptile or man!"

cried Miriam in a fury, and, catching up her knife and twine, she ran from them down the little path toward the village.

This time Dismas laughed, but Zabad did not.

"Someday," he said through tight lips, " 'twill afford me great pleasure to show yonder maiden the proof of her words!"

"Nay, there you stop!" Dismas sharply checked his laughter. "Miriam is naught to you, and you shall not harm her!"

Zabad only raised his eyebrows.

"Look you!" continued Dismas heatedly. "I have given you hospitality and shelter these many years for the sake of the service you once did me. But unless your words and actions show you to be both friend and gentleman, I will from henceforth refuse you lodging or friendship here!"

"My dear Dismas," said Zabad loftily, "you will continue to furnish me lodging as long as I desire it, yea, and friendship, too — that of yourself and of your fair sister! Have you considered how joyfully the Roman guards would arrest the man who gives shelter to the famous Blond Bandit after his clever robberies and amazing disappearances?"

Dismas' face was white and his lips tense.

"And, think you, those same guards might not more joyfully welcome the news that the infamous Blond Bandit is to be found, asleep and defenseless, in a little village near Jerusalem? Two can play at that game."

"Then," said Zabad, eyeing him steadily, "the advantage lies with him who first catches the ear of the Roman prefect."

"True. Think not that I have forgotten how you would once have left me to the mercy of the Roman guards while you ran like a ferret for cover."

Suddenly shifting ground, Zabad leaned casually against

the trunk of a near-by olive and stifled a yawn. " 'Twas every man for himself, then as always. Though, indeed, it proved that once more I had credited your Pharisee with greater intelligence than he possesses." He plucked a single spear-shaped leaf from the tree and turned it about in the palm of his hand. "Well, I will not for the present deprive myself of so secure a hiding place as your humble dwelling, particularly as you have neighbors who love you well enough not to betray me. And, I think, you will not easily call the Romans to your aid, for even you will admit that Zabad on your roof is better than Roman soldiers in your home — and Miriam's. Indeed, 'tis not likely I shall be here often, for the adventure begins to pall, and I can supply myself with all I need in far subtler ways than breaking into Roman houses and relieving them of their ill-gotten wealth. 'Tis evident that old age will soon be upon me!" He stretched his powerful lithe young limbs and laughed. "Your vines promise a good crop, Dismas."

"Aye, and what avail is it?" said Dismas bitterly, but glad to drop the subject. "Alone Ephraim and I can but care for the half of it. My helper turns his back on me just when the vines need tending; my sister is frightened into the house by a villain; and I myself stand here prating like a fool while the tares flourish."

Zabad laughed. "Indeed, 'tis as I have ever said — the farmer works and starves; the city man — well, he, too, may starve, but he need not work for the privilege of doing so. Look you, Dismas! Why do you not sell this foul bit of land and make a free man of yourself?"

"Sell the land!" Dismas almost gasped. "Nay, it was my father's land, and his father's before him, and —"

"Nay, nay, prate not your lineage into my unappreciative

ear. 'Tis not altogether a misfortune to have been early orphaned. For, look you, I can live my own life without fear of ancestral ghosts scowling upon every transaction. But I need not waste my words. You were ever unprogressive and fearful of venturing upon a new enterprise."

"And, pray," said Dismas, flushing a little, "what new enterprise have you in mind for an unprogressive husbandman like me?"

Zabad shrugged again. "Jerusalem is full of opportunities for men with a little money and much ambition. And with Zabad as your *friend*," he emphasized the word meaningly, "you need have little fear as to your success."

Dismas considered for a moment, then rather abruptly turned back to his work.

"Nay, I had best remain the poor husbandman," he said shortly.

Zabad laughed. "Indeed, is my friendship, then, so poisonous a thing? Nay, I meant not that you should do aught against that touchy conscience of yours. There are yet a few honest men in Jerusalem."

Dismas made no answer, and Zabad turned to go.

"Nay, then consider it well. At the least it would enable you to give your mother the care she needs." And throwing his mantle jauntily back over his shoulder, he sauntered down the path, while Dismas watched him with frankly envious eyes before turning moodily back to his work.

CHAPTER IX

The Galilean

RODANIM sat on the marble bench in his father's lovely little garden and stretched his legs lazily before him. It was good to be in the swim of things again, he thought. To be very frank, there were other things that were good about this life. It was good to feel fine clothes about his body, to have slept on a soft couch, to have his every little need anticipated by his father's efficient servants. But, most of all, it was intellectually good to be back, and that not only because of the resumption of his long-neglected studies. Men looked at things from an entirely different angle here. Take, for example, the case of that John whom people called "the Baptist." Their little village had been all agog over the "man sent from God." Many had insisted that the man was the Christ though it seemed he himself had denied it. The whole matter had been vague and confused.

But here in his father's circles it was different. Neariah had been one of those deputized from Jerusalem to investigate the matter. They examined the evidence carefully, in accordance with the Scriptures and traditions and even went to interview the man. He was a powerful preacher, indeed, and there was no doubt of his thorough knowledge of the Scriptures. But when confronted with the direct question as to his identity he had put them off with vague references to another that was to come after him. Evidently he had no conception of the true essence of the Messiahship. Indeed, the next day Neariah, from sheer curiosity, had returned to hear John once more and had seen him point out another to his disciples, calling him the "Lamb of God." Two or three had thereupon deserted their old master and followed the new. Neariah had made a few cursory investigations. The "Lamb of God," Jesus by name, was the son of an obscure carpenter of Nazareth. To a man of Neariah's learning it was at once apparent that the man's origin excluded all possibility of his being the long-awaited Messiah — for was Christ not to be born of David's line in David's town? So the whole thing had been scientifically handled and disposed of, and by the vigilance of the Pharisees the people had been spared the ignominy of following after yet another false Messiah who would surely have, sooner or later, led them into difficulties with the Roman officials.

Yes, it was good to be back. Indeed, it surprised him how easily he had slipped back into his old way of living. Neariah had received him frigidly enough upon his return, and had it not been for Martha, he would have turned back. But at night, when the fever was upon him, Neariah cried out for his son, and Rodanim was there to soothe and comfort him. For the first night in many weeks Neariah's troubled soul found rest in sleep. In the early morning hours he awoke to find the beloved face still bending over him, and with relief, and yet fear, in his eyes he had murmured: "Leave me not, my son, never leave me again!" And Rodanim, in pity at the wasted form and suffering soul before him, had promised. From that time on Neariah's health had rapidly mended, and this morning they had gone together to the Temple to offer sacrifices and thankofferings to the Lord.

The matter of the restoration of Rachel's property was mentioned but once between them while Neariah was still ill. It was not in Neariah's soul to be penitent. He only said: "It would have been better had the property remained in my hands, for thus the Lord would have received tithes therefrom. Therefore hold it not against me, my son, for it was in a good cause."

In another man such reasoning would have angered Rodanim, but his father had seemed so frail, so incapable of harming anyone, that he had said nothing.

"Neither will I hold it against him," he thought, surveying a bed of early anemones at his feet, "for all men make mistakes, and truly, I believe, this illness has made a new man of my father." And, indeed, it seemed so. Whether from illness or from a humbled soul, his figure seemed less erect, his eyes less stern, his smile less grim, and, above all, he could not have enough of the companionship of his son, whom he had once avoided as a nuisance and a plague.

But now that he was again appearing with his father in public, there were new problems to be met. Only this morning, as they left the Temple, he had caught the eye of Zabad as he stood talking to one of the money changers. Zabad had leaned his hands on the table and surveyed him elaborately from head to foot, with an insolence that left no doubt as to his opinions. He must speak to Miriam and Dismas before they would hear from others of his return and would perhaps be led to misinterpret it.

But what was he to say to them — to Miriam in particular? The illness of his father would, no doubt, be sufficient explanation to them for his return. Would they understand, too, his resolve to remain with Neariah? It all seemed simple enough. He now had the home and wealth he had wished to offer Miriam, and the fact that it had come to him sooner and in a different way than he had expected need make no difference in his plans. But, of course, there was one difficulty — a great one. His eyes roved over the richness of the garden, and as they came to rest upon a certain dark-red rosebush, his troubles seemed epitomized in the memory of mischievous dark eyes peeping over its budding blossoms and a childish voice saying: "Will your father be angry?"

Undoubtedly he would. Rodanim had no illusions about his father's ideas on the matter of social position. As a Pharisee, he, and his son likewise, were entitled to the highest respect wherever they appeared. The chief seats in the synagog were reserved for them, and the uppermost rooms at weddings and other feasts belonged by common consent to those Pharisees who were bidden as guests. According to the Pharisaical code, such distinctions involved certain responsibilities, and one of these was to associate only with members of their own class. Certainly it did not include marriage with the orphaned daughter of a poor husbandman, particularly not with one whose brother had personally incurred the wrath of the prospective groom's father.

But Rodanim, though anticipating lengthy and perhaps stormy objections from Neariah, had no doubts as to the eventual realization of his plans. After all, he had shown his father that he could be independent. If Neariah wished him to stay, he would do so on his own terms. It was Rodanim

who held the upper hand now, and he anticipated little difficulty in bending his aging father to his will.

But all Neariah's shrewdness had not left him with his
illness. He did not argue with his son. He listened carefully
and thoughtfully to Rodanim's plans. When the young man
had finished, he sat for long minutes in silence; and to his
watching son it seemed suddenly that his body grew frailer,
and his face pale and more haggard, as he turned pleading
eyes upon him.

"So — you would leave me again!" His halting voice was
barely above a whisper.

"Nay, Father!" Rodanim protested quickly. "Nay, indeed!
Miriam —"

"Think you Dismas' sister would live in contentment in
Neariah's house?" His eyes held a memory of their former
piercing directness.

Rodanim was prepared for the question. "We shall live
near by," he answered. "'Tis rumored that Ishtaf's house is
to be sold, and 'tis but two doors away. I shall be ever ready
to come to you whenever you desire —"

"So you will leave me again!" The voice carried such a
tone of hopeless finality that Rodanim's heart smote him. He
watched the thin hands fumbling with the nobly carved cane
his father always used of late, and the words he had prepared
would not be spoken.

"But, indeed, Father," he said at last weakly, "you had not
thought to keep your son under your roof — forever?"

"But a few years, my son," Neariah turned to him pleadingly. "Truly, had you fallen in with the merchant as you
desired, it would have required years ere you could have
taken a wife. Now give those few years to me, since I have

lost so much of you already, and thereafter you shall have a
free hand in whatsoever you wish."

And Rodanim, who had thought so easily to bend his aging
father to his will, could not resist the pleading in those black
eyes that had never once shown mercy to another's pleadings.
Not trusting himself to speak, he inclined his head slightly
and walked away, while Neariah watched his retreating
figure with a faintly triumphant smile on his wrinkled lips.

❖ ❖ ❖

Zabad, most versatile of young men, proved also to be a
good salesman. He brought Dismas a contract whose terms
were beyond Dismas' highest expectations. The purchasing
was done through a land agency that did not yet have a
buyer for it, but that would pay for an option on the land.
Dismas was to continue working it till a buyer could be found
— perhaps a month or two — at which time the balance of
the purchase money would be paid.

With more money in his belt than he had ever before
seen, and more to come, Dismas felt that his decision to sell
the land was fully justified. Nor did he hesitate from this
time on to trust to Zabad's guidance. He would keep his eyes
open, so as not to become involved in any dishonesty. But
Zabad, after all, was a businessman and, as such, would be
of invaluable help in setting Dismas up in his new life.

Old Ephraim readily agreed to take Miriam and Rachel to
Jerusalem in his cart to see a physician there. Rachel protested; she was content in her home and would rather not be
troubled with doctors and medicine. But Dismas insisted,
telling them that the harvest promised well and that a wine
merchant from the city had already made contract for it and
had paid a goodly sum in advance. Now it was only fitting

that Rachel should be provided for. He silenced Miriam's questioning glances by pressing several pieces of silver into her hand, which seemed, indeed, proof enough.

So it was that when Rodanim came to the village, he found Rachel's cottage deserted. He came upon Dismas in the vineyard and in the course of the conversation inquired about the women.

"They have gone to Jerusalem to consult a physician," Dismas told him.

"Is Rachel worse, then?" Rodanim was concerned.

"Neither worse nor better. But 'tis time she is attended to. And now I can well afford it."

"Indeed?" Rodanim's gaze wandered up and down the neat rows of vines.

Dismas laughed. "Nay, I have not found gold in the earth, nor treasures of rubies and diamonds! The matter is much simpler. I have contracted to sell the land."

"Sell the land!"

"And why not, then?"

"Nay, I — I scarcely know — but 'twas your father's, and his father's before him, and. . . ."

"Aye, aye, I know the whole tale. But you are scarcely the one to school me. Did you, then, carefully consider your father and your father's father when you gave up your home some years ago?"

"Nay, I— 'twas different, Dismas, as you know."

"Aye, different in that a Pharisee may do as he wishes, while a poor husbandman must cleave to the soil and dare not stir therefrom!" Dismas spoke heatedly, and Rodanim, uncertain what to say next, fell silent.

"I have considered it well," Dismas went on more quietly.

"Miriam and Mother as yet know nothing of the sale. The house will not be sold. They will continue to live there on the money I will provide when I take up business in the city. Zabad says. . . ."

"Zabad!"

"Aye, Zabad!" Dismas' tone was truculent again.

"Is it Zabad who has persuaded you to sell your land, and Zabad who will set you up in business? Nay, Dismas, I pray you, become no further involved with Zabad! Truly, it were better to starve as an honest husbandman than. . . ."

"Have you ever starved as an honest husbandman?" queried Dismas sardonically. "We have not all wealthy fathers to whom we can go crawling when a husbandman's life becomes burdensome!"

Rodanim caught himself up stiffly. "You — you misinterpret my action," he said. "I feared as much, therefore I came. . . ."

"You need make no explanation," said Dismas. "I have heard the whole story and am little interested in hearing the details. I am not responsible for your actions, nor are you for mine. Therefore leave me in peace, and go your way, lest anger come between us and these last years of friendship end in enmity."

Reluctantly Rodanim took his leave. As he reached the stony highway, he hesitated; then, on an impulse, he turned toward the village. Just inside the door of Rachel's home, where he had often watched Miriam's dark head bent above her sewing, he found her basket of mending. From the blouse of his tunic he drew a dark-red blossom. Surveying it ruefully because its velvety soft petals were already wilted and drooping, he laid it on the basket, where it made a splash of dark color against the drab of the woven reeds.

It was not till after having helped Rachel to bed and having seen to her comfort that Miriam noticed the splash of red on her sewing basket. It was hardly a flower any longer, but the limp velvety petals and the delicate odor were unmistakable. Instinctively she hid it in her sleeve as Dismas came in for his evening meal.

"Was — was Rodanim here?" she asked, too abruptly.

"Aye," Dismas said, looking at her inquiringly, "How knew you that?"

Miriam flushed a little. "I — I saw him on the road," she lied weakly.

"Aye, he was here," said Dismas shortly. Experience had taught him to be careful in his speech when there was something he did not wish Miriam to know.

Miriam was silent for a few minutes. Then, when Dismas seemed to be determined to say no more, she questioned him again rather hesitatingly.

"Gave he — no explanation for what he has done?"

"Nay, then," said Dismas, wondering a little. "What explanation was there to make? He saw that I knew what had happened, and he came merely — nay, indeed, I know not of a surety why he did come. . . ."

Miriam, feeling the soft coolness of the blossom in her sleeve, thought she knew why he had come, and yet. . . .

"Is it true, then? He is living with Neariah again and is not a merchant as he had planned?"

"Nay, then," Dismas was becoming irritable under her questioning. "You saw him, you say. Was he then dressed as a merchant or as a husbandman or, indeed, as anything but a rich Pharisee's son? Why all this questioning? He has gone back to his own world, and it were best we leave him there, for we shall see but little of him henceforth."

Miriam's silence was so unexpected that Dismas looked up, to find her looking at him with tear-suffused eyes and trembling lips. He sprang up as she turned away to hide them.

"Miriam, little one, what is it? Why these tears?"

Tears burst into sobs as he caught her and held her close.

"O Dismas, he lied to me — he lied and lied, and — I believed him — O Dismas!"

"Nay, then, is it such tragedy that a man should speak a little lie? 'Twas but the easiest way out for him — that he might go without complaining of the life he had shared with us. Indeed, 'twas more thoughtful of him than if he had spoken the truth."

Miriam only shook her head and sobbed the more, while Dismas looked helplessly around for aid.

"Nay, sister, come, be of cheerful heart. Rodanim was a welcome companion, but now he is gone. Come, forget him now, and be my cheerful little sister again."

"I — I shall never forget him." Miriam's tone was so woeful that Dismas almost laughed, till the import of her words struck him.

"Miriam!" He held her off aghast. "You mean — you love him? What folly is this! Nay, he is rich and a Pharisee's son and would not look to a poor husbandman's sister. Nay, it is not to be thought of! Fool that I am, to have let him live with us these years and not to have foreseen. Look you, 'tis but a child's affection! Miriam, come. . . ." But Miriam had torn herself away from him and disappeared into her own small chamber. Dismas stared after her, sighed, shook his head, and sat down to finish his meal with a troubled heart.

To Dismas the physician's recommendation that Rachel be taken to Galilee to the medicinal springs at Capernaum came as a distinct relief. Now he need not tell her and Miriam of the sale — it could all be transacted while they were gone, and he would have no explanations to make nor arguments to withstand. Moreover, in new surroundings Miriam would surely forget Rodanim. When they returned — well, things would probably work themselves out. He was not one to borrow trouble.

So matters were speeded for their immediate departure. Old Ephraim was to accompany them and see to their safety on the way. Rachel protested feebly that she wanted but to end her days here in the home that was her own, but Dismas was insistent, though Miriam seemed to have no heart either for going or for staying.

But one thing Rachel demanded with something of her old vigor. The Feast of the Passover was at hand, and these days the little family would spend together in feasting and in worship. And Dismas, in spite of his eagerness to see them off, could not but agree. But to Miriam for long afterward it seemed that these feast days had robbed her heart of its last hope.

Dismas had left Rachel and Miriam in the gallery of the Court of the Women and had gone back to the outer court to exchange money for the payment of his Temple tribute. Hardly had he left them when Rachel drew from her pouch another coin and gave it to Miriam with the instruction to have it changed, likewise, into Temple money, for the payment of Jacob's tribute. The request startled Miriam, but Rachel met her half-frightened protests with calm eyes.

"I know well that Jacob is no longer with us and that the

Law does not require tribute from him; but so I wish it. Go
you now; I will abide here and await your return."

So Miriam left her, making her way through the throngs of
worshipers that crowded the court. Almost without thought
she made her way to the Beautiful Gate, though one of the
side gates would have been closer. But her task was a dis-
tasteful one. She hated the noise and confusion of the outer
court, with the haggling of the money changers, the disput-
ing and the bargaining over the doves, the sheep, and the
oxen sold here for sacrifices, and the noise and stench of the
animals themselves. She was almost glad of the delay when
she found the steps outside the gate almost impassable. They
seemed to be mostly country folk here — Galileans, by their
tongue — and their attention seemed to be focused expectantly upon a central figure who stood upon the terrace
beneath. From her position at the top of the steps Miriam
could see Him clearly. He stood silent, unheeding of the
crowd that pressed about Him, in His hands a number of small
cords which He was busily knotting about His staff with an
almost vindictive energy. Wondering a little, Miriam pushed
her way down the steps. Were the Temple authorities now
condoning tricksters or workers of magic in the Temple
market? Surely, that was all that was needed to make the
Court of the Gentiles a full-fledged bazaar such as one found
in the city itself. It seemed incredible, but what other reason
could there be for the concentrated attention the crowd
gave Him?

On the terrace she hesitated, looking over the low wall
into the court, trying from afar to select a table less busy
than the others, and a money changer who would not haggle
and cheat and ridicule as they loved to do to those whose

clothing betrayed their country origin. As her eyes roved up
and down, they were caught by a tall striding figure, whose
crown of blond hair seemed to gleam with the same light as
the gold in the money-changers' fingers. He passed from one
table to the next, and at every table he seemed to be receiv-
ing an accounting of the trade carried on there. It was the
first time Miriam had known that Zabad had dealings with
the money changers — even more, that he seemed to be in
charge of them. But it explained a great deal. "The Bazaars
of the Sons of Annas" these Temple markets were contemptuously named in the city streets. And Zabad, as overseer for
Annas, had that high-priestly protection which enabled him
to perpetrate his almost open violation of the Law with no
interference from the rulers. With a gesture of distaste
Miriam turned away, half-minded simply to drop the silver
into the treasury without bothering to have it changed.
Rachel need not know, and since it was not required that
tribute be paid for Jacob it would matter little that sacred
money was not used.

As she stood hesitating, the noise in the court below her
seemed to swell in volume and fury. Men began shouting
and running. Through the confusion she saw that the sheep
and the oxen had broken loose from their stalls and were
running wildly into the porches and out the gates beyond.
It seemed as though a wave of anger and retribution were
sweeping through the court, and no man dared to face it.
The cattle herders tried desperately to keep their herds
together as they drove them from the Temple. Those that
sold doves clutched at their boxes and cages in frantic attempts to save their merchandise before the wave should
strike them. As the money changers sprang to their feet to

meet the oncoming menace, Miriam and the milling crowd about her could see its cause. It was slight enough. Only one Man — the Galilean whom Miriam had noted earlier on the terrace. But so instinct with wrathful energy was that Figure, and so vital in its threatened chastisement the flailing scourge He held in His hand that all were swept before Him like chaff before the wind. Not a word was said in protest, not a hand raised to stop Him. At His approach the merchants' hearts seemed suddenly to fail them and to ask in dismay: "Nay, what is it that I do here?" Even Zabad — and Miriam watched with caught breath as the two met. Zabad towered a full head above the Galilean, and he sprang forward in protest as two of his money-changers' tables went crashing to the floor. The Galilean said not a word, nor was His scourge lifted against this solitary opponent. But what His steady gaze woke in Zabad's heart none ever knew. He stood his ground a moment, then simply bowed his tawny head and walked out into the porches. In the sudden hush that followed the voice of the Galilean could be heard addressing those few money changers and dove vendors that yet remained before Him.

"Take these things hence! Make not My Father's house an house of merchandise!"

Then, as if suddenly weary, He dropped His arm, the scourge clattered to the floor, and He turned to face the multitude crowding behind Him. Wondering faces there were and gleeful ones; faces that shone with joyful approval of this lone Man, who had had the courage to end a traffic abominable to every true Israelite. But some few faces there were that frowned, and Miriam noticed near one of the gates a small group forming with much gesticulation and indignant head shaking. Evidently these men were representatives of the rulers, for there were Pharisees among them, and priests. With a shock Miriam recognized one of them as Neariah. Half listening to the hum of voices that rose about her, she let her eyes wander up and down the court in a half-reluctant search for Rodanim.

"Will they cast Him out?" queried a voice near her.

"Nay, that they dare not," the voice was gruffly Galilean. "There are sufficient of us here to cast *them* out, should they lay a hand on Him." The speaker shouldered his way down the steps to lend his aid to the Galilean's friends.

"Nay, they are wise enough not to cause a tumult. Indeed, it surprises me that the Roman garrison in the tower has not already cocked its ear and come a-running!"

Then Miriam heard no more, for a low, familiar voice sounded in her ear.

"Miriam!"

Speechless, she turned to him, but her eyes said, "Rodanim! Rodanim!" And Rodanim smiled.

"I saw you from below," he began, then stopped; for her eyes, as they left his face and took in his broad phylactery and wide-bordered Pharisaical robe, lost their welcome and dropped to her clasped hands.

"Then, it is true — you have gone back to Neariah?"

"Aye," he answered wonderingly. "Did you not believe what they told you?"

"In my heart — I did not," she said, and her voice was so low he had to bend to hear it.

But Rodanim had had enough of criticism for his actions from his former friends.

"Is it, then, so criminal in these days that a man should show honor and allegiance to an aging father?"

"Nay, that is not wrong — but a man should do it in honor and in truth."

"I told you no untruth, Miriam. All that I said was true, and if circumstances have somewhat altered my plans, I was none the less sincere. . . ." He stopped, for his tongue was patently leading him where it should not.

"Look you, Miriam," he went on. "Here is not the place for talk. But I will come to the village. . . ."

Miriam shook her head. "I go away."

"Away?"

"Aye. To Capernaum, where Mother may recover her health. . . ." She could not resist a glance at his face to see the effect of her words — and her heart stopped still at the obvious relief that was there.

"Then — I wish you a pleasant journey, and may the Lord grant healing to Rachel." His voice was lighter and almost gay, for it had suddenly occurred to him that, surely, by the time of her return he would have found a way to release himself from the promise he had given his father.

But to Miriam the moment was unendurable. Turning abruptly, she slipped away into the crowd, and though Rodanim, when he realized she had gone, started after her, even calling her by name, to the considerable amusement of the crowd about him, she was gone and he did not see her again.

CHAPTER X

By the Sea

IT WAS never more beautiful by the sea, thought Miriam, than at sunset. It was very quiet to-night; and the voices of the fishermen in their boats off shore reached her with a peculiarly heavy sound, as though the very air were reluctant to bestir itself. But it would not be long, she knew, till the evening breezes came crowding in like ripples off the sea, and, indeed, as she watched, the sharp reflections of boats and shore began to tremble and blur in the water, and she lifted her head to catch the grateful coolness. A storm might be brewing tonight, she thought, for the sky had been sultry and ominous. She had never seen anything like the suddenness with which the waters here could be lashed to a frenzy by the winds sweeping down from the surrounding hills. It had been in the midst of such a storm that she and her mother had arrived in Capernaum. In all the long journey from Jerusalem. Miriam had never been more grateful that old Ephraim had accompanied them. They had planned to take shelter at the inn until they found lodging with one of the townsfolk, and they were making their way along the outskirts of the town when the storm struck. Such a fury of

wind and rain the two women had never before experienced.
Ephraim, without a second's hesitation, had driven their
burros into the protection of the nearest courtyard. There
they had no need even to ask for shelter, for the door had
been thrown open to them, and they had been received with
a quiet Galilean hospitality such as the women of Judea had
never before encountered. Mother and daughter lived here
— Abigail and Sherah — and the warmth and comfort of their
welcome were as soothing to Miriam's troubled spirit as the
glow of the little charcoal fire and the warmth of the food
were to her body. Rachel, too, slipped upon the bench with
a sigh and gratefully accepted the cushions Abigail propped
about her.

"I, too, have known the meaning of illness," she said, noting
the paleness of Rachel's cheek and the listlessness of her
hands. Miriam, sipping the broth Sherah had brought her,
wondered at the sudden light in the old woman's eyes, as if,
indeed, her illness had been a beautiful experience rather
than a hardship. And she wondered yet more at the reluctance of the smile with which Sherah met her mother's quick
glance.

Sherah was beautiful, Miriam decided dreamily as she felt
warmth and contentment envelop her like a cloak. She was
not young, but the years must have been happy ones for
her, for the high white brow beneath the smoothly plaited
chestnut hair seemed to know nothing of trouble or anger or
sorrow. Yet in her eyes and about her full red lips there
lurked the shadow of a discontent that seemed strangely and
tragically misplaced. Somewhere, Sherah had missed that
serenity of spirit that bubbled like a spring in her mother's
heart and could not but overflow into love and kindness

toward others. The old woman bustled busily about, seeing
to Rachel's comfort, settling old Ephraim in a corner with
a large bowl of broth, and showing by her ministrations so
loving and eager a heart that Miriam and Rachel felt the
tiredness slip from their bodies as if at last they had reached
home.

And home it proved to be, for Abigail would not have it
otherwise when she learned that they sought lodging in
the town.

"God has sent you here to me," she said, "and I will care
for you. Nay," she went on, in answer to Miriam's protests,
"it is life's breath to me to minister to the sick, and it is but
seldom that I can do so; for Sherah here, my daughter, is
ever ungratefully healthy," she laughed, "and my son-in-law
is seldom here."

A shadow crossed Sherah's lovely face.

"Aye," she said, and the word was like a sigh which she
tried to stifle. "Therefore we have room sufficient for you,
and you are truly welcome." As she spoke, little bitter lines
that seemed but newly learned settled themselves upon her
face, and she turned from them abruptly to place yet a little
more charcoal upon the fire.

So Rachel and Miriam were settled in the guest chamber
on the roof, whose small window overlooked the sea. It was
by no means a wealthy home, and Miriam felt that the money
Dismas had given them for lodging could be well spent here.
But old Abigail would have none of it.

"Nay," she said, dipping water from the jar into a small
basin. "As the Lord gives us, we will share with you. There
is no need for payment."

Sherah looked displeased, so Miriam quietly handed her

the money. But Abigail's quick eyes caught the action, and she looked at her daughter with reproachful eyes.

"Indeed, Mother," protested Sherah quickly, "with Simon no longer fishing, and we left to fend for ourselves, it is but meet that we take what the Lord sends to help us."

"We have never lacked," said Abigail softly, and again with that bright light in her eyes. She said no more, but turned to carry the basin of water in to Rachel.

* * *

One of Miriam's first concerns upon reaching Capernaum had been, of course, to find a reputable physician to oversee Rachel's treatments at the springs. She had spoken of it to Sherah, but before Sherah could answer, Abigail broke in.

"We have a Physician in our coasts," she said. "He will heal your mother."

"Who is he?" asked Miriam, wondering anew at the light in Abigail's eyes, and the frown on Sherah's brow.

"Jesus of Nazareth He is called," answered Abigail. "He is a Physician and more. He. . . ."

But here Sherah interrupted.

"Nay, Mother, and how can you promise this Jesus will heal her? He is ever a busy man, surrounded by multitudes who press upon Him for help, and, moreover, who knows where He is now and to what outlandish places He has dragged those that follow Him."

But the note of bitterness in her voice did not deter the old lady.

"He will come again," she said to Miriam, "and you shall see for yourself. When you know Him, there will be no need for further explanation. But go not to other physicians, for they will but take what money you have and leave your mother none the better therefor. Only be patient and of cheerful heart, and all will be well."

So Miriam waited, but she was far from achieving that cheerfulness of heart that Abigail prescribed. It was more list-lessness than patience that bore her through the days that lengthened into weeks. She dreaded the time when they should return to Judea with its memories of Rodamin and the ever-present possibilities of meeting him in the village or in the Temple — Rodanim, whose grey eyes had held only relief at her going, and who would certainly never be con-cerned about her return. Desperately she tried to fix him in her mind as she had last seen him — tall and handsome, but very dignified in his rich Pharisaical robes, and with undis-guised pleasure in his voice as he bade her a pleasant journey. But other memories came crowding in upon her — of Roda-nim in the plain garb of a husbandman, coming in from the vineyard, tired and hungry, but with a ready smile and a teasing gleam in his eyes for the light-footed girl that waited upon him — of a withered and dried rose blossom which she still kept among her possessions, of a man who had held her hands tightly in his and had whispered that he would never forget her — and then had sent her from him with rejoicing!

It would, indeed, have been better had she had more with which to occupy her time. She would help here and there about the house, or watch Sherah at her loom, for Sherah wove the finest of Galilean homespun, the sale of which pro-vided food for herself and her mother. Occasionally she would chat with old Ephraim, who had taken up his abode in the half-empty storage loft of the small house, declaring it to be all an old man's heart could desire. Or she would watch him at his work, handing him a tool now and then as he mended the broken steps or rethatched the roof or did other repairs about the house. But her own listlessness kept her from doing more, and so constant was Abigail in her attendance on Rachel that even her mother seemed to have no need of her.

Indeed, Rachel seemed happiest when Abigail was with her. They would sit for hours over the mending or weaving, and Miriam knew by the light in Abigail's eyes that they spoke of the Physician. Sometimes she, too, would join them, and so one day she learned whence sprang that well of serenity in old Abigail's eyes.

They sat in Rachel's chamber, for Rachel was weary and lay on her couch, while through the open door came the sound of the loom on the roof, where Sherah wove.

"It was in those days," Abigail said, "when Jesus was wont to dwell with us when His work brought Him here to Capernaum. I lay ill of a burning fever, and when Simon and Andrew came, Sherah told them at once, for she was sore beset to do aught that would aid me. They then besought Jesus, and He came to me and rebuked the fever and took me by the hand. At the coolness of His touch I felt the heat leave my worn body, nor was I any longer fatigued, for as He raised me I felt life and strength flow into my veins so that I myself could gratefully minister unto them for the Sabbath meal. Therefore, because His love dwells in me, do I count it a joy and a blessing that you two came here to us, that I may fulfill that for which He restored me to life and health!"

"Does He yet dwell with you when He is here?" Miriam inquired. "Then, indeed, it will not be hard to win His help."

But Abigail shook her head.

"Nay." She hesitated a moment, then lowered her voice. "He does not force His presence upon those whose hearts are turned against Him. Yet it was not always so, for Sherah, in gratitude at my healing, wove Him a goodly robe which He yet wears. It was only later, when Simon was long absent with Him and the cares of providing food and clothing fell to Sherah's lot, that her heart was embittered within her and made hard. And yet I believe that as He came to me in mercy for the healing of my body, so He will in His own good time bring to Sherah, too, that great happiness which has come to me."

It was a wondrous story, and they listened reverently. Yet it was more than the story that held them in hushed silence. It was the glory in Abigail's eyes. Old and faded they were, etched in by deeply wrinkled, parchmentlike cheeks and brow, yet in them was a glowing warmth that spoke of something more than simple human kindness. In wonder and in awe Miriam gazed in silence, till the steady click of the loom without brought her back to reality. There was something more that she needed to know.

"Jesus helped you because you were the mother-in-law of one of His disciples," she pointed out. "How do I know that He will hear us when He comes?"

Abigail smiled. "I will tell you more of that day wherein I was healed. There had been much talk in the city that day concerning Him, for in the synagog He had healed one with an unclean spirit. Now the night was come upon us, and I came here to the guest chamber to see that all was in readiness for Him. The stars shone brightly over the quiet sea, and as I leaned over the parapet to catch their glimmer in the still depths, I heard a stirring in the street beneath as of a multitude asleep. And there I saw indeed a multitude—of sick men on their beds, of lame men with their crutches, of the groping blind and the pleading mute, of the broken-hearted and those possessed of devils — all waiting in hushed and solemn expectancy there at the door of the house. From here to the market place they lay, lining both sides of the street, and I shrank back in despair, for how could He heal so great a multitude? He was weary, and the time had come for rest, and I thought within myself, 'I will not disturb Him, for the task is too great. Let the people wait till morning, or go to the homes from whence they came. It is too much to ask of Him.' But as I rolled out the mats and lit the lamp here in this room, a voice came from within me: 'You have received His loving gift of health and would deny it to others?' In my shame I ran down the stairs and would have thrown myself at His feet, but ere I reached Him, His eyes met mine, and He nodded and smiled gently as if He knew that I was come to summon Him. So He went out into the street, and under the quiet starlit sky He walked through that suffering throng, laying His hands in blessing upon every one of them, and all were healed. — Nay, it needs not the intercession of friends to win His compassion. He will rejoice to aid you, and that more fully even than you could desire!"

"So many souls to be healed, so many bodies to be cared for!" sighed Rachel softly. "Indeed, and I would rather He would send me hence with Jacob than that I should live the lonely years through with healthy body and weary soul!"

It pained Miriam to hear her speak so, yet she had learned that any protest was of no avail. So she did not sit often with them. Her restless soul found greater interest in wandering down the little tree-shaded footpaths that led from one seaside village to the next, or in sitting by the lake on the rocks beneath her favorite clump of oleanders. Here she had a free view of the curving beach, and sometimes found in the bright sunshine, the sparkling water, and the music of the lapping waves some solace for her heavy heart.

It was not only Abigail who spoke long and sometimes tiresomely, to Miriam's way of thinking, during these hot summer afternoons. Rachel never wearied of telling her story of having seen the Christ as a Babe. To Miriam it seemed incongruous to speak expectantly of the Christ here in Galilee, for would not the Christ come in sudden splendor to the Temple in Jerusalem? And, in spite of her reluctance to return to Judea, she yet looked forward with the eagerness of her people to the time of His coming, and longed to be there in the Temple courts when He came. As her mother had said, the Babe must by now be grown to man's estate.

Some such thoughts occupied her mind as she sat one lazy afternoon by the lake. Ephraim was down on the beach, and as he limped toward her, his arms laden with a heavy piece of driftwood, she called to him.

"Ephraim," she said as he came near, "what say you would be 'the Glory of Israel' "?

Ephraim's blue eyes twinkled at her from above his silvery beard.

"Nay, then, is it such ponderous matters that cause you to bide here so long in thought? I had supposed 'twas but the dark-haired lad who caught you when you stumbled on the steps of the synagog last Sabbath."

Miriam flushed, but she did not laugh.

"Mock me not, Ephraim. Great yokels are they all here in this north country, and I will have none of them. Tell me now, What is Israel's 'Glory'?"

Ephraim set down his piece of driftwood and surveyed her thoughtfully.

"Indeed, it is not to be wondered at that those who are young do question Israel's glory. For with Roman soldiers in every town and village, with Roman tribute to pay out of every shekel earned, and Roman laws that mock at all we hold sacred, it would indeed appear that Israel's glory is departed. Yet I do believe," he paused, and his eyes wandered to the hills beyond the sunlit water, "I believe that Israel is a nation set apart, a God-chosen people, from whom shall come the Anointed One. He who shall surely redeem His people. Therein lies Israel's glory." His glance returned to Miriam's face, as if doubtful of having answered to her satisfaction.

Miriam frowned thoughtfully at the toe of her sandal.

"So I have ever been told, from childhood on, but it is a matter difficult to understand. But if one were known as 'the Glory of Israel'— he would then indeed be the Anointed One?"

Ephraim looked at her oddly. "Speak you of Jesus?" he asked.

"Jesus the Physician? Nay, I speak of one in Judea who came years ago as a Babe to the Temple. Ephraim, is it possible that the Anointed One is already among us, and we know Him not?"

Ephraim looked at her again out of the corner of his eyes, opened his mouth as if to speak, thought better of it, and silently stooped to pick up his driftwood.

"It is possible," he said at last. "But I must carry this to the house ere they lack for fuel."

Miriam watched him with affectionate eyes as he shoul-

dered his burden and limped up the grassy slope to the house.
He was ever a loyal friend and even here, so far from his
home, a sturdy and faithful worker. So helpful had he become to the household that Sherah had once remarked, with
a mirthless laugh, that, indeed, they scarcely had further
need for a husband and son-in-law about the house.

Beyond such an occasional remark, Simon was seldom
spoken of. To Miriam it seemed incredible that any man
could deliberately have left such a home to follow a wandering Physician; for had Sherah not been constantly busy and
troubled by the need of providing for herself and her mother,
she would have been as kindly and serene as Abigail herself
and far more lovely. Simon must be a dolt, indeed, and an
ungrateful wretch into the bargain, not to care for her and
cherish her as she deserved.

But all her prejudices were swept away like a breeze over
Galilee when she caught her first glimpse of Simon. Early
one morning she was sitting once more under the oleanders
idly watching the boats bobbing up and down in the water. It
had been a stormy night, and the waves were still high, although the wind had died. Farther up the beach a boat had
just reached shore, and Miriam watched in idle wonder the
number of men who embarked. There had been at least a
dozen men in that small boat, and she wondered how they
could possibly have weathered the night's storm without
foundering. In spite of their fishermen's clothes, they seemed
to be an important group of men, for one after another of
the fishermen along the shore suddenly dropped his work
and ran toward them, meanwhile shouting to his companions
to come, too. Quite a crowd had assembled there on the
beach when she saw one man leave the group and run toward

her. As he passed her, she suddenly knew it must be Simon, and, stirred by the excitement that filled the air and seemed to be sweeping the entire community around her, she scrambled to her feet and ran after him into the house. There Sherah was half sobbing in Simon's arms, while Abigail was already busy about the little charcoal fire preparing food. Feeling a little like an intruder, Miriam would have turned away, but Abigail would have none of it.

"Nay, nay!" she cried. "Come, child, sit you here and listen. And Rachel, too," as Rachel came from her room to learn the cause of the excitement.

"Come, Simon, give me your robe to lay in the sun, and sit you here by the fire — truly you are drenched to the skin. 'Twas a boisterous night — did you have a troublous crossing?"

Simon looked down at his damp clothing and smiled a bit ruefully.

"Aye," he began, but Abigail interrupted again.

"Come, sit you now first and eat, and — tell us about Him."

So they all sat while Simon ate of the food before him. But he had taken scarcely two mouthfuls before he pushed away his bread. And Abigail did not protest, for he began to talk, and marvelous were the tales he told of lepers cleansed, of lame men walking, of blind men seeing, of the sick being made well, and of the Kingdom of God that was to come. Abigail and Rachel listened with shining faces, Miriam's eyes were wide with wonder, but Sherah's face was downcast and troubled. She sat close to Simon, fingering his sleeve or the belt of his tunic, as if to reassure herself of his presence.

"So, then," she said, when Simon paused for breath, "now you are home with us again — and you will abide here, Simon, will you not? And we shall be happy as in the days before He came. . . ." Her voice faltered and died as she met Simon's astonished look.

"Leave Him? Now? Nay, Sherah, that I can never do!"

Sherah did not lift her eyes again, but her fingers twisted his girdle into a little hard knot as she replied, so low that even Simon could scarcely hear:

"My heart is empty without you, Simon!"

Simon took her hands and held them tightly in his.

"Sherah, my wife," he said. "I cannot answer you, save that there was never a Man like this. You have heard of His wondrous works — indeed, you have seen some yourself. . . ."

Sherah shook her head impatiently.

"There have been physicians before, Simon, and will be again. . . ."

"But He is more than physician, Sherah, can you not understand? Indeed, last night," his voice sank a little as if the wonder of it were still with him, "last night He came to us as we were riding out the storm — He came walking on the water, Sherah — and — I can yet scarce believe it — He called to me, and I, too — this great hulk of mine, walked on the sea as if 'twere dry land. . . ."

"Nay, Simon!" here Abigail interrupted, a glint of amusement in her eyes. "That He could walk on the water I might come to believe, but you, Simon? Nay, there you go too far!"

"As I stand before you, Mother, 'tis true!" Simon rose protestingly. "I walked as safely and as surely as I do now upon this hard clay. . . ."

"Which, doubtless, accounts for your wet robe and sodden clothing," said Abigail, dryly.

Miriam smothered a smile at the sudden rueful look on

Simon's face. Then he laughed with a frank heartiness that made her heart warm toward him.

" 'Tis a wondrous thing," his voice sobered and held once more that tinge of awe, "this walking on the sea. Look, you, there I was, walking as bravely and surely as ever man strode down a pavement, but the wind was contrary, and the waves boisterous — and — I must confess — my heart quailed with fear, and as I feared, I sank. Indeed, I should have drowned, but — He was there, Sherah, and drew me forth and brought me safely to the boat. There was never a Man like this, Sherah, believe me!"

Sherah only shook her head. "A great Man He may be, Simon," she said, "but — what of those you are pledged to provide for and keep? What of your mother and your wife? Shall they hunger and go without clothing that you may wander up and down with a Man who has scarcely enough for Himself?"

Simon looked at her in blank astonishment. Helplessly he turned to Abigail, who met his look with a little smile.

"We have never lacked, Simon," she said reassuringly.

"Nay, we have never lacked!" Sherah rose to her feet in anger. "We have not lacked because the two of us have worked till our souls cried out for rest, because we have sold that which should warm our bodies and gone about in rags that we might have a little to eat! We have not lacked. . . ."

"Sherah! 'tis enough!" cried Abigail sharply. Sherah's breath caught in a little gasp. One moment she stood, tall and rigid, her dark eyes flashing into Simon's distressed blue ones, then she sank to a bench and buried her face in her hands.

"We have not lacked, and we shall not lack," went on

Abigail quietly. "Do you go as your conscience bids you, Simon. The Lord will provide for those who follow the prophets He sends!"

Simon looked at her in wordless thanks, then dropped to the bench beside Sherah.

"Sherah," he said earnestly, "Sherah — I would have you go today to the synagog. . . . He will be there. . . . Do you come and hear Him, and you will know why I must follow Him to the ends of the earth!"

Sherah answered nothing, and with a great sigh Simon rose, took his robe from the waiting Abigail, and left the house.

Miriam hesitated. She longed to run to her silently weeping friend and give her what little comfort she could. But Abigail — there was disapproval in every line of her erect little figure. Rachel, too, had disappeared — and suddenly Miriam came to her senses with a little shock. If she wanted to bring her mother to this Physician, she must follow Simon at once and find out how it was to be done. Without stopping to think that Simon was probably in no mood for anyone's troubles but his own, she ran from the house. He was walking in great strides down the empty street — it seemed that all in the city had left their occupations to see this wonderful Man — and Miriam had to run as she had never run before to overtake him.

"Simon!" she panted, catching at his sleeve, for he seemed to be oblivious to all around him. "Simon, help me!"

He stopped and stared at her with unseeing eyes.

"I would — bring my mother to Jesus — that He may heal her. . . . Where shall I go and what must I do?"

"Find Him for yourself!" was the gruff reply, and Simon strode on.

Miriam gasped in dismay as she watched him go. But after two or three paces he suddenly wheeled and returned to her, his face almost as dismayed as hers.

"Nay, daughter, forgive me!" he cried with a little groan. "This rash tongue of mine gives me more trouble than its size would warrant. How can I help you?"

Miriam repeated her request.

"This afternoon," he answered after a little thought, "at about the ninth hour, He will leave the synagog. Do you bring your mother and accost Him then."

Miriam was about to thank him when he stopped her.

"Have I not seen you before?" he asked.

"I was in the house — with Abigail — and Sherah —" faltered Miriam, loath to bring the scene back to his mind.

"Nay, nay!" he said with an impatient gesture. "That I know. But ere that — you are not of Galilee — yet I have seen you before — those great dark eyes!"

"Aye, I know," cried Miriam, her memory revived by his words, "I was very small — you called me the little maid with great dark eyes — and you saved me from a stray camel that would have crushed me to the wall. I remember — you said the storms of Gennesaret were as nothing compared to the perils of Jerusalem."

Simon's great laugh joined hers.

"Aye, and I am ever of the same opinion. These piles of brick and stone do hem me in —" he shrugged his shoulders at the walls of the narrow street. "But I must go. Look you, little maid with the great dark eyes," he smiled at her. "Hard by the synagog is a little park of grass and flowers, and to the left thereof stands a plane tree. Do you make your way thither, and I will mark you there and bring you to Him. Nay, thank me not!" his face was serious again, and his eyes troubled. "If gratitude be in your heart, do you show it, and — bring Sherah with you!" Abruptly he turned and left her.

CHAPTER XI

A Prayer Answered

AS THE four women picked their slow way through the deserted streets of Capernaum, Abigail told them the story of the city's great synagog. Miriam listened with but half an ear, for her mind was occupied elsewhere, wondering how best to approach Jesus, yet never doubting that He would hear them and do His best to heal Rachel, for would not Simon himself intercede for them? Sherah, supporting Rachel on the other side, walked with downcast eyes and unhappy face, for she had been prevailed upon to come only because Abigail insisted that her strong arms were needed to bring Rachel to the synagog, Ephraim having, for the first time in his life, completely and irresponsibly disappeared. Miriam had no doubt he would be found in the throng about the synagog. Of the group, only Rachel seemed to be listening, nodding, and smiling in spite of her weariness at the long walk, whenever Abigail mentioned the name of the Physician who was to heal her. The synagog was built, Abigail said, by the Roman centurion whose garrison was stationed in Capernaum. Because of his wise and generous rule there had been in Capernaum few of those clashes between the Roman

soldiers and the civilian Jews which were almost daily occur-
rences in Jerusalem and other large towns. And when the
centurion had built this synagog, he had endeared himself in
their hearts to such an extent that when he was in need of
help, the elders of the city themselves had gone to Jesus and
interceded for him, that Jesus might come, and heal his sick
servant. Jesus had healed him in a most miraculous way —
simply by speaking the word there in the street. And across
the town, in the centurion's palatial home, the sick man
heard the word and was made well from that selfsame hour.

But, as they reached the fringes of the multitude eddying
about the synagog, it was evident at once that this was no
peaceful gathering. Jubilant, yes, and excited, but through
it ran an undercurrent of that old fierce rebellion that had,
time after time, thrown off the yoke of the oppressors of the
nation and made of them a people set apart. Strange words
and phrases reached their ears: "A king that would be king
indeed." "Throw off the Roman yoke." "A Moses with manna
for all." "*His* people need never want nor hunger"— phrases
that made Abigail raise her brows.

"These be never our peaceful men of Capernaum," she
said, as they won their way to the plane tree and Rachel
sank gratefully down in its shade.

"Nay, that we are not," said a young man who, seeing how
pale and tired Rachel looked, had courteously given up his
place to her. "We are for the most part from Bethsaida Julias,
though your men of Capernaum are not lacking. But we have
all eaten of the miraculous bread and fish, and now indeed
we shall have a king who will provide for his people as
never king has before!" The multitude swallowed him up as
he pushed his way closer toward the synagog.

"What means he?" wondered Sherah, her unhappy face taking on a gleam of interest.

"Indeed, have you not heard?" an old man stood at her elbow, leaning on his staff for support. "There was never such a miracle as He wrought last evening."

"Nay," answered Sherah bitterly, "that one fool should try to walk on water and nigh be drowned for his pains. . . ."

"Woman, you know not of what I speak!" answered the man with the impatience of old age. "He fed us all, I tell you. Five loaves and two small fishes were given him — 'twas my grandson with the lunch he was to have brought his father — nay, but it mattered not, since his father, too, had forsaken his shop to follow Him into the desert — and I, too, was there, though my aged limbs would scarce carry me so far. But I was there, and I sat in the grass on the edge of the crowd, and I ate of the bread my grandson provided, and so did all the rest. Five thousand and more we were, sitting there on the grass, and He fed us all. Do you doubt He would make a king such as the world has never before seen?"

"If this be true. . ." said Sherah wonderingly.

"True it is, woman," said another standing by. "I, too, was there and ate of the bread and the fish, and so did most of these about us here. Indeed, we would have hailed Him king last evening, but — 'tis a puzzling thing — His disciples He sent away across the sea, and He Himself eluded us. But now we have found Him here in the synagog and have come to hear what He has to say."

"Aye," nodded the old man. "Doubtless He will now proclaim Himself and will become our King indeed. 'Tis a good thing, in one's old age, to know that bread will never be lacking!"

" 'Tis a good thing at any age!" retorted Sherah, her face suddenly relieved. "Simon was right. Why did he not tell me? If He can thus feed His people, we shall never lack, and from henceforth I shall follow Him as Simon does. Mother, let us make our way nearer the synagog, that we may hear Him."

But Abigail shook her head. "Do you go," she said. "I will abide with Rachel that we may take her to Him when the time comes."

Rachel was about to protest, but Abigail silenced her as Sherah pushed her way eagerly forward.

" 'Tis best so. Well I know that you are tired. Simon will not forget us. He will seek us here, and bring us where He may help us!"

A sudden surge of movement in the crowd broke into Abigail's speech.

"What is it?" cried Miriam, unable to see above the shoulders of those around her.

"The congregation is leaving the synagog," answered a man near by who had climbed the low garden wall. Then, noting Rachel's pale face, he went on: "If you would see Jesus, make yourselves ready, for He will doubtless follow shortly."

"Is Simon there? Can you see Simon?" demanded Abigail.

"Him whom they call Peter? I think 'tis he by the doorway. Here, little lady, do you take my place for a moment and see for yourself." He leaped down from the wall and swung Miriam up to his place as though she were a child.

"Aye, Simon is coming," she cried to Abigail. "Sherah is with him, and never have I seen her face so lighted from within — and his, too!" She was almost jumping up and down with excitement. Then she cried out in dismay. "Stay! —

There is some argument. . . ." From her perch she saw Sherah stop suddenly as if listening to what was said around her, then turn to Simon questioningly. Evidently Simon's answer displeased her, for she turned to others about her and spoke to them. Simon tried to urge her on, but she tarried, and soon they became the nucleus of an argumentative, gesticulating group. Indeed, the entire multitude seemed suddenly to have become a disgruntled quarreling throng, and, as Miriam jumped down from her perch to rejoin Abigail and Rachel, they could hear for themselves how it had been in the synagog.

"He says that *He* is the Bread of Life," said one scornfully, "which came down from heaven."

"Nay, hardly shall He feed us on *such* bread!" said another with an angry laugh. " 'Tis ridiculous! Is not this Jesus, the son of Joseph, whose father and mother we know? How is it, then, that He says, 'I come down from heaven'?"

"He is the Living Bread, He says, and whoso eats of His flesh shall live forever."

"This is an hard saying; who can hear it?"

So the talk went, and some laughed in angry derision, and some cursed in disappointment, and some wept in sorrow, but wherever those who had heard Him in the synagog went, there the talk rose in angry surges, and as it died down, almost imperceptibly, the crowd began to melt away. By ones, then by twos and threes, then in great groups, they turned their backs on Him who had now reached the door of the synagog. In silence He watched them go, making no attempt to hold them, but on His face was such an expression of tender love and sorrow that Miriam almost wept to see Him there alone.

But Simon had reached them now, and as he helped Rachel to her feet, Miriam stole a glance at Sherah. The light was gone, and all the old lines of discontent had deepened on her face till it seemed all beauty had fled, leaving only a hard and bitter disappointment in its place. Simon's eyes were hurt and helpless, but his jaws were set, and with a little thrill Miriam knew that this man would never leave his Master.

Jesus Himself had spied their little group and moved toward them now, surrounded by yet a small group of men who seemed uncertain whether to go or stay. Among them Miriam recognized Ephraim. As they reached the broad step, Miriam heard Jesus say: "Do these things offend you? No man can come unto Me except it be given him of my Father."

Then He turned His back squarely upon His followers and came toward them. At Miriam's first glimpse into His eyes, her heart gave a great leap. For here, indeed, was the "Glory of Israel!" All the light that had shined in old Simeon's eyes, the brightness of Abigail's, and the hope in Simon's seemed to be concentrated and glorified in the eyes of this Man with the sorrowful face. And, for an instant, as He took Rachel's hand, Miriam saw an answering glory in her mother's eyes.

"Daughter, be of good cheer. My Father has heard your prayer, and it shall be answered."

Rachel gave Him the same gentle smile that her face had worn before. That was all. Sherah, watching closely, gave a sudden angry laugh, and Miriam saw her lovely lips twisted in a scorn that was ugly to see. Simon, aghast at her rudeness, caught her arm, but she shook him off.

"I go — home!" she said sullenly. Turning her back on them all, she walked with an insolent leisureliness down the street.

Simon, with hurt and anger twisting the lines of his face, watched her go and said no word. Old Ephraim suddenly left his place and joined Abigail and Rachel on the steps. Jesus turned to His little group of followers, and with added pain Miriam noticed that most of them had taken advantage of His preoccupation to steal away unobserved, till there were scarcely a dozen men left. The smile Jesus gave them had in it nothing of bitterness or surprise, only a deep and melancholy knowledge that it must be so.

"Will you also go away?" He asked quietly.

At these words Simon, still staring after the retreating Sherah, seemed to awake as from a troubled sleep. Impulsively he started forward and joined the group about Jesus.

"Lord, to whom shall we go?" he cried. "Thou hast the words of eternal life. And we believe and are sure that Thou art that Christ, the Son of the living God."

The others, murmuring consent to Simon's confession, pressed in closer. One by one, Jesus met their eyes, seeing all that was in their hearts.

"Have I not chosen you twelve?" He said at last in a voice laden with the sorrow of an evil world. "And one of you is a devil!"

Quick glances at one another, little smothered murmurs of protest — yet none dared say a word. Silently and slowly, as if to give them a little more time for decision, Jesus made his way past the synagog and down the street, whither one by one they silently followed.

"The Glory of Israel!" Miriam's heart was exultant as her eyes followed the disappearing group. "Mother, truly, I believe we have found that of which we spoke many years ago!"

She turned to the two women on the steps and abruptly

caught her breath. Rachel was lying in Abigail's arms, limp, and paler than Miriam had ever seen her, while Ephraim bent over her, holding her hand.

"Mother, what is it?" she cried, a terrible fear clutching at her heart. Rachel did not stir nor did that gentle smile leave her lips. Abigail and Ephraim turned to her, their old eyes full of sorrow for her hurt. "God has truly given your mother — the answer to her prayer!" said Abigail softly.

*   *   *

In time of trouble the heart seeks comfort in the companionship of friends, but sorrow does not always teach which friends are those in whom comfort can be found. So Miriam and Sherah each discovered in the other's despair bitter food for her own.

To be sure, so great an impression had Simon made on Miriam that at first she defended him, saying that surely it had hurt him sorely to leave his wife and his home. But Sherah would have none of it.

"Nay, nay!" she cried. "Do I not know Simon, who now must even go by another name? Can I not even now see him before His Master, claiming a special reward in His foolish 'kingdom,' for that he has left his wife and home? Nay, Simon has no regrets, nor will have, so long as that Deceiver holds sway over him."

Miriam said no more, for, while she differed in her opinion concerning Simon, she fully agreed with Sherah in her attitude toward Jesus. "Deceiver" was a most appropriate turn for Him, for, as she in her turn told Sherah, it would have been heart-rending enough had her mother died before meeting Jesus, but to have her hopes raised by the tales of His miracles, yea, and by the very words of Jesus Himself, and then to have her mother depart at the very time she was exulting in the discovery that her "Healer" was indeed the long-awaited Messiah — it was more than the human heart could bear.

So Miriam and Sherah built around themselves a wall of bitterness beyond which Abigail and Ephraim moved sorrowfully and silently, knowing that only time and the grace of God could crumble it to dust and reach the lonely hearts within.

Dismas had come in response to Miriam's summons, but he did not stay long. After they had gone without the city walls to the grave where Rachel had been laid and had wept there together, he seemed anxious to depart. Nor did he urge Miriam to accompany him. Indeed, when Miriam hesitated between Dismas' need of her and her own desire to remain with her new-found friends, Dismas let fall a piece of gossip which he hoped would settle the matter as he desired it.

"You have not inquired concerning the welfare of our neighbors," he said casually, as they sat by the seaside, watching the distant snows of Mt. Hermon like a steadfast cloud in the sky beyond.

"I — I had no care therefor," said Miriam, though as she spoke her heart began to beat wildly, for she knew of whom he would speak.

Dismas hesitated. He had no liking for inflicting yet more pain on her already bruised heart. Yet it was best that she should know, that any foolish thoughts she still harbored might be finally laid to rest.

"Ben Levi's wife has been blessed with twins, both boys," he said, carelessly flipping a stone into the water, "and it is said that Rodanim will shortly wed the daughter of Nicodemus and bring her to the village to live."

"And how fares Zadok and his aged mother?"

Dismas stole a glance at her averted face. If the news meant no more than that to her, then it was well indeed.

"Well enough, though it becomes ever more apparent that she has not many more years to live."

They fell silent, watching the little foamy ripples running up the sand at their feet. At last, with a sigh, Miriam broke the silence.

"Dismas," she said, "if it be true that you have no urgent need of me, then I will abide here with Sherah and Abigail, for they have proved true friends to me, and my heart is heavy at the thought of returning home — alone."

So Dismas, having accomplished that which he desired, gave her money and departed alone for Jerusalem, not bothering even to stop at the vineyard now tended by other hands, nor at the little, neglected stone house in the village.

CHAPTER XII

Return to Judea

So the wintertime of rain and cold swept by, and as the pale pink of spring began to tinge the almond trees again, the hearts of the faithful in Israel turned to thoughts of the Passover Festival. Preparations for the great pilgrimage were well under way. Money changers had set up their booths in every little town and village, roads were being repaired, and outside the towns the sepulchres were whitened, that no pilgrim might inadvertently pollute himself.

Nor was it only the faithful in Israel who prepared for the feast. From outlying Roman garrisons as well as from the towns and villages surrounding the Great City, troops were ordered to duty within its walls. Fort Antonia, that great tower overlooking the Temple itself, was crowded and tense with expectancy, from the Procurator himself, shaking his head over his winecup, to the lowest foot soldier, energetically polishing his helmet for the glory of the Roman Empire, and to the confusion of upstart Jews who might conceivably get out of hand in the excitement of the Paschal week. For this was the time when national feeling ran high, when the hated yoke of the Romans pressed heavy and hard, when

the people were ready to hail with fervor and with rioting
the advent of any new prophet who held up before them
Israel's old dreams of a great and mighty independence.

In far-off Galilee, Miriam's heart, too, remembered a little
of its former joyousness. For the festival time was a happy
time, and its happiness through all the years had fixed itself
almost as a habit, so that in spite of the sorrows and dis-
appointments of the last two years she looked forward to it
with a little inward glow. Moreover, she was going home,
and the pain that she felt at the thought of returning without
her mother was nearly offset by the pleasure she felt in being
able to offer Sherah and Abigail hospitality for the feast days
in her home in Bethphage. As the preparations went forward,
she thought with more and more pleasure of the vineyard
with its neat stone walls, of the little shady plot under the
fig tree, and of the stone house in the village, where she had
spent so many happy years. And when inevitably the painful
vision of Rodanim appeared within its memoried walls, she
suppressed it with housewifely worries as to whether Dismas
would have kept the place neat and clean, that she would
not be ashamed before her guests. Surely, knowing that she
was coming, Dismas would have had one of the neighbor
women give it a thorough cleaning. She had sent word to
him, but one could not always be sure that he had received
it. She herself had not heard from him for several months and
had felt uneasy about it, for he had up to then faithfully sent
her monthly letters and money that she should not lack.
Abigail reassured her. The times were evil, and likely his
messengers had met with mishaps that delayed them or had
perhaps themselves pocketed the money. It was impossible
these days to know whom one could trust. Nevertheless, had

it not been that the Passover was so near, Miriam would have
sent Ephraim to search out Dismas and discover whether
aught was amiss.

So it was that Miriam's heart almost stood still as in the
dusk of a warm spring evening the little party entered the
courtyard of her home some days before the Passover. She
noted with concern the unswept pavement, the broken
bench, and the dusty threshold beneath the closed door.
Sherah and Abigail stood behind her in silent sympathy,
while Ephraim, leading the pack mule, shook his head in
consternation.

"Good friends," Miriam turned to them uncertainly, "there
is somewhat amiss. Do you abide without, while I — I shall
see how it is within. . . ." Her voice choked a little. She
turned almost hesitatingly, pushed open the door, and
entered.

Across the room a figure sprang to its feet, and a man's
voice, low and tense, reached her ears.

"Shut the door!"

Startled, Miriam only stood and stared. In the dusty gloom
her fear-stricken eyes could note but two things: that the
man who spoke to her was not Dismas and that one of his
hands was clutching at the knife in his belt.

"Shut the door!"

Mechanically Miriam obeyed, but she felt that she could
never again move a muscle as the man left his corner and
limped toward the center of the room. He peered at her
closely, then he suddenly stopped and shook back his coal-
black hair in a gesture oddly familiar, while his hand dropped
to his side.

"Little Miriam!" he said, still in that low, tense voice. "Nay,

I should have thought you would return ere long."

"Zabad!" There was no mistaking the blue eyes and bold features, in spite of the coal-black hair. "What do you here? Where is Dismas?"

"Nay, so many questions from so fair a questioner do overwhelm me!" He kept his voice low, as before, but Miriam recognized and resented the old-time mockery in his drawl. But his next words were short and clipped. "Whom have you there without?"

"None but old Ephraim, and two Galilean women who were to be my guests — but I cannot bring them here. . . ." Her bewilderment gave place to dismay as her eyes, grown accustomed to the gloom, took in the dusty floors, the untidy shelves and cupboard, and the cobwebs hanging thickly in the corners.

"That you assuredly cannot," agreed Zabad, but his voice held more than housewifely concern over the condition of the rooms. "You will depart with them at once — you have friends in the village who will shelter you. They know that Dismas is gone and the house neglected. They know *not* that I am here. And they must not be told. Do you comprehend?"

His voice was threatening, and his hand once more crept to his belt. Miriam's mouth was dry, but she did not move.

"Where is Dismas?"

"Come you alone in the morning, and I will tell you. But haste now, your friends grow restless." And, indeed, Miriam could hear Ephraim calling, and sounds of fumbling at the latch of the door. Zabad's voice was suddenly harsh and snarling. "Get you gone, lest I add yet another sin to my record!" He crouched low, and Miriam saw his face twist in pain as he sprang aside, for the door was opening behind her.

"Miriam, child, what then?" Ephraim's voice was troubled. "See, here is Samuel, come with news of Dismas and with offers of hospitality for the night. It is not meet that you stand thus alone in the dark. Come, child!"

Mechanically, Miriam stepped out and closed the door behind her. From beyond the low wall, Samuel's kindly face smiled and nodded at her, though his eyes, too, were troubled.

"Aye, girl, come you with us. My good wife, seeing you arrive, sent me at once to bid you welcome, for, says she, likely Miriam does not know that Dismas is away, and, surely, the house is not fitted for guests after standing so long empty."

"Where is Dismas?" Miriam's mind and tongue seemed capable of no other expression.

"Belike in Jerusalem, my child. 'Tis true, he has not been in the village for many months, yet he has been seen now and again in the city, and doubtless all is well with him. I marvel that he has not sent you word of these things, though he was ever close-mouthed and not given to talk. But come — in my house there is food and warmth and rest for all, and though it be but humble, yet 'tis gladly proffered." And he led the way to the neighboring house by the crossroads, whither Abigail and Sherah led the stunned and unresisting Miriam.

❋ ❋ ❋

In spite of her weariness Miriam slept little through the long hours before dawn. From her kindly neighbors she had learned that Dismas had abandoned their home in the village almost immediately upon her departure, had sold the vineyard, and taken up residence in the city, and probably a business also, for those of the villagers who had seen him had reported that Dismas must indeed be prospering, for his clothing and manners had been such as a poor man could ill afford. Samuel did not add that the tall blond Zabad had invariably been Dismas' companion, nor that Dismas himself had been surly and almost rude to his former friends and acquaintances so that after a time they neglected to seek him out and avoided him with as wholehearted a dislike as he seemed to entertain for them.

It was, of course, now clear to Miriam how it was that Dismas could have so regularly and generously sent her money during her long stay in Galilee. And though her heart ached at the thought of her father's vineyard being tended by stranger's hands, still she could not judge Dismas too harshly, for it was for his mother's sake he had done it. That this, too, had been in vain only added to her bitterness.

But now she must find Dismas and see how it was with him. That, Zabad had promised to tell — and now, for the first time, her thoughts began to dwell upon Zabad. And as she recalled the coal-black hair that was once so golden, the limping gait where once had been only arrogant swagger, the low voice, tense with something as close to fear as Zabad would ever show, and the face twisted in sudden pain — as these things returned to her in the deep dark before the brightening of the dawn, she felt a fear growing in her heart that all the memory of Samuel's reassuring words could not allay. Zabad was a fugitive; Dismas was in a like case, or worse. She felt suddenly as sure of that as if she herself had seen the Roman guard lay a heavy hand upon his shoulder and lead him away to the frowning towers of the Fortress Antonia. It was only the danger of waking

Sherah and Abigail on the mats beside her that kept her quiet and apparently sleeping, though her hands were clenched till the nails drove into the flesh and she felt cold drops of perspiration on her forehead.

As the first streaks of dawn lightened the little window high up in the wall, Miriam threw back her rug with a sense of relief that she could at last be about the task that lay before her. Cautiously, so as not to awaken her companions, she rose, caught up her cloak, for the spring mornings were chill, and descended to the lower rooms, where she found her hostess already awake and bustling about. She looked at Miriam questioningly.

"I go to my house," said Miriam, her voice faltering a little. "And I — I would be alone. There are certain of Mother's things that I would attend to."

Leah only nodded, for she was ever a silent woman. But her heart went out in compassion to this slight girl with the pale face and the great shadowed eyes that surely had not slept that night.

"Stay not overly long," she said, "for it is not well to be thus alone in sorrow. Within the hour you will find nourishment here, and later we shall go with you to your home and see to that which must be done."

So Miriam stepped out into the chill morning under a sky aglow with the sunrise. But there was little glow or warmth in her heart as she lifted the latch of her neglected home and entered.

Zabad had been watching for her. He closed the door after her and fastened it that it could not be opened from the outside. Why was it not fastened last night? thought Miriam as he motioned her to a seat on the bench.

"Even the wariest among men do occasionally lapse into carelessness," said Zabad, as if reading her thoughts. " 'Twas only my fool's luck that it was you that came last night and that you entered alone."

He leaned against the door and regarded her as she sat, and his eyes had lost none of their boldness.

"You do grow ever lovelier, little Miriam," he said, and, because she had heard the words before in other tones, she winced.

"You were to give me word of Dismas," she said coldly. "Where is he?"

"In Jerusalem."

Miriam bit her lip in exasperation.

"Then doubtless I need but to go there and find him," she said, rising and drawing herself up to her slim height.

But Zabad's broad shoulders were barring the door, and there was a mocking light in his blue eyes.

"Nay, fair maiden, this once you shall not run off like a frightened chick. Sit you there and listen to me."

"I will listen to naught save that which concerns Dismas," retorted Miriam stubbornly.

"You shall hear of Dismas when I so choose to tell you, not before. And I choose now to speak first of myself."

Because there was nothing else to be done, Miriam seated herself again upon the bench, but in spite of her anxiety her head was high and her back very straight.

But for once the words did not come easily to Zabad. He cleared his throat several times, then finally burst out in irritation: "Name of a turtle, must you sit there as forbidding as the gods my father bowed to? I do confess that my robe is torn and soiled and has lost some of its richness, and black hair is doubtless less becoming to me than the original gold. Yet I know of perhaps a dozen maidens who would not sit there as cold as the snows of Hermon when Zabad chose to speak with them."

"I am not accustomed to giving audiences to thieves and fugitives," said Miriam bitingly.

"Yet in a few minutes you will be wishing that your brother, a thief, were a fugitive as well." His voice had a snarl in it, as if glad at last to have found a weapon to wound her.

His words had all the effect he could have desired. Her forebodings of the night before swept around her like a whirlpool, and she clutched at the bench as if to save herself from being engulfed in its depths. Words would not come; she could only look up at Zabad with terror-stricken eyes.

He smiled sardonically. "Truly, I had thought the news would unbend that back and bow that head!"

"I — I believe you not!" gasped Miriam, struggling to her feet. "It is a lie! Dismas. . . ."

"Verily, it is no lie, but as true a word as I have ever spoken. And lest that be no assurance to you, let me ask but a question. Where, think you, came all the money sent to you and your mother in far-off Galilee?"

"Dismas sold the land. . . ."

Zabad laughed. "Is that what they say hereabouts? Nay, but you have not had time sufficient to note whose men they are that work in yonder vineyard or who it is that extorts money from the villagers with his now completed wine press."

"Neariah?" The whisper tore through Miriam's throat.

"Aye, and not alone that ancient wreck of righteousness,

but his son and heir, our friend Rodanim, who with his
father's property has inherited all his sanctimonious cunning
and, indeed, has somewhat improved thereon."

"Never would Dismas have sold the land to Neariah,"
faltered Miriam. Overwhelmingly she realized how her heart
had, unacknowledged even by herself, been placing its last
hope upon Rodanim, who, according to Zabad, had now
acquired her brother's property as ruthlessly as he had once
thrown aside her love.

"Not willingly, of a truth. Nor to Rodanim. But the two
of them have ways and means. . . . In any case, think you
that flea-bitten parcel of dust would market at a price to
provide what Dismas has given you? Nay, Dismas has long
since been in business with me, and were he not **the clumsiest**
fool that ever handled other people's money, all would yet
be well. . . ." He shook back his hair with an impatient
gesture.

"It is no flea-bitten parcel of dust," protested Miriam, her
reeling mind clutching at the one thing she could dispute.
" 'Tis well watered and. . . ."

"Oh, aye, aye — 'tis the veriest piece of paradise on earth
— but all that alters not the fact that it is no longer yours,
that Dismas is in prison, and that you are left desolate, with
no means of livelihood and none to care for you."

With all her strength Miriam fought to bring her mind
into some reasonable order, to bring out of this chaos some
one thing to be done, some key to the puzzle, that, once
found, would draw the other pieces into orderly rows beside
it, whence she could pick them up and lay them neatly into
place. But she could not find it. She only stood there, looking
up at Zabad, too helpless even to speak. But Zabad waited.

"Help me," she said at last. "What shall I do?"

Zabad grinned. It was the question to which he had been looking forward throughout the night. He limped to the bench and drew her unresisting down beside him.

"Look you, Miriam!" His voice was eager. "In ten days' time there leaves from the port of Joppa a fair vessel whose captain I know, and he has promised me safe passage to Alexandria. On my bidding he will take you, too, as my wife. I have money and jewels sufficient that poverty need never affright us. There in Alexandria will be new markets, new opportunities, and in a short time I will build you such a house and give you such luxuries that your heart will rejoice and you will forget the unhappy years that lie behind you."

If Miriam had expected Zabad to lay her puzzle, neatly finished, in her lap, she saw now how mistaken she had been. It was rather as if he had taken her carefully hoarded pieces and scattered them helter-skelter about the floor. But one vile piece she yet held in her hand, and shudderingly she threw it after the others.

"Never would I wed a thief," she said with clear finality.

"Sisters of thieves do rarely make a better match," said Zabad negligently, but there was a glint of anger in his eyes.

And at last, upon the bewilderment and the fear and the terror, came the shame, and Miriam bowed her head upon her hands, while Zabad sat quietly and let her weep. When she could weep no more, he brought her Dismas' wine in a little cup that had been her mother's, and she drank it and set it upon the table with unsteady hands.

"Where is Dismas?" she asked dully.

"In the prison at the Fortress."

"What will become of him?"

Zabad did not answer.

"I will go with you," she said, still in that dull, lifeless voice, "if Dismas, too, accompanies us."

Zabad's satisfied smile changed to a sudden frown.

"Tell me not that it is impossible," she went on, without looking at him. "You have ever been able to accomplish that which honest men could not. For Dismas' life I will give you my own — and for naught else."

Zabad made no reply, and Miriam did not raise her eyes. At last he rose to his feet.

"The thing can be done," he said. "I would not hesitate, were it not for this troublesome leg of mine. But it shall be done. Give me but this day here in your house; see that none disturbs me. This night I shall go to Jerusalem and lay my plans."

"Tonight begins the Sabbath." Miriam raised her eyes in protest.

Zabad looked at her quizzically and broke into a laugh. She flushed hotly, and in spite of her resolution her heart shrank within her at the manner of man she had promised to wed.

"Give me seven days' time," he went on. "Dismas shall be released by then; we shall meet you here by night and make our way at once to Joppa, where we shall be well provided for. Till then, do not fear; all will be well." With an almost courtly air he opened the door for her. She passed through silently, eyes downcast, and heard it close behind her as she gratefully breathed the blessed air of the clear spring morning.

CHAPTER XIII

The Son of David

MIRIAM had little difficulty in dissuading Leah from her neighborly intention of helping set the little cottage to rights. She wanted none to touch her mother's things, she said, unless she herself were by, and she felt too ill to undertake the task that day. Her plea of illness needed no corroboration beyond her pale face and shadowed eyes, but Abigail, seeing the trouble within them, guessed that the illness was rather of spirit than of body. Her quiet voice and cheerful words did as much for Miriam as did the comfortable cushions upon which she reclined and the refreshing drinks which Abigail brought, and in this kind atmosphere the band of terror about her heart relaxed somewhat, and she slept fitfully.

Sherah found more than enough to occupy her in the kitchen with Leah, for preparation must be made for the Sabbath, and the presence of so many unexpected guests brought more work than she could easily do. Yet she would not hear of their seeking shelter elsewhere.

"Nay," she said cheerfully. "It is but neighborliness, and I would prove but a poor friend indeed were I to let you go. I have no mind to let others in the village do better by their neighbors than I. After the Sabbath we will see that Miriam's home is restored to order, and when that is done, then you may go with my blessing."

So it was that, after the longest Sabbath Miriam had ever known, she found herself amid a welter of brooms and brushes and dusting cloths, striving to bring order and cleanliness out of the chaos that had once been her home. She moved as one in a dreadful dream; a dream made the more hideous by the knowledge that any awakening would but add to its horror. That she had little heart for the work was clearly apparent to Abigail and Leah, who kept up a cheerful chatter in which even Sherah joined in an attempt to lighten their young friend's sad heart. Ephraim and Samuel, too, busied themselves with the repairing of such things as had broken down from long neglect. To Miriam it was hollow mockery, this diligent garnishing of a home that would never again be hers. But she dared not let her friends think otherwise. As the morning wore on, she found more and more tasks that would take her out into the sunny courtyard or up upon the roof, away from the determinedly cheerful bustle and chatter within.

And there was much of interest to be seen outdoors, much to keep her thoughts from dwelling on the future. For where the two roads met just on the other side of Samuel's house, the roads were alive with pilgrims from Bethany and Jericho going up to the city for the feast. So it would be all the week, and so it had been for days before, for many could find no lodging within the city and went as far as Bethany, and even beyond, for their night's rest. Yet today the crowd seemed strangely undecided, for some hurried toward the city, as though bearing messages thither, and some loitered by the fork in the road, looking expectantly back down the road to Bethany, speaking to other pilgrims, who, in their turn, slowed their pace and seemed to be waiting.

It was while Miriam was thus watching the crowd, wondering what it was for which they waited but too listless to inquire, that she saw two men approach the door of Samuel's house. She had only time to notice that one of them seemed somehow familiar when she realized that they were not waiting for entrance into the house. They were loosing Samuel's colt which was tied there by the door. Familiar or not, they had no business loosing Samuel's colt, and she ran in quickly to tell Samuel. In a moment the two men became the center of an excited, gesticulating crowd, and Samuel himself was pushing his way toward them, demanding indignantly, "What do ye, loosing the colt?"

Miriam did not hear the answer. But from the steps behind her she heard a sudden gasp from Sherah, and she knew at once why it was that one of the two men had appeared familiar. But Samuel was returning, and on his face was written a wondering excitement.

" 'Tis the Master, the Prophet of Galilee," he cried. "He comes this way to the city, and the pilgrims wait for Him. Others have gone before and have told His friends in the city. Come, let us join the throng and see Him as He passes by!"

Without a moment's hesitation Abigail and Leah dropped their work and followed Samuel to the road. Miriam looked about her, but Sherah had disappeared. Then, because anything seemed to her better than that futile work in that desolate house, she, too, followed.

The crowd was waiting. Simon Peter had spread his robe

over the colt's back and had brought him to Jesus, who was approaching now up the rocky road, accompanied by pilgrims from Bethany. As He mounted, a child threw a flower before Him on the road. Another fell beside it. Pilgrims began tearing down branches from the roadside trees, and even from the gardens which they passed, and strewed them in His way. More flowers and palm branches plaited and twisted formed a rough matting in His way. Some even tore off their cloaks and stretched them along the path, making a colorful momentary carpet as He approached.

From the steps of Samuel's house Miriam watched as the procession approached. Simon Peter appeared dazed, as, indeed, did the whole group of His disciples, who most nearly surrounded Him. Evidently the enthusiasm of the multitude caught them by surprise. Jesus Himself sat silent, unmoved and unastonished. The adulation of the crowd neither pleased nor displeased Him, yet, as He came opposite her, Miriam felt that He saw in the upraised faces about Him something that none else could see, something immeasurably sad, some heavy burden that His heart yearned to lighten. And, again, in spite of herself, her heart went out to Him as to One in whom lay all of trustworthiness and helpfulness. Almost without volition she took her place as the multitudes prepared to move on toward Jerusalem.

"What, then, has this Man done to warrant so royal a welcome?" It was a rustic of the rustics that asked the question, thought Miriam as she turned to see. It seemed incredible that one should know nothing of the Man. Yet he seemed sincere.

"Nay, how is it that you know not?" marveled another. "Have you not heard of His miracles, how He has made the blind to see and the dumb to speak, the deaf to hear and the maimed to walk?" His voice went on, but Miriam hardly heard him. It was true. Jesus was a great Man, a Prophet sent from God, and she, who had closed her heart to Him these many months, was willing to admit, here in this jubilant throng, that she had been wrong. He had wrought great things, and if He had failed with her mother, indeed, it proved only that there were limits to all men's power. He was gracious and kind, and He would have helped if He could. Miriam caught her breath at the sudden rush of joy and relief that swept over her. She suddenly felt that all the help she needed lay in this Man of Galilee, and the shifting of her dependence from Zabad's doubtful shoulders to His seemed already accomplished.

A new sound aroused her. They had moved but a few feet from Samuel's door. But around the bend of the road ahead arose a great shout as the welcoming pilgrims from Jerusalem caught sight of those from Bethany. All movement was halted again till the confusion had abated somewhat, and those from the city turned to lead the jubilant procession. The shouts of the people were resolving themselves into a mighty antiphonal chanting of the ancient Psalms of David. "Hosanna to the Son of David: Blessed is He that cometh in the name of the Lord!" Miriam reached up and caught one of the palm branches the young men were cutting from the trees and passing out among the people. The man behind her had resumed his speech, and, as the crowd still stood waiting for those ahead to begin the triumphant procession, she turned eagerly to hear him.

"Aye, and lately He has even raised one from the dead; Lazarus of Bethany, who lay four days in the grave ere He came to call him back to life. Nay, 'tis a wonder that has stirred all Jerusalem and Judea; and you knew not thereof?"

Miriam felt once more as though she were caught in a whirlwind that threatened to tear her soul from her body.

"This cannot be!" she faltered. "No man has the power to raise from the dead, nay, nor even to stay the hand of death from those that yet live!"

"This Man has!" insisted the man. "Nay, and if you believe me not, go there about the group that most closely surround Him, and there you will find Lazarus himself, he who was once four days dead."

Blindly Miriam turned and pushed her way to the edge of the crowd. More by feeling than by seeing she passed Samuel's house and went on to her own. As the closing verses of the great Hallel echoed against the rocky hillside, she pushed open the silent door and closed it against the joyousness without. Her palm branch fell to the dusty floor as, with a great sob, she ran across the room and threw herself down before the stony figure of Sherah, sitting upon the bench. She buried her head in Sherah's lap, and her sobs drowned out the fading chant of the people, while Sherah's one finger played listlessly with a ringlet of her dark hair.

❖ ❖ ❖

The dungeon in which Dismas sat was not darker than his thoughts, nor were the damp, fetid walls and the tread of the occasional sentry outside the door more depressing. Yet he had in these last days somehow achieved a certain calm that enabled him to think clearly and without the panic that had invested his first weeks here in this dim hole.

He no longer blamed Zabad for his plight. It was his own doing and that of none other. He had even ceased to consider the bitter fact that, had the Procurator, Pilate, not felt, as usual, so uncertain of his position as to feel impelled once more to make an example of one of his hated Jewish subjects, his sentence would undoubtedly have been less severe. All these considerations vanished like the valley mists before the glaring sun of the fact that in a few days he was to face death, and that for death he was totally unprepared.

He felt now even no bitterness that death was to come to him so young. He would not have been prepared had he been allowed to live out his four-score years and ten. Eventually for him death would have meant the same condemnation that faced him now, and in his heart he knew that had he been granted the years of a Methuselah, he would not have used them so that he could have faced his last hours in peace and confidence.

Two things, indeed, he had for which he was grateful: that Rachel was dead and that Miriam was in far-off Galilee, where she would likely not hear of his shame till it was too late for the hopeless agony of trying to aid him. At least, it was not on his conscience that his crimes had caused his mother's early death, though, indeed, he admitted grimly that he had given her little enough cause for rejoicing over her son.

Desperately he tried to recall Rachel's teachings concerning the thing that faced him now. There was Job, for instance, who in spite of all his troubles, was confident that after his death he should see God. But Job was a righteous man, "perfect and upright, one that feared God and eschewed evil." Rachel's teachings had surely never envisioned in her son a soul as black with crime as his had become.

"Though your sins be as scarlet, they shall be as white as

snow." From somewhere in the depths of his memory the words of the old Prophet stirred a new life within him. It was Isaiah who had thus prophesied of the Messiah, of the One who should bear His people's griefs and sorrows, upon whom should be laid the iniquity of all men. Like an answering echo there came to his mind the words of a later Prophet, spoken not so long ago that he could not remember the vigorous condemnation in His voice: "If ye believe not that I am He, ye shall die in your sins."

Dismas had heard little more, for he had been already late for his appointment with Zabad in the outer courts of the Temple. Indeed, at the time he had not cared to listen, for this Man had earned Zabad's undying hatred by His purging of the Temple courts from the merchandise and money changers there under Zabad's management. Yet now those few words came to him clearly, and he realized that this Man who had spoken was laying claim to being the Messiah who should wash His people white as snow. Dismas did not pray, for he felt that he had forfeited all right to communion with the God of his fathers, but with all his heart he wished that he might, just once before he died, have speech with this Prophet of Galilee.

The outer door was opening. Dismas sprang to his feet and peered through the small grating of his own cell door. Other eyes peered through other gratings, trying, as he was, to see what transpired in the narrow passageway, for it was not yet time for their evening meal. It was a break in the monotony, and whether it augured good or ill was a matter of immediate concern to all the prisoners.

It was a shuffling, senile old man whom the guard preceded down the aisle. He indicated Dismas' grating and went on down the passage. The old man was loud in his greetings and lamentations.

"Nay, Dismas, my grandnephew, son of my sister's son, how is it that I find you thus? Here your mother languishes with the fever, and your brothers loll in idleness, nor will your sisters spin and weave, and I — nay, my heart is bad, and my bones are rheumy, and I have a very devil within my vitals. . . ." the old man's querulous voice went on and on till one by one the faces at the neighboring gratings disappeared. The complaints of an old man were more wearisome than solitude, and Dismas might have thought so, too, had not Zabad's blue eyes looked at him so steadily from under the tattered gray cloak. He managed to make some appropriate replies, but so great was his astonishment that it was some time before he realized that Zabad was trying to give him something.

It was a jewel. Almost Zabad threw back his head and laughed at the distaste on Dismas' face.

"I will have none of your thieving," he whispered fiercely and thrust it back into Zabad's hand.

"Be not a fool!" Zabad kept up his loud complaining, whispering his messages when to all indications the old man had to stop for breath. "I have bribed the guard. . . . This night your door will be left open. . . . You have but to walk out. . . . The outer gate the guard will unlock for you when you present him with this jewel."

Slow hope was dawning in Dismas' haggard face.

"Indeed, I — I comprehend not. You — you would free me?" Zabad's warning glance kept his voice down to a whisper. "Nay, I — why do you risk such danger? If you were recognized here. . . ."

"I should likely share your cell and your sentence. . . . But you understand now how 'tis to be done?"

"One thing I understand not." Dismas spoke slowly. "It is not mere friendship that moves you thus to danger. Were there not gain in it for you, you would leave me to rot and die and consider yourself well rid of me. What is it that you wish of me, beyond sharing your crimes and eventually coming again to this same pass?"

"Only that you be your own sweet self and accompany me to Joppa, where the three of us shall take ship to Alexandria."

"The — three of us?"

"Aye."

"Then — you have told Miriam. Is she in Bethphage?"

"Anxiously awaiting your arrival."

"That I may break her heart with further crimes — almost I am persuaded to remain here."

"Nay, and if you are not a very fool of fools! In Alexandria we shall start anew. And think not that I cannot even now substitute hope for certainty and lure Miriam to Joppa and Alexandria without you. Indeed, I marvel that I did not do so at once. 'Twould have been a great deal simpler, though Miriam is not easily deceived."

"Miriam has promised to go with you in return for my freedom. Is it not so?"

"Aye, and if you are fool enough to reject my offer, she shall accompany me nevertheless. Make haste. The time is short, and I have no desire for further foolery."

"I understand you. Give me the jewel."

With lightning strength Dismas seized Zabad's extended arm and bent it back against the iron bars.

"Ho, the guard! The guard!"

The unexpected shout from Dismas and the surprising pain in his arm brought stark panic to Zabad's mind. With an oath and a wrench that left his arm hanging limply by his side he freed himself and ran blindly down the passage — full tilt into four armed guards whom Dismas' shout had aroused. They stopped him there, and wondered that it took so much to beat so aged a man into insensibility and submission.

* * *

Rodanim took his ring from his fingers and laid it on the parchment before him with a gesture of finality. The last document had been signed, and now the matter was settled, irrevocably. All the properties Neariah had had recorded in his son's name, Rodanim had signed back to his father; all save one — the vineyard that had been Dismas', which he himself had bought from Zabad.

Rodanim was well aware what had been his father's motive in turning his property over to his son. Neariah had seen Rodanim grow restless as the months passed in the luxury and loveless righteousness of his father's home. And he had known that there was no surer way to bind his son to him than by making him responsible for his father's welfare. So Rodanim had become not only manager, but outright owner of his father's estates. And Neariah had never before congratulated himself so highly upon his astuteness as when Rodanim had outbid all Zabad's prospects and had bought Dismas' property for himself. Never from his home in the village did he view the rich vines and completed wine press without a sense of satisfaction in his son's achievements.

But it was to be short-lived; for Rodanim was once more preparing to leave him. There was no reason whatever why

Neariah could not manage his own affairs. Indeed, in the
last year he had seemed to recover all his old strength and
vigor. The old man throve on opposition. There was no tonic
more stimulating to his soul than a crusade for Pharisaic
righteousness, and he had it now in full measure. Rodanim
could not repress a rueful half-chuckle as he recalled how
at the last Feast of Tabernacles Neariah had turned on
Nicodemus like a hawk on a lamb. It had been concerning
Jesus of Nazareth, of course. Since the time of his ordination
to the Sanhedrin, Rodanim could not remember that any
other issue had so absorbed its members. Nicodemus' unfortunate remark came on the heels of that lame excuse offered
by the Temple officers when they came back empty-handed
from their commission to seize Jesus at their earliest opportunity. "Never man spake like this Man," they had said. It
had been pointed out to them, clearly and carefully, how
none of the rulers or of the Pharisees were deceived by this
Man, but only the superstitious rabble, cursed by their
ignorance of the Law.

And then Nicodemus threw his surprising little thunder-
clap into their midst. "Does our Law judge any man," he
asked, "before it hear him, and know what he does?"

It was nothing more than any righteous, rigid Sanhedrist
might have said under the circumstances. But it deceived no
one. There was a little pause, a sudden hush as the devastat-
ing knowledge came to each of them that their ranks were
divided, that one among them — and who could tell how
many more? — had fallen under the Deceiver's spell and could
no longer be counted among the faithful.

But it did not take Neariah long to recover. With biting
sarcasm he turned on the man who was once his friend and

said: "Are you also of Galilee? Search, and look; for out of Galilee arises no prophet!"

Nicodemus made no answer. Neariah had placed his point neatly. For this insinuation that Nicodemus was ignorant of the Scriptures, like a simple Galilean, was a point best calculated to prick deeply. Nicodemus was one of the most ardent students of the Scriptures; indeed, he had been known to neglect the traditions themselves in his search for Scriptural truths. Rodanim, watching, had been suddenly glad that he had never confessed how the teachings of Jesus in the Temple had interested him.

The meeting broke up in a confusion of ill humor. Nicodemus stood where he was, and no man took him by the hand or bade him a good evening. Rodanim, because he had come so near to making the same mistake, felt a sudden impulse to speak to him, to ease the stricken loneliness that seemed to envelop him. As he turned abruptly out of line, he collided with another man, the broad-shouldered Joseph of Arimathea, who seemed, too, to have made a sudden swerve toward Nicodemus. But the two men now looked at each other with startled eyes, each apologized profusely as if trying desperately to keep the other from guessing his intent, and presently, arm in arm, they left the Temple chamber together.

One good thing resulted from the rift between Neariah and Nicodemus. Rodanim no longer had to fend off his father's none-too-subtle attempts to interest him in Nicodemus' daughter Ruth. Indeed, Neariah would have forbidden his son even to call at Nicodemus' home if he had dared. For, out of some perverse spirit of independence, Rodanim found himself thereafter more and more often in the home of Nicodemus. And when, one evening, he found the Arimathean there, also, he was not greatly surprised. The three of them talked long and often, and frequently Nicodemus' wife and daughter made a quiet but interested audience. The Prophet of Galilee was their sole topic. That, and the old prophecies; and, as Nicodemus read them and they compared them with this living Man of God, it seemed to Rodanim more and more that here indeed was the Anointed One. Yet He had not been recognized by the leaders of Israel. Those whose business it was to hail the Messiah upon His advent and present Him to the people, rejected this Man of Galilee as a deceiver of the people. The three Sanhedrists in their evening discussions were cool and impersonal. They weighed the evidence objectively. They did not commit themselves.

But now Rodanim had made up his mind independently of his two older companions. He believed in this Man of Galilee. The words that He spoke in the Temple were true and came of God. And he resolved to hesitate no longer. The Sanhedrin were resolved that Jesus must be put to death, and He would need all the friends He had in the next few months. Jesus had been warned of the secret resolve of the Council; Nicodemus had seen to that. Now all that was necessary was to keep Him out of Jerusalem, perhaps in the back country of Galilee, till His following included enough influential men to turn the tide of opinion among the leaders. Rodanim determined to be one of the first of these. A few days only he would wait till, as a last act of filial love, he had eaten the Passover with his father. Then he would leave him to follow whithersoever the Messiah might lead.

CHAPTER XIV

"People Stood Beholding"

MIRIAM found little solace in the once beloved ritual of the Passover Festival. To be sure, she wore her festive dress at the evening Paschal meal, which they shared with the company of Samuel and Leah, and in the morning she attended with them the service in the Temple and mingled there with the throngs of people come for the festive offering of the first day of the Passover week. But as the splendid service unfolded, the conviction grew stronger and more despairing within her that all this was not for her. As the prayers of the people rose with the fragrant cloud of odors from the golden altar of incense in the Holy Place, Miriam could not pray. As the white-robed priest approached through the golden doors of the Sanctuary and took his stand at the top of the steps of the porch; as the threefold benediction fell like the peace of God upon the souls of the worshiping multitude, Miriam's heart shrank within her.

These were God's people, these hushed and silent worshipers; like Abigail and Sherah beside her, they would return to their daily duties refreshed and sustained, with heart and mind dedicated anew to the service of the Living God. Not

so Miriam. For her, life would soon become a horror of shame
and deceit. The only thanks she could offer on this holy day
of thanksgiving was a wretched, semiconscious gratitude
that Rachel had not lived to share it. She had thought much
of Rachel these past days since her unexpected encounter
with the Prophet of Galilee — Rachel, with her gentle smile
that saw only the good and would not acknowledge the evil,
whose life had been near to perfection, who never would
deny her God and her people as Miriam was about to do. It
could not be — it was hideous unreality — dear God, it could
not be! Rachel would have found a way — a better way.
Rachel would have — Neariah!

She almost cried aloud when she saw him. He was in the
court below, almost directly beneath her. The service was
completed, the throngs of people were moving restlessly, and
fearful lest she lose him, Miriam turned abruptly from her
companions and made her way down the broad staircase
with irreverent haste.

As she went, her thoughts ranged themselves very clearly
in her mind. She would not speak to Neariah. She would
only keep him in sight, and, sooner or later, Rodanim would
join him. What a desolate fool she had been, not to go to
Rodanim at once! Why should she have believed Zabad's
lies, even for a moment? Rodanim would have helped her;
she knew it as surely as she remembered the truthfulness of
his gray eyes and the warmth of his smile. But now it was
too late to seek him out at his home in town or village.
"Seven days," Zabad had said on the eve of the Sabbath.
Tonight, or at latest the next night, he would be waiting at
the cottage, waiting for her to redeem her promise. She
must keep Neariah in sight till he led her to Rodanim.

It was not an easy task. Neariah and his companions had no difficulty in pressing their way through the crowds. The faithful gave subservient way to the Pharisees. But for a slender young woman, not daring herself to be seen, it was a task requiring all her attention and slight strength. Nor was it any easier when they reached the city streets, for the crowds seemed to become even denser as they progressed. They were nearing the city gate when Neariah and his friends came to a halt. The way had simply become impassable.

It was not a festive crowd that thus choked the streets. They were for the most part silent and subdued as they watched what seemed to be a procession approaching the gates. Miriam could not see what it was that attracted their attention, nor was she greatly interested. She had to keep Neariah in sight and, at the same time, send darting glances here and there lest Rodanim be near and yet escape her. She could hear the steady tread of feet that betokened the Roman soldiery, and she caught glimpses of a cross bobbing up and down above the heads of the people — nay, three crosses! She shuddered involuntarily. It was a fearful punishment, this Roman mode of crucifixion. She hoped they were not Jews that were thus led to execution.

But evidently they were — at least one of them. For a man behind her spoke in the harsh tongue of Galilee. "Aye, there He is! See — our own Prophet of Nazareth! And how woefully they have mistreated Him! Are there not among us such as could deliver Him?" The words were bold, but the voice was subdued and murmurous, as though fearful of being overheard.

"Nay," his companion's voice was equally hushed. "When the Romans and our own Sanhedrin agree together, what can we poor countrymen do? And, indeed, it may be that He *has* deceived us and done that which is guilty of death, for they are learned men."

It came to Miriam with a dull comprehension that it was Jesus of Nazareth here who was about to be crucified. Had she been less concerned with her own anxieties, the news would have shocked her in its terrible contrast to the memory of her last sight of Him. But Neariah had apparently had enough. For some minutes he and his friends had been talking heatedly, evidently angered by something in the procession. Now, just as a group of women at the gates burst into loud cries and lamentations of sympathy as the condemned men drew near, the Pharisees turned back, retracing their steps, so that Miriam had to turn abruptly aside to avoid them. Even as she did so, she doubted whether Neariah would have recognized her even had he seen her, for his black brows were knit, his eyes were dark with smoldering anger, and his lips thin with a cold determination. Nothing would have turned him from whatever purpose he had in mind just then.

It was not without a certain wonder that Miriam followed the delegation of Pharisees through the teeming city streets to the magnificent palace of Herod. It was here, in this royal abode, that Pilate preferred to stay rather than in the barren fortress of Antonia. Was it possible that Neariah would intercede with the Roman Governor for the life of the condemned Jesus? Or perhaps for one of the others whose crosses she had seen laboriously bobbing above the heads of the crowd in the streets? It was not likely. The Pharisees had little compassion for any man; certainly not for the Man of Galilee, who had so thoroughly and so publicly denounced them before their faces in the Temple.

They waited a long time outside the Praetorium. The Pharisees did not enter, of course, lest they become defiled during the feast days. But Neariah sent in messenger after messenger demanding that Pilate come out to them. As always when something unusual occurred, a crowd began to gather about the group. It was a respectful crowd — for these men were Pharisees — but curious, and Miriam had no difficulty in finding out what was going on.

Pilate's refusal to see Neariah was curt and ill-humored. "I have washed my hands of the affair. Why do you trouble me further?"

Neariah finally presented his grievance through a messenger. They had seen the title which was to be affixed to the Galilean's Cross. It was not accurate. Jesus had been condemned not because He *was* King of the Jews, but because He had *said* He was King of the Jews. It was a small matter, but one of great importance in the impression it might make upon the casual observer.

Pilate's reply was curt and final: "What I have written, I have written."

The Roman messenger made no attempt to disguise his scorn as he closed the gates in the Pharisees' faces. Nor could the people quite conceal their delight at the baffled rage with which Neariah shook his fist at the heavy brown walls that towered above him. He swept the crowd with a baleful glare, then turned abruptly and strode furiously off, followed by his equally irritated associates.

They argued heatedly among themselves as they proceeded down the streets. Then they separated; one stopped at the palace of Caiphas, the high priest. Another hurried off in the direction of the Temple. Neariah and another kept

steadily on to the place where they had met the procession
on the way to execution.

All was quiet there now, though the streets were far from
deserted. Outside the gates the gardens and orchards were
dotted by the white tents of pilgrims who had failed to find
shelter within the city walls. Just off the broad highway rose
the barren knoll of Golgotha, and upon its crest, the three
newly erected crosses with their dreadful burdens stood in
silhouette against a storm-darkening sky.

Miriam hesitated as the two Pharisees began to climb the
hill. Her heart quailed at the thought of viewing more nearly
the scene on the hilltop. But Neariah and Rodanim were
never long separated — all Jerusalem knew that. She would
more readily find him with Neariah than by searching for
him in the town at a time when every home was any man's
home, when Temple services and festal processions kept the
entire population on the move. Doggedly she lifted the hem
of her robe and began the short ascent.

As on the streets, the people here, passers-by on the highway attracted by the scene, were quiet and subdued. Indeed,
it was a heart-rending sight, one that would evoke sympathy
and grief at any time — and this Man had had many friends.
Only the soldiers, drinking huge draughts of the wine with
which they had provided themselves, seemed to find entertainment in this King of the subject Jews, whom they so
despised and hated.

The people made way for the Pharisees. Their presence
here was somewhat unusual. Pharisees did not ordinarily
sully themselves by attending criminal executions. All eyes
were upon them as they made directly for the center Cross.

Here they stopped, surveying the silent Sufferer before

them, while Neariah began slowly nodding his head up and down, a sardonic smile on his thin lips.

"Nay, then," he said in a voice easily heard by all the spectators. "Thou that destroyest the Temple and buildest it in three days, save Thyself! If Thou be the Son of God, come down from the Cross!"

His companion's voice rang out in mocking laughter. "He saved others; Himself He cannot save!"

"If He be the King of Israel, let Him now come down from the Cross, and we will believe Him," shouted a voice from another corner, and Miriam in her watchfulness for Rodanim noted that others of the scribes and elders had climbed the hill and were mingling with the crowd.

The people were not slow to respond. The indifferent roused themselves to follow the lead of their masters; the curious leaped at the prospect of further entertainment; the vindictive heaped scorn upon scorn; and the sorrowful shrank within themselves and offered no protest.

Even he that hung on the further cross turned his groaning maledictions from the soldiers below him to the Man who hung by his side.

"If Thou be Christ, save Thyself and us!"

Something within Miriam sprang to sharp and painful attention at the sound of that voice. She could not identify it, but somehow the whole focus of her existence seemed to have whirled to a point on this pain-racked figure.

But the third man, who hitherto had hung silent and absorbed in his pain, now roused himself and called angrily to his companion.

"Dost not thou fear God, seeing thou art in the same condemnation? And we indeed justly, for we receive the due

reward of our deeds; but this Man has done nothing amiss."
Then he turned to the silent Figure on the central Cross and
said more softly: "Lord, remember me when Thou comest
into Thy kingdom."

And so Miriam knew, and the day turned to whirling blackness about her. But through that concentration of pain and
despair she heard the voice of the Galilean — a voice of
majestic and pitying love — as He spoke to her brother:
"Verily, I say unto thee, Today shalt thou be with Me in
Paradise."

Dismas said no more, but a look of inner contentment,
such as Miriam had never seen in him before, spread over
his pain-racked face.

Miriam did not move. Like a wounded animal she
crouched low there among the spectators and could not
bring her numbed mind to form a coherent thought. The
people about her moved as though in a glassy nightmare. A
group of women — led by a man whom she recognized as
Simon Peter's companion that bright day not long ago when
they had loosed Samuel's colt — approached the center Cross
and fell on their knees in sorrow before it. Miriam stirred,
and the thought crossed her mind that she might join them
and thus bring herself nearer to her brother's cross. But the
voice of the Galilean stopped her. He was commending to
the care of this disciple one of the women — His mother.

Gasping for self-control, Miriam drew back. She could not
go to Dismas. She could not add to his suffering by letting
him see her there, in shame and hopeless agony, alone, without friends. She would wait here till the end, and she would
see where they buried him, for his body would not be allowed
to hang over the Sabbath. Later she would do for him what

she could. Now she could do nothing; it was best to leave him alone.

There were other women standing some distance off, watching. Those who had come to bid farewell to the Galilean now moved away to join the others, while, with tender solicitude, the disciple led His mother down to the highway and into the city.

Motionless, Miriam waited. The world seemed to be growing dark and darker with a nameless terror. Once she caught a glimpse of Neariah. He was looking uneasily at the sky. After all, he was an old man and needed to watch his health. He had no mind to be caught in such a storm as the one now brewing. He began the descent to the highway.

Dully Miriam rose to follow, then checked herself. There was no longer need for Neariah, no need for Rodanim. Only she must sit here and wait. The world grew blacker and blacker, and she could not tell whether her own senses were failing her or whether Nature itself were mourning with her. Long she sat, and once she heard the Galilean cry out above the uneasy jeers of the soldiers. And she saw one run to bring Him a little wine from a sponge on a reed, and she yearned to cry out, that Dismas, too, might receive this small comfort. And again she heard the voice of the Galilean, but could not tell truly whether it was that or the ominous rumblings and mutterings that rose on the wind, culminating suddenly in a shock that stirred the ground where she sat, swayed the crosses before her terrified eyes, and cracked in searing light upon the crest of the distant Temple like the avenging finger of God Himself. And yet she sat and waited.

Presently, as the darkness lifted somewhat and the dust abated, the few remaining watchers on the hill bestirred themselves. Another deputation was arriving with orders from the Governor. They had been expected. The evening of the Sabbath, a high day, was approaching, and the three sufferers would not be allowed to hang there much longer. Not, indeed, that their punishment would be mitigated by a merciful shortening of their sentence. First, by way of compensation, their bones were to be broken. Then the thrust of the spear put an end to what remained of life.

Uncertain as to what was about to happen, Miriam stood up for a clearer view. As the brutal club crushed her brother's legs and his agonized screams tore through the murky air, all self-control left her. Pressing her hands to her eyes, she turned and ran stumbling down the hillside, screaming like the condemned men behind her, clawing at those who in compassion would stop her, crying out in terror and despair, till she finally sank into black and merciful unconsciousness in the arms of one who caught and held her till she gave up the struggle in agonized relief, for the face which bent over hers was the face of Rodanim.

CHAPTER XV

Peace

MIRIAM could have slept if Neariah had gone away. The faces about her were, for the most part, kindly faces. Rachel, with her gentle smile, Sherah, lovely and cool, Abigail, her soft face wrinkled in tender solicitude, and other women whom she had never before seen. She could not always tell whether they were real or dream faces, but whenever Neariah's black brows and forbidding eyes frowned down on her, she knew. He was real. For beside him there sprang up always two other faces: Zabad's, scornful and mocking, and Dismas' twisting in an agony of pain and remorse. And there was always a third Face, pain-racked as the others, but with eyes full of promise and a great love. Miriam longed to turn to Him, to hear from His lips why these things must be, but Dismas was screaming in her ears, and Neariah's laughter was drowning out all sound and sense in a horrible whirl of nothingness that threatened terribly to engulf her. But always a hand was held out to save her, a strong hand which she clutched with all the strength of her fragile being. And she would wake in a cold terror to find Rodanim beside her. He said nothing, but only sat watching her, stroking her

177

hand and smiling reassuringly whenever her eyes opened. So she would close them again in peace, for all the terror was gone then, leaving only a numb pain and a great weariness.

Once, as she woke, she noted that the lamp beside him had grown pale with the light of morning. And again a lovely young girl brought him food and drink. Miriam guessed her to be Nicodemus' daughter, for the girl could not quite hide the pain in her eyes as she watched Rodanim clumsily trying to eat without disturbing the small still hand in his own. But she was too tired to remember why there should be pain in Nicodemus' daughter's eyes at anything Rodanim might do.

Later she noticed her surroundings. It was a small, well-furnished room in which she lay. From an adjoining chamber came the sound of voices; soft voices, subdued and oppressed as with a great sadness. There was a sound as of much coming and going, but none brought cheerful tidings to lift the melancholy of those voices. The curtain in the doorway to the hall was drawn, and she was glad, for it was comforting to sit here thus with Rodanim. As she stirred, he bent over her, and her questioning eyes went from one to the other of his, as if knowing that somewhere within their grey depths lay the only hope life still held for her.

Now she noticed Sherah sitting quietly near by; Sherah, with a strange look of uncertainty on her lovely face. Sherah had always been so sure of herself. Noting that Miriam was awake, she spoke softly to Rodanim, bidding him go and rest while she sat here in his place. Rodanim looked questioningly at Miriam, and she smiled faintly in return, and only later remembered that once she had thought never to smile again.

So Rodanim arose stiffly from his chair, stretched his legs, kissed her hand before he released it, and went out through the curtained doorway.

Sherah sat quietly in his place, and Miriam closed her eyes again. But she did not sleep. There was something she must tell Sherah. It took all the effort of which she was capable to form her tongue into the words she must say — and then the effort was, after all, too great. She sighed, and Sherah looked at her questioningly.

"Sherah!" She was surprised at the weakness of her voice.

"Aye?" Sherah reached for her hand and held it. It was not so large and warm and comforting a hand as Rodanim's, but it was strong and sure.

"He — is dead!"

"I know, dear friend, I know!" Sherah's eyes were misty as she bent over the small figure on the couch.

But Miriam shook her head impatiently. "Nay — I meant not — Dismas." The name threatened to envelop her once more in those nameless depths of pain, but she shook it off and tried once more. "I meant Jesus — the Christ!"

"Aye?" Sherah drew back once more.

"Simon will — come back to you now."

Sherah made no reply, and Miriam was too tired to try again. She dozed off but woke again with a start, glad to find Sherah still by her side. There was yet more she had to say to her.

"How — came you here — Sherah?"

"Mother was there — by the Hill and would not come away. I could not leave her. We knew not you were there, till — till you ran to Rodanim. Then we hastened to your help. Rodanim brought us here. It is the home of John Mark, one of Jesus' followers, and it seems all His friends and disciples have been in and out this Sabbath to mourn with one another. Indeed, and a more anxious lot I have seldom seen, for they fear that the rulers will seek them out next and destroy them, though we have with us three of the rulers themselves: Nicodemus, Joseph of Arimathea, and young Rodanim. Truly, 'tis. . . ."

"Then — Simon is also here?" It took a great deal of effort to interrupt Sherah, but Miriam well knew she was talking only to avoid the question.

Sherah stopped her nervous chatter and fell silent, but Miriam would not be denied an answer.

"Did he not — welcome you? He loves you, Sherah."

"Aye — but Simon has — other troubles. Since his Master died he has not ceased to weep and reproach himself. He was braver than most — for they all scattered like silly sheep when Jesus was taken. But Simon followed after and watched how, in the palace of Caiaphas, He was condemned. But he was recognized there by the servants as a Galilean and accused of being one of His disciples, whereupon Simon denied it; for, indeed, it was no concern of them that asked. 'Twas no more than the rest, too, would have done, yet Simon reproaches himself beyond measure, for it seems the Galilean prophesied before that it should be so. He will neither eat nor sleep, nor can any persuade him — for, indeed, none blame him. Nay, none would know thereof had not Simon himself made it known — and therein again is he more courageous than others would have been. But he will not have it so. I — I cannot see him thus much longer, and — I know not what to do."

It was as though the torrent of words had suddenly shattered the dam of Sherah's calm, and she dropped her head to her hands with a half-stifled sob.

It was Miriam's turn to give comfort, and at her light touch Sherah threw back her head and smiled faintly.

"See, now, I must not trouble you with my slight woes. Nay, and you must rest. Here is drink for you, and a little medicine, that the fever may leave you and you may sleep."

Obediently Miriam drank what Sherah offered, then sank back on the pillows. But she was not finished.

"Sherah?"

"Aye."

"Dismas believed on Him — on the Christ."

Sherah made no reply.

"He promised — that Dismas would be with Him — in Paradise. Think you — could He truly have been — the Messiah?"

Sherah bent low and smoothed back the curls from Miriam's hot face.

"Nay, dear friend," she said at last. "Would I could comfort your heart! But how, then, could He be any greater even than Dismas — or any help to him — He that died the same death?"

But Miriam shook her head. "Nay — He was a greater — than Dismas."

But now weariness overcame her again, and she gratefully closed her eyes.

It was Abigail who sat by her bed when she next awoke. She was busily mending by the light of the lamp, whose glow betokened another evening. Miriam watched the age-gnarled hands weaving the thread to and fro in the flickering light.

"I have dreams," she murmured. "Are you but a dream, Abigail?"

"Nay, that I am not, little friend," Abigail's laugh was

cheering. "And that you may have proof, here is a little broth
that you must drink, lest your strength return not." She laid
down her mending and uncovered a steaming bowl on a
table near by.

"Nay, wait!" Miriam shook her head. "First I would know
— I have such dreams — and sometimes — Mother is here beside me. Tell me, friend Abigail, do I dream — then? Mother
is not — here?"

Tenderly Abigail brushed the curls from Miriam's moist
brow. "Nay, my child, your mother has long since gone to
her eternal rest. Yet if you dream of her, 'tis surely in blessing
that she comes to you!"

"Aye — I knew 'twas but in dreaming — and I am glad. I
would not have her here — now."

"Perchance, then — our Lord did well when he granted
her prayer so many years ago?"

"Aye, He did well." And then, because Abigail's waiting
eyes had lost none of their serene glory, Miriam added: "He
knew, Abigail — and if He had not died — verily, I think I,
too, would have come to believe on Him — as Dismas did."

"He will return, dear child, for His kingdom shall have no
end. Do you believe that, and you, too, shall have a part
therein. It may be many years, or many ages, but He will
return, though we may not see Him again on earth."

Miriam said no more, and presently, because her hand
shook so when she tried to hold the bowl, Abigail held it for
her as she drank deeply of its heartening contents.

❖   ❖   ❖

There was a stir of excitement in the air when Miriam
awoke from the sleep of a dream-troubled night. So heartening was it to wake to the streaming sunshine and the song

of a lark outside the window that almost she wished never to sleep again, never to think or to dream again, only to lie there in the warming sunlight and listen to the melody without.

She was alone, and, even as she wondered what might have lightened the melancholy of the muffled voices she heard in the adjoining room, Abigail entered. She was cheerful as ever, yet in those eyes that had never lost their confident light there appeared, if possible, a yet more glorious hope. She could not keep her good tidings to herself.

"Dear child," she breathed. "It does indeed seem that — our Lord is alive again. He is risen, and some of our women have seen and talked with Him. He is risen, indeed, and all our sorrows are ended. Dear Miriam, now. . . ."

But Miriam caught her hands in her own and noted how, for the first time in her experience, the aged hands were trembling.

"Nay, nay, good Abigail!" Miriam drew her to a seat on the couch. "You do dream, for thus it cannot be!"

"Aye, so say they all! But the tomb is empty, for even Simon and John bear witness thereto. But only to the women did He appear, not to the stiff-necked and hard-headed men who will not believe. Would God I had been with them this early morn!"

"Was it for me you stayed?" questioned Miriam softly. Abigail nodded, and she went on soothingly, for never had she seen Abigail so wrought up. "Indeed, I am doubly sorry, for — you are not one to see visions, and, mayhap, had you been there, these others could not have thought to have seen Him."

Almost pettishly Abigail drew her hands away.

"Nay, you are as stubborn as the rest. With the Christ risen, and the empty tomb before them, they do but cower behind locked doors, saying that the rulers have but stolen His body that they may lay blame on His disciples and likewise persecute them. Nay, and our Master did well that He showed Himself first to the women, for I do believe these stupid and hardhearted men would have cast Him out from among them for very fear — all save John."

"Does John, then, believe this thing?"

"Truly, I know not. Yet since he has seen the empty tomb, he has said nought, but there is a waiting hope in his eyes that was not there before."

"But Simon has seen it, too, you say. Yet does he believe? Simon would be among the first, were it truly so."

"Simon *does* believe." Sherah stood in the doorway, her face troubled. She carefully set the steaming bowl she carried upon the low table before she spoke again, and then it was with an effort. "Simon, too, has seen visions, saying that this dead Galilean has appeared to him and spoken to him."

"Simon — has seen him?" In hushed wonder Abigail rose to her feet. "Nay, I must have speech with him," and she sped from the room.

Sherah said nothing as she worked about the table, but Miriam would know more.

"This — cannot be, Sherah," she said, but it was more of a question than a denial.

Sherah shook her head. "Nay, it cannot be. Yet people have seen visions ere this, and I thank God that such has now come to Simon, for it has roused him from his despair and there is hope within him. But that the Galilean is indeed alive and risen — that cannot be."

Miriam spoke very carefully. "If it were so, Sherah — if this Man who died there — with Dismas — were alive again — then, truly, He must be the Son of God!"

All Sherah's troubled uncertainties flung themselves out in a torrent of angry words. "Nay, would then the Son of the Living God have given Himself to the shame and suffering of the cross? Would He not blast those who laid hands on Him by the very words of His power? Aye! and if this Galilean is indeed alive, where does He keep Himself? Why does He not mingle with those whom He led in His lifetime rather than appear in visions to some few distracted souls whose wits are foolish with grief? Nay, why does He not appear to you, here, or to me? We should soon know whether it were vision or Man that stood before us!"

In the dead silence that followed her outburst Miriam's voice came, gentle and subdued.

"How, then, should He appear to you — or to me — we who in life resisted Him when He would have come to us?"

Sherah made no reply, and Miriam, too, ate her morning meal in silence.

It was a long day for Miriam. With returning strength she realized that she must make plans for the dreary future. To live in the little cottage in Bethphage was now impossible. That she would find a kindly welcome with Abigail and Sherah in Galilee she well knew. Yet now that Simon would undoubtedly return to the home he had left, she could not but feel an intruder in their re-established circle. Perhaps she had best stay in Bethphage after all. But the once-happy memories of Rachel and of Dismas smote her bruised heart with such pain that she cowered under the covers in almost physical fear. She would have wept that she alone of that

luckless family had not been taken — but the tears had all
gone from her.

Perhaps she should stay here in Jerusalem and work as her
mother had done. With a sudden new anxiety she realized
that from henceforth even food and clothing would be de-
pendent upon her own efforts. So there was no further question in the matter. She had no skills in any but the common
household duties. She would find occupation in one of the
homes of the rich in Jerusalem. Nor would she be entirely
friendless, for Bethphage was near by, and she could depend
on any of her mother's friends for needed help. And even in
Jerusalem there was — Rodanim. Rodanim had come to her
when she had most needed him, and he would never fail her.
And yet — there was a little question within her that would
not be subdued. He had not actually come to her; it had been
pure blind accident that had led her frantic rush into his
arms. And though he had sat there through the long night
while she fought her way back to life and sanity, where was
he now? Why had he not so much as come to wish her well
these past two days? As she finally forced herself to put the
long suppressed question into words, she realized that what
she hoped of Rodanim was more than mere friendship in
time of desperate need. Her heart was as unreasonable as
ever, she told herself, for any difficulties that had come between them years ago were by now increased a thousandfold.
Yet when she wanted to analyze those difficulties, to set them
down in convincing order before her mind, Rodanim's face
with the kindly gray eyes and the teasing smile broke all her
looming obstacles into fragments.

"I do not wish to disturb you but. . . ."

Miriam looked up in surprise to see one of her obstacles

CHAPTER XVI

Appointment in Galilee

N EARIAH died that night. By morning all Jerusalem was aware of its great loss. In the synagogs and in the Temple the leaders went about with rent garments and ashes strewn upon their heads. Nor was it all outward show. Already they sorely missed his leadership. When the soldiers guarding the grave of the Galilean came with frightened tales of visions and an empty tomb and were openly bribed to report the body stolen while they slept, there were those who shook their heads, declaring that Neariah in his day would have found a better way. Nor did it seem likely that his son would become fully a worthy successor to his father. Under his father's tutelage he had made a favorable beginning in his work in the Sanhedrin, but now that Neariah's hand had slipped from the reins, Rodanim had already flouted Pharisaic tradition and robbed his father of the respect due his memory by personally quieting the wails and wild flutes of the hired mourners in the funeral procession and by cutting short the oration at the grave which Rabbi ben Zadok had been at such pains to prepare. To tell truly, the good Rabbi *was* becoming somewhat long-winded, and, surely, none who observed

Rodanim's pale face and haggard eyes could doubt for a moment his genuine sorrow. Nevertheless, it was evident to all that Neariah's death had left a gap in the ranks of the Pharisees too big for his son to fill.

This, of course, did not prevent them from fulfilling one of the most binding directions of the scribes — that of comforting the mourners. From sunrise till sunset the courts and apartments of the house of Rodanim echoed to the scurrying feet of servants and the subdued voices of those who came to mingle their tears with those of the household.

It was with a great deal of hesitation that Miriam joined the throng of sorrowing visitors. Indeed, had it not been for Abigail, she would not have gone. But Abigail was surprisingly insistent that in this case everything be done in order and according to tradition, and if there was a scheming little chuckle in the depths of her aged heart, she kept it carefully hid from Miriam.

The chamber of mourning with its torn draperies and its upset chairs and couches was well filled when Miriam and Abigail arrived. In the doorway they met Nicodemus and his daughter. Ruth bowed to them, but said no word, and Miriam guessed that in her heart she had taken final leave of her love for Rodanim.

In spite of her insistence that they were but doing the correct and proper thing, even Abigail was somewhat abashed in this well-dressed and arrogant Pharisaical company. True, they were all here to mourn, but Abigail's bright eyes noted that the rent places in their garments all came carefully short of the rich broideries and fringes that adorned their robes. Nor did their humility extend to their eyes or their bearing as they negligently gave way to these two insignificant women. Miriam, anxious to finish the ordeal, almost pushed her way to the head of the room, where the mourners sat. Rodanim, with a half-absent air, was listening to another Sanhedrist, who claimed his attention, and did not notice them. So Miriam spoke first to Rodanim's aunt who, sitting beside him, looked as frightened as ever.

"May the Lord of consolations comfort you!" Miriam began in the ancient formula. But then she stopped, for, at the sound of her voice, Rodanim turned abruptly, and his somber face lit up with a joy that set her own heart wildly beating. Yet he said no more than he might have said to any in the room: "Blessed be He who comforteth the mourners!" and, as they passed on, he turned to speak to one of his servants.

It was in the little vestibule that this same servant stopped Miriam and Abigail, begging them attend his master in the garden. Wondering and half reluctant, Miriam would have refused, but Abigail wound her aged fingers firmly into the hem of the girl's veil and led the way, so that she must, perforce, follow.

They had waited in the garden but a few minutes before Rodanim and his aunt came out to them. Abigail of a sudden became intensely interested in the herb garden that grew on the opposite side of the court, and Martha, graciously fulfilling her duties as a hostess, promptly led her thither. Miriam, with confused and painfully beating heart, would have followed, but Rodanim, a little smile playing about his lips, drew her reluctant hand through his arm and led her to the marble bench under the pomegranate tree. Once seated, he did not release her, but held her small hand tightly in his own, resisting her halfhearted attempt to draw it away.

"It rejoices me greatly, little Miriam, to see you thus in restored health," he began.

"It — it was not of the body, this illness of mine," replied Miriam faintly, "but of the heart."

"And therefore I do rejoice the more, for healing of the heart is not given to the ordinary physician."

He paused as if waiting for her reply. Miriam hesitated, but the new happiness within her would not be quelled.

"Rodanim," she said earnestly, forgetful of her shyness. "Do you know that the Galilean — the Christ — is arisen?"

Softly he said: "You, too, my beloved!" and the words as he spoke them seemed almost a prayer. "Tell me more. Did you see Him?"

"Nay, I saw Him not, but I heard His voice, and it took the pain from my heart and the sorrow from my soul, and I am well again!"

Rodanim sat staring at the pool at his feet, a thoughtful half-smile on his lips. Miriam leaned forward eagerly.

"Rodanim — I must know — how was it you were there that day — on the Hill?"

Abruptly his eyes swung back to hers, and there was a grimness about them that made her draw back.

"You thought I came to mock, as did — my father?"

Miriam could only nod, miserably, but with the admission came the overwhelming knowledge that she had been wrong.

"Know then that of all men I am most cowardly and unworthy, because though I had come to believe, I did not acknowledge Him — till it was too late!"

In the face of this unexpected self-criticism Miriam sat silent and astonished.

"I came to the Hill," Rodanim continued, more quietly, "with Nicodemus and Joseph of Arimathea, to claim His body, that in death we might do Him the honor we had neglected to give Him in His life."

"And I prevented you," said Miriam softly.

Rodanim shrugged his shoulders. "For Him it was too late. For you — it was my joy and pleasure to do what I could."

"But it is not too late, Rodanim! He is risen, I tell you, and alive, and has appointed His disciples to meet Him in Galilee."

"That He is alive, I believe. I have heard it from others ere this. But — think you — He would have one in His kingdom who sat with His enemies, who would not acknowledge Him when hatred and persecution were His lot, but, now that He is risen in glory and has proved Himself victorious, would come kneeling at His feet like a despicable hypocrite?"

"Think you He would receive one who, in her trouble, refused to accept His blessings?" asked Miriam softly. "I do not know, Rodanim. But I go to Galilee that I may learn."

For a few minutes Rodanim sat silently beside her, head bowed in thought.

"When the days of mourning for my father are over," he said at last, "I, too, will go to Galilee to find Him."

There seemed nothing more to say. At length Miriam stirred restlessly.

"You have guests, Rodanim," she reminded him.

"I have dismissed them," he said shortly. "Surely, it is a son's privilege to mourn in solitude if he so desire it."

There was a faint gleam of the old mischief in his eyes as he spoke, but the lines about his mouth deepened in pain.

Miriam spoke softly. "I truly grieve, Rodanim, that this sorrow has come upon you."

Rodanim shook his head. "He showed me little love or

kindness," he said. "Yet he was — my father. And his last act
was of such blasphemy and revilement that — the thought
of it shrinks my heart within me!"

"Did he not — speak to you, after he was hurt?"

Rodanim shook his head. "He lay in a stupor those three
days. Only once, shortly after Nicodemus had come with the
great news, did he seem to rouse. I told him then, hoping
that he might understand: 'Jesus, the Galilean, is risen from
the dead!' He looked at me in momentary astonishment,
whispered, 'He is risen?' and sank once more into unconsciousness. He spoke no more." He paused and flicked a
fragment of a flower petal from his knee. "I could only pray
then — and hope now — that in those hours that he was with-
drawn from us his heart knew and acknowledged the truth."

They fell silent again. There was no sound but the splash-
ing of the little fish in the pool, and Miriam realized that
Abigail and Martha had retired to the house and left them
there alone. Once more she stirred restlessly, and Rodanim
turned to smile gently down on her.

"Dear Miriam," he said, "here we have talked long, and
yet I have not said all that is in my heart. And I have held
your hand this long while till it must be nigh crushed with
my holding!" So saying, he caressed the hand softly, then
transferred it tenderly, but none the less firmly, to his other
hand, while his free arm encircled her waist and drew her
to him.

"Nay — nay, Rodanim," protested Miriam feebly, frightened at the rush of feeling that overcame her at his touch.
"Nay, you must not!"

"Little Miriam!" his lips moved softly at her ear. "Long
ago I would have had you share with me what little was

mine. Now I have much, but it is but ashes upon my tongue if you do not accept it as yours. Sweet Miriam, do not draw away! See, there are but thirty days of mourning here yet prescribed, then I would have you come to me, as my wife and mistress of my household. . . . Nay, nay, sweet child, why do you weep?" Aghast, Rodanim held her from him and stared at her in such consternation that Miriam almost felt a laugh rising behind her tears.

"It — it cannot be, Rodanim." She shook her head. "You are kind, indeed, and do me great honor — but it cannot be."

"Why, then?" he demanded. "Miriam, surely, you have not learned to love — some lout of a Galilean fisherman!"

"Nay, nay, dear Rodanim!" she smiled at his dismay. "Nay, it is not that. It is — this, Rodanim," she straightened herself, and there was no mirth in her eyes as she forced them to meet his. "I would not have it said among your great and noble friends — that Rodanim's wife — and the mother of his children — was sister to a man who lies in a criminal's grave!"

She rose abruptly then, for she had said the final word, but Rodanim caught her sleeve.

"He will not lie there long," he said gently. "I have already made application that his body be given over to me, that I may lay it in an honored grave."

She paused a moment, then turned to him again.

"For that I thank you," she said simply. "You are overgood to a common country maiden." She would have gone then, but he still held her sleeve, and she could not, with dignity, tear it from his grasp.

"Abigail is awaiting me," she said, with a touch of annoyance in her voice, for now that all was said she would go quickly, before the ache in her heart became unbearable.

Rodanim, his lips twitching, watched her in silence, then laughed with a joyousness he had not felt these many years. Half perplexed and half offended, Miriam drew herself up to her full height, her brows contracted in a swift frown, and, dignified or not, she snatched her sleeve from his fingers and turned down the path. But he was beside her in a moment and once more caught her close.

"My beloved!" He held her till she lay still in his embrace, then kissed her unresisting fingers. "Know, then, what my friends — aye, and my children — will think of their mother and Rodanim's wife." All laughter and teasing was gone from his voice as he went on. "They will be proud to speak of her as the sister of the one — the *only* one — who in that dark hour on the Hill still knew and recognized the Man on the Cross beside him, as the Messiah, the Son of the Living God!"

✿　✿　✿

"He has appointed us to meet Him in Galilee."— It was good to leave the bloodstained, tumultuous city, good to leave the anguished memories and the pain-racked Hill for a fresher, freer air, for the green of Galilee and the blue of the northern sea. As the little band passed through city and town and village their number grew, for everywhere they spoke of the wonders that had come to pass — not loudly, but friend to friend and believer to believer. There were no glad hosannas and tumultuous shouting as they made their way ever northward, but in their hearts was a shining hope that found its highest fulfillment when finally, in the Galilean mountains, they knelt at His feet in hushed adoration and listened to His words. The Christ was risen indeed, and from henceforth all that saw and heard were to spread His message of sin forgiven and punishment atoned to the uttermost parts of the earth. And Sherah — Sherah, too, bowed her head in acknowledgment that this Man had a greater claim than she, and she laid no more obstacles before the feet of him who was to be so powerful a rock in the building of Christ's kingdom.

It was after the appearance of the Christ before the assembled throng of five hundred, while the spirit of His presence still seemed to linger upon them, that Miriam heard a low voice speak her name, and felt a familiar hand take her own in its clasp. With a thrill of joy she turned to Rodanim.

"Once I heard of His saying, 'Let the dead bury their dead'," he explained. "I knew not then what was the meaning of His words, but I know now and have come to follow Him."

Miriam only nodded and smiled, but her heart was full of a great peace.

It was not many days later that, early one morning, Miriam and Sherah picked their way over the pebbly beach down to the sea. Simon had gone a fishing that night, and they were come to see what fortune he and his companions had had. It did not surprise them greatly to find Rodanim there before them, for it seemed he was ever present where Miriam was to be found. Moreover, he, too, had heard of Simon's fishing expedition and had come to see the result.

"For," he said, as they settled themselves on Miriam's favorite rocks under the oleanders, "I do believe that the Lord is more likely to make His appearance again where His disciples are; and where Simon Peter is, there the rest are not far off."

"But, I fear, not for long," Sherah's quiet voice broke in.

Miriam looked up quickly, but there was neither triumph nor joy in Sherah's face.

"What — do you mean?"

"He has spoken much to me of this matter. In his heart, he says, he will ever venerate and love the Christ above all that heaven or earth could offer him, but — he feels himself no longer worthy to be one of the chosen Twelve. Therefore, as you see, he has once more gone a fishing, as he did in the years before the Lord was known to him."

Miriam sat in stunned silence, but Rodanim sensed that the story was not finished.

"What did you say?" he asked gently.

"I — tried to dissuade him" — Sherah's voice was unsteady — "for I feel that my former hardness of heart may have had somewhat to do with his decision. But now that I know this Jesus to be the Anointed One of God, I do bitterly regret my willful blindness and would do all in my power humbly to help Simon serve his Master. But now Simon will return to his old life — and therein, I, too, am punished, that Simon may not serve where his heart is."

There seemed very little that could be said. Miriam laid her hand on Sherah's and said, "Mayhap the Lord will not let him go, dear friend."

Sherah clasped the kindly hand in gratitude, but her misty eyes were turned toward the sea, where Peter's ship was coming into sight. Silently they watched as it came near the land, and the voices of the fishermen came to their ears with the clarity of morning. "They have caught little or nothing," said Sherah, "or Simon would ere now have shouted to us of his success."

Gradually all three became aware of another Watcher upon the shore. He walked to the water's edge and called to those in the boat.

"Children, have you any meat?"

At the sound of that voice, Miriam's body stiffened, and she clutched Rodanim's arm. Instantly alert, he, too, watched that Figure upon the sand.

"Cast the net on the right side of the ship," He directed them, "and you shall find."

Almost mechanically the men drew forth their net and cast it once more into the sea. All but one; John, sitting in the prow of the vessel, did not move. Now, as the shouts of the men pulling on their well-filled net rang across the water, he grasped Simon Peter's arm and leaned over to speak to him. Abruptly Peter dropped the corner of the net he had been clutching, snatched up his coat, wrapped it about himself, and plunged into the water.

"Nay, again?" There was love and tender laughter in Sherah's voice as they watched the dripping figure emerge from the lake and kneel at the feet of Him who stood there. But the boat with its dragging net was not far behind. Evidently at the Lord's command, Simon Peter ran to meet them and dragged the heavy net upon the shore. Then, silently and in reverence, they drew near to their Lord, who, as He had so often done in days of greater familiarity, gave them to eat of the bread and fish broiled upon a small fire of coals at His feet.

The three watchers on the rocks, knowing in their hearts that all were welcome before the Lord, joined the hushed circle. As they partook of the miraculous food, Jesus drew Simon Peter apart and spoke to him alone. Sherah had eyes for none but the two who talked together so earnestly, and Miriam and Rodanim, unashamedly clasping hands, watched, too. There was another who hovered near — John, who seemed desperately anxious to hear all that might fall from his Master's lips, yet hesitated to intrude in what was obviously a private conversation. Watching, they saw Peter's head bowed in utter dejection, then lifted at last in passionate expostulation. And, as the Lord spoke on, his powerful figure straightened, and his shoulders squared as if taking upon himself a joyous burden not to be laid down while his life should last. As renewed vigor and determination seemed to flow through his great body, Sherah spoke softly to her companions.

"Simon has received that for which his heart has yearned. And I — that I may make amends for my sinful blindness — will go with him, as God gives me strength, to the ends of the earth, that we two together may serve our Lord in gladness all the days of our life!"

Jesus had turned to go. As Peter rose to follow, he noticed the hovering figure of John near by and, with a sudden rush of sympathy, drew the Lord's attention to him. But Jesus, after a few words, continued on His course. Yet the incident had given Sherah time to reach her husband's side. Peter's rugged face lit up in fulfillment of his last desire as, with clasped hands, they followed the Master down the sunlit, pebbly beach.

Acting Out

"Have you flipped?" Kathy whispered to her.

"Bug off, cuzzy wuzzy," Deena told her. "I thought you'd like the new me."

That made Kathy stop and think. She was always complaining that Deena should loosen up. But now that she was acting differently, Kathy didn't like it. It was too bizarre, and it definitely was not Deena—everything she did looked kind of . . . off kilter.

"Is this like in that movie *Invasion of the Body Snatchers*, where alien life forms take over people's bodies and the people start acting really weird?" she asked.

"Do you think it's weird to act just like you do?" Deena asked her. She'd picked up Kathy's tape player from the front hall table and was now shaking to the beat of the ThunderMongers on the headphones.

Cranberry Cousins
LOVE LETTERS

BY CHRISTIE WELLS

A Troll Book

Acknowledgments

Many thanks to Suzanne Weyn for all of her help on bringing Kathy and Deena to life and for her creative contributions to this book.

Library of Congress Cataloging-in-Publication Data

Wells, Christie.
    Love letters / by Christie Wells.
       p.   cm.—(The Cranberry cousins; #5)
     Summary: After a young journalist unknowingly causes friction between Deena and Kathy, he again unknowingly unites them in a common cause as the cousins try to sabotage a suspected relationship between him and Kathy's mother.
    ISBN 0-8167-1504-1 (lib. bdg.)   ISBN 0-8167-1505-X (pbk.)
    [1. Cousins—Fiction.]   I. Title. II. Series: Wells, Christie. Cranberry cousins; #5.
PZ7.W4635Lo 1989
[Fic]—dc19   88-16938

A TROLL BOOK, published by Troll Associates
Mahwah, NJ 07430

Chapter 1

Lydia Scott thumbed through the Cranberry Inn's reservation book. "I have some good news and some bad news," she told her daughter, Deena.

Deena stumbled backward slightly, unbalanced by the tall stack of fresh dryer-warm towels she was about to take upstairs to the guests at the inn. "Let's have the good news first," Deena requested, blowing a strand of long blond hair away from her blue eyes.

"The good news is that we're booked solid again this weekend. The bad news is that we're booked . . . "

" . . . solid again this weekend," Deena finished the sentence. She understood her mother's ambivalent feelings completely. It was great that the inn was finally doing business, but no one had imagined they would have so many guests at once. Deena felt as if she'd run up and down the stairs a million times in one week alone!

Still, it was a dream come true. When her mother and her aunt Nancy had decided to reopen the old inn they'd inherited, they weren't sure they could make it a success-

1

ful business. They had no real experience in running an inn—but Nancy had been a waitress and Lydia knew accounting, so they figured they at least had a fighting chance.

Deena and her mother had moved to Cranford from Boston, where they'd been living ever since her mother and father divorced. Widowed Aunt Nancy and Deena's cousins Kathy and Johnny drove all the way in from San Francisco with all their earthly belongings in a beat-up red van. They'd officially opened their doors last Thanksgiving, but up until now they hadn't exactly been overwhelmed with business.

Then two things happened. The first was that they'd been visited by a cranky old gentleman who reserved a room for the weekend. To their surprise, he turned out to be the author of a book called *A Guide to New England Weekends*.

He included the Cranberry Inn in his review of good places to stay, saying: "Though its renovations are not complete, and the staff is somewhat discombobulated at times, I recommend this inn highly for the warmth with which it greets its guests, making all who arrive feel as if they were a welcome family member returning home."

The second thing to happen was that summer came at last, after the long New England winter. The summer brought droves of tourists—all of whom seemed to have read *A Guide to New England Weekends*. This was all wonderful, except that Nancy, Lydia, and the girls quickly discovered they weren't prepared for the demands of so many visitors.

"I wish all these people didn't expect to be treated like

a welcome member of my family," Kathy grumbled as she clomped down the stairs balancing a clanking tray of dirty dishes. "Nobody in our family has breakfast delivered to their room upon request," she added, stopping to rearrange the dishes on the wobbly tray.

"Shhhh!" Deena hushed her cousin. "Someone will hear you."

"Oh, excuse me, Miss Congeniality, but some of our beloved family members upstairs are in a royal snit because there are no clean towels. You'd better move your buns up there pronto before a riot breaks out."

Deena rolled her blue eyes at her cousin. "I'd be glad to," she said. "I do try to think of our customers as guests in our home."

Deena wished Kathy had a little more team spirit. After all, they were both fifteen. That was certainly old enough for them to pitch in and try to make the inn a success.

It wasn't that Kathy didn't work hard; she did. But Deena wished she would do it with a bit more gusto, really get into the challenge, the way Deena did. That wasn't Kathy's style though. It seemed to Deena that Kathy only got enthused about two things—rock music and her boyfriend, Roy. Deena just wanted Kathy to realize that there was more to life than zipping around town on Roy's motorcycle while listening to the latest song by Nuclear Waste on her headphones.

And then there was Kathy's appearance—the ton of black eyeliner, the too-tight jeans, the long brown hair, chopped short on one side and in layers on the other, the long dangling earrings. Deena didn't think that exactly fit

3

the image of wholesome New England hospitality that their guests expected. But whenever Deena suggested a change, Kathy told her to bug off.

"I'd like to take a shower before noon," an irate guest bellowed from the top of the stairs. "And I need a towel."

"Hark. I hear one of our delightful family members calling right now," Kathy said with mock sweetness.

Deena straightened her posture and took on an expression of endless patience and kindness. "I, for one, am happy to serve our guests."

"You're delivering towels, Deena, you're not Mother Teresa ministering to the poor," Kathy snapped.

"Oh, you don't understand, just let me through," Deena huffed, shifting her grasp on the towels and heading toward Kathy on the narrow stairs.

"Hold on, would you, I—" Kathy shouted as Deena tried to squeeze by. It was too late. Deena had jostled Kathy's tray, sending it crashing down the stairs. Cups and plates rolled and smashed at their feet, spraying the wall and stairs with jam and leftover coffee and milk.

"I asked you to get out of my way," Deena said defensively.

Kathy looked at her cousin with murder in her eyes. "Give me a towel to clean this mess up," she growled.

"These towels are for the guests," Deena said, turning to go.

"Well, I need one!" Kathy shouted, trying to grab the top towel from the stack. Deena stepped backward to avoid Kathy's reach, but she stumbled, sending the entire stack of towels flying onto the steps.

"Now look what you've done!" cried Deena, scram-

bling down the steps to retrieve the towels. "All these towels will have to be rewashed."

"What *I* did!" yelled Kathy. "What *I* did!"

"Hush, girls," Deena's mother scolded, hurrying to the front hall closet for a dustpan and broom.

"Towels!" cried the man from upstairs. "I'd like a towel sometime today." Deena looked at her mother with panicked eyes. Lydia quickly looked through the towels until she found two that weren't in terrible shape.

She rubbed the coffee stains off the corners with her fingers and folded them quickly. "Take these to him," she told Deena, handing her the two towels.

"Mother," Deena whispered, horrified, "these have coffee stains on them."

Lydia Scott sighed. "He won't notice, and if he does, he'll think it's rustic old inn charm." Deena looked doubtful but carried the towels up to the complaining man.

Kathy took the dustpan from her aunt and continued to sweep up the broken dishes. "Sorry, Aunt Lydia," she apologized.

"I wish you girls would call a truce," Lydia said wearily, "at least until your mother gets back next week. We're short staffed even when she's here. With her gone I really need your help. I know you and Deena don't always see eye to eye, but please try a little harder."

"O.K., I'll try," Kathy promised, wondering if Aunt Lydia understood the magnitude of the sacrifice she was asking.

"Thank you," Lydia said, returning to her reservation book. "I'm going to ask Deena to do the same."

Kathy used one of the dirty towels to soak up a puddle of coffee on the stairway carpet. She thought about her mother in New York. She's probably having a great time, Kathy thought as she restacked the tray with the few broken dishes.

She was really proud of her mother, who had finally gotten her book of poetry published. *Out at the Inn* was a tremendous success. Now Nancy was in New York seeing her publisher. Reporters for the local paper had been calling the inn all week, trying to set up interviews with her when she returned. Nancy might not have been famous by New York or Hollywood standards, but locally she was big news.

Nancy Manelli had always dreamed of being a successful writer. She'd had a few short stories published and even had a play produced in San Francisco a long time ago—but they hadn't brought her any fame, and they certainly hadn't paid the bills.

That was one of the reasons why she'd brought the family to Cranford. She was sick of waitressing nights and hoped the inn would give her a less grueling way to make a living while she pursued her writing. The other reason was that she said San Francisco held too many memories of Kathy's dead father.

Now everything Nancy had hoped for was finally happening. Everyone at the inn was thrilled for her, but just a little sorry for themselves. Being one person short this last week had been a hardship, and Nancy wasn't due back from New York for at least one week more.

Vrum! Vrummmmmmmmmmmmmmmmmmmmmm. Kathy heard the sound of Roy's motorcycle as he pulled into the front driveway. She put the tray on a table in the front hall and ran out to meet him.

"Hey," he greeted her, pulling off his helmet as he climbed the wooden steps of the front porch.

"Hey," she said cheerily. "Am I ever glad to see you. Between the guests and Deena I'm about to tear my hair out."

Roy plopped down on the cushioned white wicker chair on the porch and ran his hand through his short, spiky brown hair. "Any news from your mom?" he asked.

"She called the other day. Everyone's making a big fuss over her. She sounded happy but tired."

"Yeah, I still can't believe she wrote a book. I never actually thought that people wrote them, you know?"

"Well, where did you think they came from?"

"I don't know," he admitted. "I never really thought about it." A funny idea lit up his face with a smile Kathy loved. "Maybe I thought the stork brought books and left 'em in a cabbage patch for librarians to go pick up in the morning."

"That's actually a very imaginative and creative concept, Roy," said Deena, coming out onto the porch carrying a large cardboard box.

"Think so?" Roy asked. "Hey, maybe I'm a poet and I don't know it."

"But your feet show it—they're Longfellows," Deena added.

"What?" Roy asked, scrunching up his brow.

"Longfellows, get it? There's a poet named Longfellow and large feet could also be called Longfellows."

7

Roy looked down at his feet seriously. "Do you think they're big? I'm a size eleven, but my brother is a twelve. I have a cousin who wears a size thirteen, and my father, now there's a guy with big feet, but me, I don't—"

"That's how the rhyme goes," Deena interrupted in an exasperated tone. "I didn't mean you personally had big feet, Roy."

"Then why did you say it?" Roy asked, confused. "I don't get it."

"Never mind, she's always saying weird stuff," Kathy cut in. "What's in the box?"

Deena's face radiated enthusiasm. "This," she said, reaching into the box, "is my entry in the Cranford Library's Young People's Art Show. It's due this Monday. I hope I'll have it finished in time."

"I can't believe it," said Kathy dryly. "We're finally getting to see the top-secret project she's been working on out in the garage."

Deena pulled out a strange-looking papier-mâché statue about two feet high. It was brightly painted in orange, yellow, and red. "What do you think?" she asked.

"What is it?" asked Kathy, narrowing her eyes. "Does it have seven eyes, or do I need glasses all of a sudden?"

"It's my statement about brotherhood, and sisterhood, of course. The seven eyes represent the eyes of all mankind. The paint is still tacky so I want to let it dry out here on the porch."

"Hey, it's got seven arms, too," Roy noticed. "I'd like to have this guy on my side during a volleyball game."

"You're missing the point," Deena insisted. "This represents life and humanity."

8

"Then how come it has a big orange nose?" Kathy wanted to know.

"That's just the kind of nose it seemed to me all of humanity would have," Deena answered, starting to get annoyed. "I should have known you couldn't appreciate art."

"I like art," Kathy snapped, suddenly very irritated with her cousin. "But that thing isn't art."

"I'd like to see you do better," Deena challenged. "It's easy to criticize. You're the one who's always doodling. Why don't you enter something in the contest? The first prize is fifty dollars."

"I'm not interested," Kathy answered adamantly.

"O.K., O.K.," said Deena. "I thought you liked to draw."

"I'm not interested, that's all," Kathy repeated.

At that moment Kathy's younger brother, Johnny, came running around the side of the inn and bounded up the stairs. "Wow, neat!" he cried when he caught sight of the statue in Deena's hands.

Deena beamed at him. "Out of the mouths of small children come the truest responses," she said happily to Roy and Kathy.

Johnny looked at the statue, leaning his head first to one side and then to the other. "Can I have it?" he asked Deena.

"I'm flattered, Johnny," Deena replied sweetly, "but this is my entry into an art contest."

"Too bad. I wanted to set it up in the middle of my action figures and pretend it was a monster from space that they had to destroy."

Deena sighed. "I give up," she muttered as she carefully positioned her statue in a sunny spot on the porch.

"Here comes the landscaper," Johnny said, pointing to a beat-up blue pickup truck making its way up the bumpy road toward the inn.

"He's got someone with him," Kathy added. She stood on the porch steps and shielded her eyes against the sun. "It's Mom!"

Kathy ran to meet the truck, followed closely by Johnny, Roy, and Deena. Nancy Manelli smiled at them as she climbed down from the front seat of the truck. Her long brown hair was tied back in a braid, but wisps of hair fell loosely around her face. She reached out to embrace Kathy and Johnny, who almost knocked her over with their hugs.

"You weren't supposed to get here until next week. What happened?" asked Deena.

"Oh, I just couldn't take any more. It was exciting, but I got tired of all the phonies," she explained happily. "Besides, I was lonely for you guys, so I got on a train at six this morning and here I am."

She turned to the thin, deeply lined man dressed in overalls who sat behind the wheel of the truck. "Thanks for the lift, Abe. I appreciate it. You can go inside and talk to Lydia about the money we owe you."

"Sure thing," he answered pleasantly. "Glad I happened to be down at the station."

Roy pulled Nancy's suitcase out of the back of the truck. "What's it like in New York?" he asked.

"Oh, it's like a big whirling machine that never stops—it's very different from Cranford, you can bet on that," she said as she walked up toward the inn, her arms

10

around her two children. "Let me see how Lydia is doing, and then I'll tell you all about it."

Nancy stood in front of the inn and took a deep breath. "Boy, it smells good here," she said. "I'm so glad to be back where there's peace and quiet."

Chapter 2

"Nancy!" Lydia ran out of the kitchen, wiping her hands on the long white apron she wore over her slacks and blouse. "Welcome home." Nancy hurried toward her sister and hugged her warmly.

Deena stood in the doorway and watched. It seemed to Deena that Aunt Nancy and her mother were as different as two people could be. Her mother was blond and fashionable. She was always neatly dressed and had an air of calmness about her. Deena could never imagine her mother doing anything that wasn't reasonable and well thought out.

Aunt Nancy was the exact opposite. Tall and dark, she seemed to move in three directions at once. She had a casual style of dressing that Deena figured was the result of having lived in California and having been a hippie way back in the sixties.

Deena sighed, seeing her mother and Aunt Nancy walk hand in hand toward the front sitting room as they chatted happily. Different as they were, the two women were so affectionate with each other.

Deena had always wished for a sister. With a pang of sentimentality she looked over at Kathy, who sat perched on one of the front hall tables, swinging her legs. Would she and Kathy ever have that sisterly feeling toward each other? Deena sighed. Probably not in this lifetime.

"Come, come," Nancy beckoned everyone into the sitting room. "I brought souvenirs for everyone. Nothing much, just a little something."

She sat on the big couch and opened her suitcase at her feet. "For Lydia, a souvenir of my trip to Bloomingdale's."

"Dusk Song, my favorite perfume!" cried Lydia. "I've looked everywhere, and they just don't sell it around here. Thank you, Nancy."

"For Johnny," she said, pulling out a cellophane bag with something green in it.

Johnny read the package. "A five-foot blow-up dinosaur!" he exclaimed. "Thanks, Mom, it's the best! I won't need your art project anymore, Deena."

"Two sweat shirts, one for Deena and one for Kathy." She reached into her suitcase and pulled out two folded sweat shirts. She handed the blue one to Deena and the yellow one to Kathy.

Deena unfolded hers and looked at it. "Thanks," she said glumly.

"Yeah, thanks," Kathy echoed, with an equal lack of enthusiasm.

Nancy looked up at them. "I'm sorry, girls, I thought you'd like ... wait a minute." Her eyes lit up with under-

13

standing, and she took the sweat shirts back from each girl. "The blue one is for Kathy and the yellow one is for Deena. I got it mixed up."

"Thank you!" Deena cried, throwing her arms around her aunt. The yellow sweat shirt had the words "New York City Ballet" written in script across the front and a silkscreen print of ballet toe shoes in a line at the bottom.

"Great!" shouted Kathy. Her sweat shirt sported the words "The ThunderMongers—Live at the Ritz." "Did you see them?" Kathy asked. "Did you really go to the Ritz?"

"I saw them one night with some friends, and I also saw *Swan Lake* at Lincoln Center."

"You're weird, Mom," said Kathy. "How can you like both things?"

Nancy looked at Lydia and laughed. "Just weird, I guess."

"I thought Nuclear Waste was your favorite group," Johnny said to Kathy.

Kathy looked thoughtful. "Nuclear Waste is great, but I think the ThunderMongers have more power. I'd say I'm more into the ThunderMongers these days."

"I'm not finished," Nancy said. "I have something for Roy."

"You didn't have to, Mrs. Manelli," he mumbled, looking embarrassed.

"It's to say thanks for repairing the porch last week," Nancy said. "It's just a token." She handed him a khaki green vest. He turned it over and read the words stitched into the back. " 'Born to Ride.' All right! Thanks, Mrs. M."

14

"That was really sweet, Mom," said Kathy, glad that her mother had come to appreciate what a nice guy Roy really was, despite his scruffy exterior.

"Now I have a surprise for you," Lydia said, smiling at Nancy. "A number of them, actually."

"What?" Nancy asked, settling back on the couch and starting to look worn-out from her long trip.

"Well, apparently news of your success has gotten out around here, and in the last few days I've had at least eight phone calls from different papers and magazines wanting to come to the inn and interview you."

"They want to interview me? That's too far-out to be real," said Nancy. "I feel like I've stepped into somebody else's life."

"You're a local celebrity, Nancy," Lydia said. "Enjoy it. I told them you wouldn't return until next week, but they keep calling anyway. Now that you're home, I'll just tell them to come on down."

"Wait a minute now," Nancy said, sitting forward and pressing her hands to her chin pensively. "I'm not sure that I want my life made so public."

"Mom!"

"Aunt Nancy!"

For once the cousins were in total agreement. "You have to do this, Mom," Kathy urged. "You're going to be famous."

"I suppose it's flattering, but I like my privacy."

"Be practical," Lydia urged. "You get a royalty check based on how many copies of *Out at the Inn* they sell, and interviews are like free advertising for your book. Once people read about you, they'll be curious to read your book."

15

Nancy laughed good-naturedly. "I can always count on you to point out the practical thing to do," she said.

Lydia smiled back at her. "That's right, everyone always says I'm the sensible one, so listen to some more sensible advice. These interviews will also be free advertising for the inn. Between the write-up in *New England Weekends*, and your fame, we may be able to keep the inn jumping the way it is now all through the winter months."

"You have to do it," Deena pressed. "This is your opportunity to express your feelings to the world. Isn't that why you became a writer?"

"I'll do it. I'll do it," said Nancy, laughing. "I know when I'm outnumbered."

The news brought a round of applause. "I hear the phone. I'll bet it's one of the reporters calling back right now," said Lydia happily as she ran for the phone.

"I'm dying for a shower," said Nancy, lifting herself wearily up off the couch. "It's hot already and traveling always makes me feel so grungy."

"You'll have to wait a few minutes," said Deena, suddenly jumping to her feet. "I have a bunch of towels still in the dryer. I'll go check on them."

Johnny followed his mother upstairs while Deena went to attend to the towels. Kathy and Roy sat alone in the front room.

"Hey, I almost forgot the reason I came over here," Roy said. "I came to tell you that I won't be around for a week or so."

"How come?"

"My great-uncle Malcolm down in Florida died the

16

other day. I have to go down to his funeral with the family."

"I'm sorry," Kathy said, putting her hand over his sympathetically.

"Yeah, thanks. He was ninety-seven, so I guess he had a full life. My father has to do some stuff about Uncle Malcolm's estate and all, so he's not really sure how long we'll have to stay there."

"I went to Florida when I was small," Kathy said. "It's pretty nice. You'll like it. It'll be a total drag around here without you, though."

Roy's face lit up. "I'm not looking forward to going, but I'm glad you said you'll miss me."

Kathy pushed him playfully. "Of course I'll miss you. I'm going to miss you like crazy."

"Me, too," said Roy, taking Kathy into his arms. She looked up at him and smiled. Then they kissed, holding on to each other tightly.

"Excuse me!" It was Deena. "I just came back for my sweat shirt. Sorry."

Roy jumped back, red-faced. "No problem, Deena. I was just going, anyway."

Kathy glared at her cousin, more than half suspecting Deena of intentionally interrupting the kiss in the name of proper behavior. "Don't go, Roy," Kathy said. "Have some lunch, at least."

"No, I really have to pack and all. We're leaving tonight."

Kathy walked Roy to his bike. She was suddenly struck with a terrible feeling of loneliness as she watched him strap on his helmet and pull on his leather gloves.

"Write to me, O.K.?" she said, throwing her arms around him.

He held her around the waist and kissed her quickly, bumping her forehead with his helmet. "I'll miss you," he said.

"See you in a week or so." Kathy gave Roy's hand one last squeeze and then watched as he rode off down the road away from the inn.

Kathy trudged back onto the porch, missing Roy already. She was about to walk into the inn when she saw Deena sitting on the rocking chair fussing with her statue. "Were you spying on me again?" she snapped.

"I wasn't spying," Deena answered without taking her eyes from her project. "But now that you mention it, I do think you could be a little more discreet. We do have guests here, you know."

Kathy's eyes went wide in mock surprise. "We have guests?" she shouted, pretending this was startling news. "Where has my head been? I hadn't even noticed." Kathy put her hand to her forehead dramatically and staggered back against the porch railing. "Thank you, Deena! Thank you! I thought we were all alone here at the inn, just me and you. It was a thought too horrible to bear, but now that I know we have guests, I'm so relieved!"

Deena looked at Kathy sharply. "Oh, stop acting like a lunatic," she huffed. "You know what I—"

Just then a man and woman who were staying at the inn walked out the front door and stood between the two girls. They wore identical madras plaid shorts, identical canvas hats, and identical red T-shirts. They both had cameras and binoculars around their necks. "Grand day for bird watching," the man stated, slapping his big belly enthusiastically.

Kathy, who was standing behind him, opened her eyes and mouth wide in a comic expression of disbelief at the couple's outfits.

Panicked that her cousin was about to explode with laughter, Deena stepped forward. "Yes, we have some lovely birds here in Cranford. This is a very popular bird-watching spot."

"Is that so," gushed the woman. "I told you we'd come to the right place, Herman. What kind of birds do you see here?"

Deena had no idea. She liked to look at the birds, she'd even taken the binoculars out once in a while, but she'd never looked up the names of the birds. She had to say something, though, because she could see Kathy turning red with repressed laughter. Deena wanted to distract the man and woman before they noticed her, so she pressed on desperately. "Oh, the basic New England birds. I saw a nice red one."

"A cardinal?" the woman asked.

"Yes, a cardinal. Cranford is the cardinal capital of New England."

At that Kathy whooped with laughter and staggered into the inn, holding her side.

"Don't mind her," said Deena, ushering the bewildered guests down the steps. "She's a little unbalanced, never really been right in the head. Enjoy your bird watching—and remember, while you're here we want you to think of the Cranberry Inn as your home."

Deena was still standing on the porch waving to the

19

bird watchers when an old blue rust-splotched Mustang rumbled up the drive. Deena recognized it as one of the three cars used by Cranford's one and only cab service, CranFords.

The car pulled up and a tall man in a rumpled beige sports jacket got out. "Hey, kid," he addressed Deena brusquely, "this is where Nancy Manelli lives, isn't it?"

"This is the Cranberry Inn, yes," Deena said stiffly, affronted by the man's tone. "I'll see if my aunt is available. And whom may I say is calling?"

"John Blackman, *New England Journal*."

Deena gave him a dignified nod. "You may sit on the porch and wait," she said, indicating the wicker chair to her left.

"Sure, kid, sure," the man mumbled, sitting down. "Just don't take all day about it, huh?"

Deena found her aunt Nancy running down the stairs, wearing an old gray sweat suit with her wet hair still caught up in a towel. "There's a man here from *The New England Journal*," she told her.

"Oh, no!" Nancy wailed. "Tell him to wait."

"Nancy," Lydia called from the reception desk. "A woman from *The Cranford Gazette* said if she doesn't come over now she'll miss the last edition, so I told her to come on by."

"But Lydia, I'm not ready—"

"Mom," Kathy called from the dining room. "A guy from something called *The New England Literary Life* called. He wanted to book a room for the weekend. We had a cancellation, so I gave it to him, O.K.? He says he's writing a thing on you for his magazine. He's checking in at two."

20

"I'm freaking out. I'm freaking," Nancy muttered tensely. "I'm going to stay calm, though. No matter what, stay calm. Deep breaths, Nancy."

"Hello, John Blackman here," the man said, striding confidently through the front door. "And you must be Nancy Manelli." He walked up to Nancy, whose hands flew up to the towel on her head. "I recognize you from the picture on the back of your book. I've been assigned to do a piece on you for *The New England Journal*'s book section. I've been calling all week and they kept telling me you weren't here. I figured I was getting the runaround, so I just came on down to see for myself."

"I was away, Mr. Blackman, and I'm really not prepared to talk to any reporters right—"

"Excuse me," said a woman with a wild perm and thick glasses. "I'm from *The Cranford Gazette*. I have an appointment to speak to Nancy Manelli."

"I was here first, lady," John Blackman cut in.

Lydia tried to make peace between the two reporters, who immediately fell into a heated argument over who should interview Nancy first.

Deena stood back and watched. Kathy came up quietly behind her. "Things are certainly exciting here in Cranford—cardinal capital of the world," she said, laughing.

"I wish you could be more helpful," Deena chided, "instead of making fun of me because I take an interest in our guests."

"Here's a helpful idea, Deena," said Kathy, still smiling. "Since you're so devoted to keeping our guests happy, why don't you put on a bird costume and go flap around in the woods? They'll think they've spotted the

21

rare squawking dodo. It's the least you can do for our beloved guests."

"You're the bird-brain around here—why don't *you* do it?" Deena snapped.

Deena and Kathy were so busy bickering that at first they didn't notice the young man, wearing a blue summer sports jacket and jeans, who came into the hallway. "I know I'm early," he said to Lydia, ignoring the feuding reporters. "I'm Doyle Donnelly from *New England Literary Life*. I made a reservation for tonight."

"And another thing that bugs me about you . . . " Kathy was midsentence when Deena went pale and clutched her arm. "What? What's the matter?" Kathy asked, alarmed at her cousin's sudden strange behavior.

Deena's eyes were wide. "Turn around and look at what just walked in the door."

Kathy turned around slowly. She saw a tall young man in his early twenties with blond hair and tortoiseshell glasses. "So? I see a guy with blond hair and glasses. He's kind of cute, I guess. What's the big deal?"

Deena looked at Kathy as if she were insane. "That is no guy," she whispered in an awestruck voice. "That is an Adonis."

"A what?" Kathy asked.

"Adonis—the golden-haired Greek god of love."

Chapter 3

Kathy looked at Doyle Donnelly again. He was cute, but a golden-haired god of love? "You're nuts," she told her cousin.

Deena was too awestruck to be offended. She gazed at the young man in disbelief. When Deena daydreamed about her future she always imagined herself with a man who was handsome, yet cultured—manly, yet sensitive. And here he was! It was as if he'd walked right out of her imagination. Everything about him was perfect: the jeans, the glasses, the way he ran his hand through his golden hair and shifted from one foot to the other with appealing nervousness. Perfect.

Unfortunately for him, Deena was the one and only person paying any attention to him at all. "Excuse me," he said again, raising his voice to be heard over the bickering reporters. "I booked a room for tonight."

"Of course, Mr. Donnelly," Lydia said, "We're all a little topsy-turvy right now. You'll have to forgive us."

"It's really O.K.," he answered, handing Lydia his credit card. "I'm in no hurry."

"Deena, please show Mr. Donnelly to room six," Lydia called.

"Huh?" Deena asked, still entranced.

Kathy nudged her. "Show Adonis his digs," she whispered. "This is your big chance."

That roused Deena. "Oh, of course," she sputtered. "Please come this way, Mr. Donnelly." She beckoned him to follow her up the stairs with a graceful, theatrical flourish of her hand.

"Please call me Doyle," he said, laughing. "The only person who ever called me Mr. Donnelly was my thousand-year-old Shakespeare professor in college, and I almost didn't graduate last month because of him. Besides, every time I hear someone say 'Mr. Donnelly' I look over my shoulder for my father."

Deena laughed, just a touch too uproariously. "All right, Doyle," she said, leading him up the stairs. "I hope you'll consider yourself a member of our family during your stay at the Cranberry Inn."

Kathy rolled her eyes. When Deena latched onto an idea, she really beat it to death. If Kathy heard her invite their guests to be members of their family one more time, she was going to be sick—and the summer was just beginning.

She noticed that her mother had taken the two reporters into the sitting room. They'd apparently compromised and were doing a joint interview. Lydia was going over their bills. Kathy realized she was suddenly at a loss for something to do—a fact she'd learned not to announce. Her mother or Aunt Lydia was always able to find a job for her to do around the inn.

Kathy walked outside and sat down on the front porch steps. She held her face up to the sun, shutting her eyes so that the light made colorful patterns inside her lids. She heard the slight swish of the trees in the breeze and the buzz of some nameless insect. There was always so much clamor inside the inn, it was good to sit alone for a minute.

The pleasure of peacefulness held its allure for another four minutes, and then Kathy grew restless. What was she going to do with Roy gone, and her friend Ellecia away at camp? The band she sang with had even decided not to perform this month—too many conflicting vacation and camp schedules. She didn't quite wish that school was in session—that was too extreme— but she wished for something exciting to do.

She got up and wandered around to the back of the inn where Johnny was sitting on the picnic bench. He'd blown up his new dinosaur and set it beside him as he played with a pocket electronic football game. A little electronic song beeped out of the plastic case in his hand.

"All right! Touchdown!" he cried.

"Cranford's biggest sports fan scores again," she said, laughing.

"Look, Kathy," he said, holding the game out for her to see, "it has little electronic cheerleaders."

Kathy inspected the hand-sized game and saw the tiny black figures of cheerleaders moving their little electronic arms to the tune of the beeping song. "Neat," she said.

"You can get a field goal or a touchdown on this," Johnny told her. "Want to try?"

Kathy took the game and tried her luck. After several

attempts she got a touchdown and heard the electronic victory song. "You're getting it," Johnny encouraged.

She didn't have the heart to admit that the game bored her, so she played a few more games until she couldn't stand it any longer. "Do you miss your friends from school?" she asked him, putting the game aside.

Johnny sat and thought about that one. "Nope," he decided.

"I thought you liked the kids at school."

"I do, but I don't miss them because I see them all the time. A bunch of us play ball at each other's houses. When they're not around, there's lots of stuff I can do around here by myself."

"You're lucky," said Kathy. "Most of my friends have jobs or are away on vacation or at camp. What do you do when no one's around?"

"I don't know. I have my action figures, and this game. I have the kittens to play with. And sometimes I hang around in the woods and look at stuff."

Kathy looked at her brother. He was lucky to be so self-sufficient. "What do you look at?"

"There's always neat things, like weird bugs, and the other day I found this strange flat stuff that looked like it was a shelf growing out of a tree. Deena said it was a poisonous mushroom."

"How come you showed Deena and not me?" Kathy asked, hurt.

"I don't know. I think you were out with Roy, and Deena is interested in nature and all, and you're not."

Kathy had to admit that was true. She still thought of herself as a city person and more or less ignored the forests around her. The only time she'd paid any attention

26

to nature was when she and her father took walks in the park back in San Francisco. Her father had been an artist, and sometimes they would go out sketching flowers and trees together. That seemed like a long time ago to her now.

It was also true that she was busy—especially with Roy—and she wasn't all that interested in what anyone else in her family was doing.

Johnny went back to his electronic game. "Want to play another?" he asked, but from the tone of his voice she could tell he was just being polite.

"No, it's O.K., you play," she said. "I'm going to see if Mom's finished with her interview."

Kathy wandered back up to the inn and saw that her mother was still embroiled in talking to the reporters. Quietly she crept into the sitting room and took a chair behind her mother.

"I tried to use the force of nature as a symbol for the strong emotions I was feeling after my husband—" Nancy interrupted herself when she sensed Kathy's presence. She turned and smiled at her daughter uncomfortably. "This is my daughter, Kathy," she told Mr. Blackman and the woman from the *Gazette*. "She's been a big influence on my life as well as my work," she added, laughing nervously.

Mr. Blackman and the woman nodded curtly in Kathy's direction. "Kathy and her cousin Deena have made a name for themselves, too," Nancy continued. "At school everyone calls them the Cranberry Cousins."

"Mom, don't tell them that," Kathy pleaded, cringing at the mention of the dreaded label, which both Deena and Kathy detested.

"Oh, come on, Kathy, it's cute," Nancy protested, "and these people want to know about our lives."

"You were talking about the nature imagery in your poems," the *Gazette* woman cut in, clearly uninterested in the current topic.

"Oh, well, I don't know. Maybe I'm making a big deal over nothing. I just write what comes to me."

"Some of the poems are very sensual," Mr. Blackman pressed. "Surely the image of the wind rushing through the pines at night means—"

"Don't be such a dolt," the *Gazette* woman hissed. "Her daughter is sitting right here."

"It's O.K.," said Nancy, "Kathy's cool. It's true, when you're this close to nature, those are the images you tend to use when expressing your feelings. Nature seems to mirror so much of what's going on inside me—the growth, the change. And nature is so instinctive, so sensual, that it's a powerful way of talking about those things, too."

"I just wanted to say hi," Kathy said, jumping to her feet, suddenly uncomfortable. "I didn't mean to interrupt. Sorry."

"You can stay, Kathy."

"No, really, I have to leave anyway. Go back to what you were doing."

Nancy reached out and squeezed her daughter's hand. Kathy headed for the kitchen. She had to admit that the thought of her mother writing "sensual" poems, even if they were about pine trees, made her feel strange. She somehow couldn't see her mother that way. She was still Mom, and that wasn't the kind of stuff moms were supposed to write about.

It was Kathy's day to set up the cold buffet lunch, and she was almost looking forward to having something to do. "You're in luck," Lydia told her. "It's so beautiful out there, no one's here for lunch. Grab yourself a sandwich from the kitchen if you're hungry."

Kathy opened the big refrigerator in the kitchen and picked through the assortment of cold sandwiches that had been prepared for lunch. She settled on a salami sandwich and grabbed a tuna on white bread to bring to Deena.

Since she'd promised Aunt Lydia that she'd try to get along better with her cousin—and since she had absolutely nothing else to do—Kathy decided that maybe now was a good time to give it a try. Deena wasn't a total horror; she meant well and she had her moments of being almost fun to be with...sometimes...occasionally. Wrapping the peace-offering sandwich up in a napkin, she went to look for Deena.

She climbed the stairs to the third-floor bedroom they shared to see if Deena was there. "Typical," Kathy muttered, seeing that despite the morning's harried pace Deena had managed to make her bed and straighten up her side of the room. Kathy's side looked like a cyclone had blown through it, miraculously leaving Deena's side untouched. "I swear she just does this to make me look bad," Kathy grumbled to herself.

"Now where could that little neat freak have gone to?" Thinking she heard Deena's voice, she walked down a flight of steps and listened at the second-floor landing. She heard Deena talking in that shrill tone she used when she was especially full of herself.

Kathy followed the sound of Deena's voice downstairs

29

and out to the front porch. Deena was standing dramatically in front of Doyle Donnelly, performing a poem that Kathy recognized immediately as being one of Deena's own.

" . . . and the morning lark, up from his rest, sings from his feather'd nest. The thrilling song he sings to me is of our many-colored humanity."

Doyle sat back in his chair and applauded enthusiastically. "Very expressive, Deena," he said.

Boy, is this guy ever polite, Kathy thought. Deena hadn't read Kathy one of her poems since Kathy had announced that hearing Deena's poetry made her feel as if her head was being pushed through a vat of mashed potatoes.

Deena spotted Kathy standing in the doorway. "I was just telling Doyle that your mother isn't the only writer in the family."

"I brought you some lunch," Kathy said, presenting the tuna sandwich and suppressing the urge to make a crack about Deena's writing.

"How sweet," said Deena, unwrapping the napkin, "but you forgot about our guest here. Would you like this sandwich, Doyle?"

"No, please have your lunch," he answered pleasantly, propping his feet up against the porch railing.

"I'm not really hungry," Deena said, putting the sandwich down beside her. "Would you like to hear another poem?"

"Sure," he replied with genuine interest. "Your work shows a lot of promise."

"Thank you," Deena said, looking down modestly. "My English teacher says more or less the same thing, but she's just an academic. You're really out there, toiling in the word fields, planting the seeds of literature."

"I wouldn't say that." Doyle laughed. "I was lucky to get this job right out of college. Writing this story on Ms. Manelli will be my first really important assignment. I'm incredibly thrilled to be here."

"Well, you just relax while you're here," Deena said flirtatiously. "Because you know our motto. Every guest is a welcome—"

"No, don't say it!" Kathy shouted, covering her ears. "Let me get out of here before you finish that sentence, or I think I'll lose my mind."

Kathy ran down the front steps of the inn still holding her ears. When she was safely out of earshot, she looked back at the porch. She saw Deena showing Doyle her statue. From her elaborate gestures she could tell Deena was explaining its deep meaning to him. Well, so much for hanging out with Deena.

Kathy returned to her room by way of the back door. She pushed a pile of clothes off her bed, plopped down, and decided to write a letter to Ellecia at camp. Ellecia had been practically dragged, kicking and screaming, to a camp in Vermont called Camp Tall Trees.

"Help! Losing my mind from boredom," Kathy wrote. "Also suffering from acute Deena-itis: a dreaded disease that attacks the nerves, causing nausea, headache, and an intense desire to scream."

Then she filled her friend in on her mother's trip, Roy's departure, and about all the work there was to be done at the inn. "How are you managing to keep the blue streak in your hair at camp?" she inquired, expressing a worrisome thought that had occurred to her late last night. "Want me to mail you some color spray, or did you stock up before you left? If you need any other necessities, lipstick, eyeshadow, blush, just let me know and I'll send them." Kathy addressed the envelope to Camp All Creeps. But fearing it wouldn't get there, she crossed it out and wrote Tall Trees.

She spent close to an hour decorating the envelope with her colored markers. Then she spotted her new ThunderMongers sweat shirt on the bed and decided to try it on. "Intense," she said, pushing the sleeves up stylishly and admiring herself in the mirror.

She pushed her layered hair away from her face and stared at her reflection in the mirror. "Looking a little pale, kiddo," she said to herself. She reached onto her dresser, which was a jumble of make-up, jewelry, and magazines, and grabbed some blush and vivid red lipstick. She applied it with a few quick strokes and finished the look with some gray eyeliner and mascara. "The country-girl version of the famous Manelli look," she said, pleased with the results. Then she settled back with an issue of *Spin* magazine and read about a few of her favorite rock singers.

"Time to start setting up for dinner," Lydia called from the second-floor landing at about five o'clock.

"Okedoke," Kathy answered, stepping out of her room and looking down to where her aunt stood with a large basket of blueberries she'd been picking from the backyard bushes. "Get Deena to help you," Lydia added, seeing that her daughter wasn't with Kathy.

"Blueberry muffins for breakfast tomorrow?" Kathy asked, bounding down the steps toward her aunt.

"Blueberry cobbler for dessert tonight."

"Great!" Kathy went out to the porch and found her cousin still there, sitting cross-legged in front of Doyle in the midst of yet another poem.

"Oh, lost is the time of heroes of fable, of men so true, gallant, and able. Oh, now is the time . . . "

"To set the table," Kathy finished.

Deena scrunched her face at her cousin. "You have no appreciation of poetry, do you?"

"Sure she does," Doyle disagreed.

"What do you mean?" Deena asked incredulously. "She thinks *Mad Magazine* is high art."

"Look at her sweat shirt. The ThunderMongers' songs have the most poetic, passionate lyrics I've ever read. The words could stand alone without the music as great poetry. Everybody down at Yale was into them."

Kathy wrinkled her nose at her cousin in a "so there" expression. She didn't admit that she only liked the group because their music had a great beat and their lead singer was totally adorable. "I've always said that about the ThunderMongers," she said.

"You know which song kills me," Doyle said, sitting forward animatedly in his chair. " 'Gorilla Journeys.' It's like something that Rimbaud would have written if he was alive today."

Deena narrowed her eyes and folded her arms angrily. She was sure that Kathy didn't know anything at all about the poet Rimbaud.

"I always thought of it as being more like Longfellow's work," Kathy replied, quickly shooting a laughing glance at her cousin.

"That never occurred to me, but you may be right. Certainly the constant references to nature would be in keeping with Longfellow's work."

"She had never even heard of Longfellow until this morning when I mentioned him," Deena chimed in, unable to bear Kathy's game any longer.

"You were talking about Longfellow this morning?" Doyle asked, sounding impressed. "What were you saying about him?"

"Yes, Deena," Kathy urged, "tell Doyle what you had to say about Longfellow. It was truly fascinating."

Doyle looked at Deena expectantly.

Deena pressed her lips together and glared at her cousin. "I was simply retelling the classic old rhyme—You're a poet and you don't know it, but your feet show it, they're Longfellows."

"Uh-huh," said Doyle, "cute. Anyway, Deena, you should listen to the ThunderMongers. The words would really blow you away."

"Girls, set up for dinner, *now*!" Nancy called onto the porch.

"I guess she's done with her interview," commented Kathy, turning to go inside.

"I hope she'll make time for me this evening," said Doyle, following Kathy. "I loved her book, and I can't wait to interview her."

"You know, she bought me this ThunderMongers shirt. She saw them while she was in New York," Kathy said, letting the screen door slam behind them.

"Wow, I'll have to ask her about that."

"Yeah, she liked them a lot, saw them at the Ritz and everything."

34

Deena sat on the porch listening to Doyle and Kathy's voices fade as they walked toward the dining room. "You're dead meat now, Kathy Manelli," she grumbled. "This is war!"

Chapter 4

"Deena, stop slamming the plates down on the table. What's the matter?" Lydia asked her daughter.

"Nothing's the matter," Deena said in a voice full of false sweetness. "I love being forced to share every aspect of my life with a cousin whose biggest thrill is tormenting me. It's great, really."

Kathy was setting a table on the other side of the room. "What did I do? I can't help it if the guy likes the ThunderMongers. Is that my fault?"

"Oh, get off it!" Deena shouted. "You're such a liar. You can't pass up a chance to make fun of me, can you? You always have to get your little remark in."

"Girls, please," Lydia interrupted. "Can you continue this at another time? Dinner is in ten minutes and the tables are only half set. Hurry it up."

Kathy and Deena continued setting the tables with a vengeance, each one slamming plates and setting glasses down with a thump. They worked from opposite sides of the room until they met in the center of the large dining room with only one large round table left.

"Creep," Deena mumbled under her breath as she set a plate down next to her cousin's silverware.

"Twerp," Kathy grumbled back.

"Weirdo," Deena snapped.

Kathy looked up and laughed. "Anyone who writes the flaky poetry you do better think twice before calling someone else weird. That poor guy looked like he was going to lose his mind if you read him one more poem."

"He appreciated my poems," Deena insisted.

"I don't know; I heard a news report that said a stranger was seen running through Cranford, totally demented, screaming, 'Make her stop! Make her stop!' It sounded like Doyle to me."

Deena had had enough. "Just lay off me!" she shouted, grabbing Kathy by the sleeve of her sweat shirt.

In a minute Lydia was between them. "Deena, let go of Kathy this instant. Have you gone crazy?"

Just then Nancy walked into the dining room with her arm around Johnny. Doyle was walking on the other side of her. "Lydia, Doyle is going to do a cover story on me and the inn for his magazine."

"Did that Blackman guy and the lady leave?" Kathy asked.

"Yes, they're gone. I was nervous at first—it feels odd talking about yourself. Once I got going, though, I couldn't stop. Maybe I am a secret egomaniac."

"I hope you'll keep talking for the next few days," Doyle said. "I have lots of questions to ask you."

"From talking to you this last half hour I'm sure I'll enjoy it," Nancy said. "If you'll excuse me, I want to check on things in the kitchen."

"I guess you'll want to know lots of background information about the inn and all of us," Deena spoke up. "I'd be happy to help you with any of that."

"Thanks, Deena, that would be great. It was really fun hanging out with you this afternoon."

"I'd be happy to help you with any of that," Kathy whispered behind Deena in a mincing imitation of her cousin's voice.

"Just shut up," Deena hissed, looking up quickly to make sure Doyle couldn't hear them. She was relieved that Doyle had walked off to a far table and sat next to the bird-watching couple.

Lydia, however, was within hearing range. "That's it," she snapped. "I cannot take this bickering another minute. I've asked you girls several times to try to get along. Now I'm angry. The two of you will confine yourselves to your room for the rest of the evening or until you can be civilized. Dinner will be sent up to you."

"But . . . but . . . I didn't do anything," Kathy balked.

"She's been on my case all day," Deena objected.

"I am not listening to another word of this squabbling. Do as I say," Lydia insisted in a voice that didn't invite further discussion.

Kathy knew it was no use trying to get her more easygoing mother to rescind the punishment. The sisters had made a pact to present a united front as authority figures. If Lydia made a rule Nancy thought was too strict, she upheld it just the same. Likewise, if Lydia thought one of Nancy's rules was too lenient, she went along with it anyway.

Kathy and Deena trudged up the stairs together. "You know we were having blueberry cobbler—your favorite—for dessert tonight," Kathy grumbled.

Deena just stuck her nose in the air in an expression of wounded dignity. This was all really too much. Kathy was bad enough, but then to be sent to her room like a baby! "I just pray that Doyle doesn't find out I've been sent to my room," she said. "He'll start to think of me as a child."

Deena lay down on her bed and picked up a copy of *Jane Eyre* she'd started two nights before. She was up to the part where the heroine hears strange, sinister laughter coming from the attic of the mansion.

In minutes she was engrossed in the story. Her mind had left Cranford, and she was wandering the dark halls of the creepy old English mansion. She felt as if she were beside Jane, holding a candle, ready to turn the key which would unlock the secret of the strange cackling laugh in the attic.

Blam-blam-blam-blam-blim-blam-blim-blam-blam! The opening drum solo of Kathy's ThunderMongers tape blasted Deena out of England. "This is 'Gorilla Journeys,' that song that could have been written by Rambo," Kathy explained as she gyrated around the room in a frenzied dance all her own.

"Turn that off!" Deena yelled, jumping to her feet. "And it's Rimbaud, not Rambo."

"That's what I said, isn't it?" Kathy continued, still dancing to the beat.

"I can't read with that on."

Kathy turned the stereo down. "Hey, this is the stuff that Mr. Wonderful thinks is the greatest."

"How can you even make out the words?" Deena asked.

"You can't," Kathy admitted; "you have to read the words in the cassette box." Kathy turned the tape up again and went back to her dance.

"Please use the headphones," Deena begged.

"I can't dance as well with them on," Kathy shouted over the music, "but since you said the magic word *please*, I'll do it." Kathy batted her eyelashes obnoxiously at Deena. "Just for you, cuzzy wuzzy."

"Thank you," Deena replied stiffly.

Kathy put on the headphones and continued to bop around the room. The music was so loud that Deena could hear the throbbing beat even through the headphones, but she decided not to press for total victory.

Deena lost the desire to read. She wanted to write in her faithful companion, her journal, instead. She wanted to write all about Doyle Donnelly.

"I feel just a pinch disloyal to Ken," she wrote. "He is off being a counselor at a tennis camp and hasn't written me all week. But I feel that Doyle was destined to come into my life. One can't fight destiny."

Deena noticed that the thumping had stopped. Kathy was lying on her bed with her feet up in the air, painting her toenails a bright purple. "You might have better luck if you sat with your knees up," Deena couldn't stop herself from pointing out.

"You might have better luck if you sat with your knees

up," Kathy mimicked in that horrible voice that Deena loathed.

"Suit yourself," Deena said with a sigh, going back to her journal. "Doyle is so clearly the man I've been dreaming of," she wrote. "We spent a glorious summer day today, exchanging ideas, communicating, and feeling the once-in-a-lifetime harmony that can only come when kindred spirits meet. I can't believe that he did not also sense the special electricity that we generated as we spoke from noon (almost) to eventide. (And why would he have spent so much time with me if he didn't like me?)"

Deena sneaked a peak at her cousin and saw that she had taken her advice and changed positions. Kathy looked up and stuck her tongue out at Deena, sending her back to her journal.

"And I don't believe Doyle really does like the stupid ThunderMongers. I'm sure that he was just being nice to Kathy out of politeness. If Johnny had come along, he would have talked to him about sports. That's the kind of versatile, humane young man he is.

"I realize that Doyle and I are seven years apart, but I feel that my maturity makes the actual years much less. Besides, when I'm twenty-one and Doyle is twenty-eight, the difference will seem nonexistent."

Deena closed her eyes. She pictured them both in their twenties, sitting by a fireplace somewhere, reading love poems out loud to each other. The fire threw a golden glow on her long blond hair as she read a sonnet she'd written in honor of their first wedding anniversary. Doyle, overcome with love and admiration, pulled her to him and they kissed there by the roaring fire.

"Wait for me, Doyle," she wrote, scribbling feverishly in her journal. "Don't give up on me because I seem young now. We have so much to share."

"You're really hot for this guy, huh?" said Kathy, leaning over her shoulder.

Deena slammed the journal shut. "Don't you have the slightest respect for a person's privacy? Just today you accused me of spying on you and you got all upset, even though I don't have the slightest interest in your affairs."

"I'm not having an affair, I just kissed Roy good-bye," Kathy said defensively.

"I didn't mean affair in that sense—oh, never mind."

"Look, Deena, it's not like I crept in here and looked at your boring old journal. You were writing like a lunatic, and I wanted to see what had you so worked up."

"As if you couldn't have guessed," Deena snipped, feeling embarrassed.

"Deena, I have to tell you that I think you're making a mistake. That Doyle guy isn't interested in you. He probably has some Yale girlfriend somewhere who makes you look like a baby to him."

"I suppose you *don't* seem like a baby to him?"

"That's not my point," Kathy protested, "but, yes, now that you mention it, I do have a certain worldliness that you lack."

"Hah!" Deena hooted. "That's a laugh and a half."

There was a rap on the door. "Dinner," Nancy called, walking in with a tray full of food. "How are you two surviving up here?"

"As usual," Kathy said, digging into the meal of fried chicken, corn, and french-fried potatoes.

"You brought up the blueberry cobbler— thanks,

42

Aunt Nancy," said Deena, spotting the much-loved dessert under a napkin.

"You're welcome. I expect the both of you to pay me back by staying off each other's cases tomorrow. You're driving Lydia totally bonkers."

"O.K.," Deena agreed glumly. "What do you think of Doyle?" she asked, eager to change the subject.

"He's a sweet boy, very bright, ambitious. I like him. Why?"

"Deena has the hots for him," Kathy blurted out.

Nancy smiled. "I can sort of see how you'd feel that way. He is attractive. He's got a lot of boyish charm. I think you have good taste, Deena."

"Thank you," Deena said primly, feeling vindicated.

"Good night, you two," Nancy said, stepping into the hallway. "Get all your feuding done tonight so we can have good vibes tomorrow, O.K.?"

"Deena," Kathy said with her mouth full of chicken, "I think it's truce time. I feel a little guilty about tormenting the feeble-minded, and besides, I don't want to spend the whole summer stuck up here with you."

"Likewise," agreed Deena, "but since you can't even call for a truce without slipping in an insult, I propose that from now on we simply avoid each other whenever possible."

"Fine with me," snapped Kathy.

Both girls read in silence for another hour, then turned off the light. Deena knew Kathy had gone off to sleep by the heaviness of her breathing. But she couldn't relax. She played every word that Doyle had spoken over and over in her head, looking for hidden meanings or new insights into his character.

After two hours of this she decided to go down to the kitchen and get some milk. She entered the hall. It was flooded with light from the full moon. She could hear the clanking of dishes and the voices of her mother and aunt laughing and talking downstairs but upstairs everything was quiet.

Awed by the beauty of the silvery light, Deena walked over to the window at the end of the hall and looked out. "Hi, Mr. Moon," she whispered in the way her mother always had when she was small and they would look at the full moon together.

After a minute her eye wandered down to the yard. There, sitting alone at the picnic table, which was illuminated by the moon and the backyard spotlight, was Doyle.

Deena gasped at the sheer romance of the image. She looked closer and saw that he was writing something on a stack of papers he'd taken out of a ring binder. He stared up at the moon for a few minutes, then put his hand onto his forehead, as if some great sadness had weighed it down.

"See you in the morning," Deena heard Aunt Nancy say to her mother.

"Good night. I'll lock up," her mother replied.

Deena watched as Doyle returned to his writing. She saw him speak to someone, undoubtedly her mother, who called to him from the back door. Deena knew the ritual— her mother didn't lock the doors until she was sure everyone was in. If someone wanted to stay out late she gave them a key.

Would Doyle stay out there all night, writing till dawn? No, Deena watched as he gathered his papers back into the binder. "You dropped one," she whispered lovingly when she saw one white sheaf of paper float unnoticed to the ground.

Deena heard Doyle come in and climb the steps to his room on the second floor. Her first impulse was to run down and tell him he'd dropped a paper. But then he'd know she was up here staring at him. Besides, she just couldn't go running after him in her nightgown.

Deena had a better idea. She'd get the paper herself and then tell him she found it in the morning. That would give her a natural reason to talk to him.

Deena waited ten more minutes for the inn to become completely quiet. When the last shower was turned off and no more footsteps could be heard, she tiptoed down the steps, wondering why they had never seemed so creaky to her before.

I'm just going to pick up a paper for a friend who's lost it, she told herself rationally. If I don't get it, it'll blow away. Still, she couldn't fight the feeling that something thrilling was about to happen. She felt like Jane Eyre wandering the halls of the old mansion at night.

She let herself out the back door and pulled her nightgown closely around her, surprised that it had gotten so cool. She looked to the spot near the picnic table where the paper had fallen. She didn't see it.

There it was! The paper shone white in the moonlight among the leaves of a blueberry bush it had blown into. Stepping gingerly on her bare feet, she made her way to the bush and plucked the now berry-smeared paper from its branches.

I shouldn't read this; it's private, her conscience told her, but she was seized with an overwhelming curiosity.

Without checking in with her conscience a second time, she looked at the paper in her hand.

Of course he'd have perfect penmanship, she thought, admiring the neat yet artistic slant of his script. She read the words and realized it was a middle page of a letter to someone.

"How can I ever hope to earn your love?" the top line read. "Your untamed spirit. Your wild grace. These thrill me to the marrow of my bone."

It's probably to some girlfriend at home, Deena thought, suddenly depressed at the thought. She read on. The words of love seemed endless. Each line painted an image of passion that made Deena breathless.

In the last paragraph Deena read, "What fate drew me to this inn? I will never know. All I know is that from the moment I saw you I was overwhelmed. Your charm and wit made me instantly at ease. Your graceful beauty astounds me."

Deena's eyes glistened with tears of happiness. She was the one who told him to feel like this was his home. She clutched the paper to her chest and twirled around, alone there in the moonlight.

"He loves me," she whispered to the summer breeze.

Chapter 5

"Oh, what a beautiful morning!" Deena sang, throwing the window to her room open wide. "La,la,la,la, la,la, la."

Kathy had thrown her pillow over her head to block out the morning light. She peeked out from under it at the sound of Deena's singing. "Would you please shut . . . " she started, but then remembered their truce and pulled her head back under the pillow like a turtle returning to its shell.

"What was that, Kathy?" Deena asked sweetly. "Did you say something?"

"Nthmmmblspkmmmmmmtmmmmmmmmm" came the sound from under the pillow.

"I'm sorry, say it again," Deena requested, walking to Kathy's bed and lifting the corner of the pillow.

"I said I'm not talking to you!" Kathy shouted. "Remember, we agreed last night? It was your idea."

Deena placed the corner of the pillow back down over Kathy's head and thought a moment. The discovery that

47

Doyle shared her feelings had brightened her mood quite a bit since she proposed that they have nothing to do with each other. Now she was feeling friendly toward the whole world and had lost her desire to feud with Kathy.

She bent down and picked up the corner of the pillow again. "I think you misunderstood me," she said. "I was merely suggesting that we try to avoid confrontation. I didn't mean we shouldn't talk to each other."

"Yes, you did, and I like the idea," said Kathy, reaching up and yanking the pillow from Deena's fingers. "Nwmmmpfbmmml," she finished, clutching the pillow to her head.

"Pardon me," Deena said, kneeling at the side of the bed and trying to talk under the crack in the pillow. "I didn't get your last remark."

"I said, now leave me alone," Kathy growled, flipping the pillow up for just a second.

"I see," stated Deena, standing up and dusting off her nightgown. She studied her cousin for a minute more and then her face brightened. Nothing could dampen her good mood this morning. "I know you're not a morning person, Kathy, so I'm not angry with you. It must be hard to face each new day with puffy eyes and a sour temper, but I know you can't control it. It's just the way your biological time table is set up. Being a morning person myself, I love to see a new day break. The glory of the rising sun, the—"

A muffled scream from under Kathy's pillow cut Deena short. Deena just shrugged her shoulders and started to get ready for breakfast, humming her favorite song from *West Side Story*, "I Feel Pretty."

Deena plugged in her electric rollers. By the time she

returned from the bathroom, they were hot enough to use. While her hair was up in rollers, she looked through her drawer full of neatly folded clothing. It suddenly seemed to her that everything she owned was awful.

She pulled out a madras short-and-shirt set. "Too babyish," she decided. A blue cotton jumpsuit was dismissed as looking too frivolous. Her favorite Calvin Klein Bermuda shorts suddenly looked dingy to her.

Deena decided that her new Lee jeans were the only things that really looked attractive enough on her, so she convinced herself that it wasn't too warm to wear them. "And I know just the shirt," she said, digging for one of several Literary Greats T-shirts she'd ordered through the mail. It had a picture of the author Ernest Hemingway on the front.

She tied a blue scarf neatly around her neck and put on tiny red ceramic rosebud earrings. She unrolled her hair, which fell to her shoulders in big loopy curls. After running a brush through it and clipping up one stubborn strand of hair that wouldn't take a curl, she inspected herself in the mirror. "Hmmm," she mused, "still a trifle too young."

Deena went over to Kathy's dresser. "Yuck," she whispered, inspecting the jumble of stuff on the dresser top. She picked up a mascara and fished through for a lipstick. Purple Passion certainly won't do, she thought, rejecting a tube. Finally she picked out a pink gloss.

"Hey, get away from my stuff!" Kathy yelled from the bed.

"I just wanted to borrow a little make-up. Sorry," Deena apologized. "I'm truly sorry. It won't happen again."

"Just ask next time," Kathy grumbled, turning over in bed.

Deena inspected her total appearance. "Perfecto," she whispered, smiling at herself in the mirror.

She took the piece of paper she'd retrieved from the yard out from under the pillow. Closing the door quietly behind her, Deena walked down to Doyle's room on the second floor. She looked around, kissed the paper quickly, and then knelt down to leave the paper leaning gently against the door.

Suddenly the door opened and Deena found herself staring at a pair of brown Top-sider deck shoes. She looked up at Doyle. "You, uh, found this, and I left it in the yard," she sputtered nervously.

"What?" he asked, holding out his hand to help her to her feet.

Deena took a deep breath. "I mean I was out taking a walk this morning, and I found this in the yard. I thought it might be yours."

It was Doyle's turn to look flustered and pale. He took the paper from her quickly. "I was just trying out some ideas, I, um never expected anyone to read it, I—"

"Oh, I didn't read it," Deena assured him. "I would never read something that belonged to someone else. I just thought that it probably was yours because . . . because I knew it wasn't mine . . . and Aunt Nancy writes in a bound notebook and other than that nobody else around here writes . . . not a word, ever. So I just narrowed down the possibilities, and I . . . "

"Thanks, Deena," Doyle said, seeming to regain his composure.

"I would be glad to see anything you've written, if you

wanted me to see it, that is," Deena said, unable to keep from gazing lovingly into the blue eyes behind his glasses. How boyish and handsome he looked early in the morning, she thought. She noticed that he hadn't shaved yet, and the blond stubble on his cheeks made him look rugged and sexy.

"Sure," he said, "I'll show you some stuff later, maybe after lunch. This morning your aunt and I are going to have our first interview."

"I can't wait to see your work, Doyle," Deena said, clutching her hands together to keep them from shaking.

"I was going down for breakfast; want to join me?"

"Breakfast, darn," Deena said, realizing that it was her day to find out who wanted breakfast sent to their rooms and to serve it. "I can't, but I'm looking forward to lunchtime. I want to see everything you've written. Everything."

Deena ran downstairs and got the list of people who'd requested breakfast be served to them. Her body delivered the trays, but her mind was already five hours ahead, imagining how things would go with Doyle when they sat and discussed his "poetry" this afternoon.

In her fantasy he'd hand her the love letter saying, "Read this, it will tell you everything." After she read it, she'd take his hand lovingly and assure him that she felt the same. He'd take her in his arms and kiss her.

Kathy was true to her word and didn't speak to Deena all morning. She, too, seemed to have something on her mind as she went about her business, delivering towels and then pouring coffee at the buffet breakfast in the dining room.

"Peaceful coexistence at last," Lydia said with a sigh. "It's wonderful."

"I think it's too quiet around here," Johnny complained as he zoomed around the dining room tables holding his model plane over his head.

"Hmmmm," Deena agreed absently as she helped clean up the tables, having delivered all her trays. She'd hardly noticed that Kathy was avoiding her. Right now Doyle was the only person in the world to her.

Deena was glad she had chores to occupy her until lunch. She had to finish cleaning up from breakfast, retrieve the breakfast trays, and help her mother put together the basket lunches for the guests who'd asked for them. While she was at it, she decided to pack an extra basket and slip in two plastic-wrapped plates of blueberry cobbler.

Close to noon, Deena caught sight of Doyle coming down the stairs. "I packed us a picnic basket," she chirped brightly. "I thought we would go to a pretty spot I know down the road, and while we ate lunch I could read whatever it was you wanted me to read."

He pulled out a large manila envelope. "I have the stuff here, but I'm afraid I can't make the lunch. I have to call into my office or I'll be in hot water, and I'm not sure how long it will take. My boss says she wants to hear exactly what I'm doing since this is my first big story and all."

"Can't you call after lunch?"

"They close early on Friday, summer hours."

Deena's shoulders dropped in disappointment, but then she realized what was behind it. Why, he's shy, she thought. He's too embarrassed to be there when I read what he's written about me. How sweet he is.

She reached out and took the envelope from him. "I understand perfectly," she told him, smiling kindly.

"Great," he said, heading for the front desk phone. "Let me know what you think."

"I'm sure I'll just love it," Deena replied, confident that she would.

She went out to the front porch and looked around for a private spot where she could be alone with her love letter. She walked around to the back of the inn and saw Kathy sitting alone at the picnic table looking through some papers in her blue school folder from last year. Deena wondered what Kathy was doing, but she was too eager to see what her envelope contained to stop and find out—besides, Kathy probably wouldn't speak to her, anyway.

Deena walked to a narrow dirt path that began the trail into the woods which surrounded the inn. She walked for a few paces and then sat down on the trunk of a fallen tree along the way. With trembling hands she opened the envelope and pulled out the papers.

Something was wrong. The words on the pages were typed. Maybe he typed it up this morning, she hoped. But no, each page had a title and none of them resembled a love letter. " 'Ode to a Whale,' " she read the title in a low, shaking voice. Quickly leafing through the pages she read more titles: " 'A Winter Walk,' 'The Free Life,' 'Thoughts While Moose Watching in Canada.' "

She looked inside the envelope again to see if her letter had gotten stuck. Nothing. Deena was confused. Where was the letter he wrote to her?

A horrible thought made Deena sit up straight against the tree trunk. It hardly seemed possible, but what if the letter hadn't been meant for her! But surely it had. Who else had told him to think of the Cranberry Inn as his home? Maybe the line about his soul being welcomed home was just poetic license, though. What if he had just meant the person made him feel at home, as in feel comfortable?

Then an even more atrocious thought hit Deena like a sledgehammer. What was Kathy looking at all by herself there at the picnic table? Was it possible? No. Yes. Anything was possible with man-killer Kathy around, she thought with growing fury. Could Doyle have written the letter to her?

Deena stuffed the papers back into the envelope and hurried out of the woods. Kathy was still at the picnic table. As Deena got closer, she saw that Kathy was smiling at whatever it was she was looking at. It wasn't a *Mad Magazine* kind of smile, either. It was a loving smile, the kind of smile Deena rarely saw on her cousin's face.

"What are you doing?" Deena demanded.

"I'm not talking to you, remember?" Kathy said, flipping the folder shut abruptly.

"What were you looking at?"

"None of your business, do you mind?" Kathy answered, getting up to go.

"I want to know what's in that!" Deena shouted, yanking at the folder under Kathy's arm.

"And I said it was none of your business!" Kathy yelled, using her free hand to give Deena a shove that sent her sprawling onto the ground.

"I can't believe you pushed me!" Deena cried as she sat on the ground, her eyes filling with tears. Kathy was already halfway back to the inn. She didn't even look back to see if Deena was all right.

Deena remained on the ground, trying to sort out all that had happened. Maybe she was jumping to conclusions here. Perhaps Doyle just wanted to see how she'd react to his poetry before giving her the letter. That thought made her feel better for all of a minute. But then what was Kathy being so secretive about?

Deena got up, brushed off her jeans, and headed back to the inn. The bird-watching couple stood on the porch talking to another man and woman who were staying at the inn. Today the bird watchers were dressed in matching kelly-green pants and yellow polo shirts. "Here she is," said the woman. "This is the lovely girl I was just telling you about. You don't often see young people as courteous as she is."

Wiping the scowl from her face, Deena smiled quickly and then resumed her march up the steps.

"Dear, could you tell us where—"

"Sorry, no time," Deena answered curtly, letting the screen door slam behind her. Deena couldn't waste a minute on chitchat. She was busy hatching a plan. If there was only some way to find out what was in Doyle's mind, then she'd know where she stood.

There was no one in the reception area. Deena knew her mother was probably in the office going over bills as she did every Friday. She peeked into the dining room and saw Doyle and Aunt Nancy sitting at a table continuing their interview.

A small black tape recorder sat on the table and recorded everything Nancy said. Doyle was also writing as

Nancy spoke. Deena sighed at the sight of his handsome profile and earnest expression.

Jennie, the college student from up the road who'd been hired to help with the maid duties during the summer months, came down the stairs holding a bundle of dirty linen, which she threw in a heap at the bottom landing.

"Whew, it's getting hot," she said to Deena, who was still standing in the doorway. "I wanted to go to the beach with my friends, but there's so much to do. I'm never going to get out of here."

Deena looked at the slim, red-haired girl. "I'll help you, Jennie," she volunteered. "I'll do the rooms on the right side of the staircase, and you do the ones on the left."

"Sure you don't mind?" Jennie asked.

"Absolutely not. I don't have anything else to do to-day, anyway."

Jennie gave Deena the keys to the rooms she was to clean. "I've already thrown the clean linens you'll need on all the beds," she told her.

"No problem." Deena followed Jennie up to the second floor and waited for her to turn into room one. She waited until she heard the sound of the vacuum in the room and then headed for room six, Doyle's room.

She unlocked the door, feeling like a criminal. His dresser was neatly arranged—she admired that. A portable typewriter sat on the desk by the window. His comb and brush were to one side, his deodorant, after-shave, and a bag of disposable razors to the other.

She opened the aftershave and sniffed it. Yes, that was

the woodsy, spicy smell that she'd noticed on him. She put some on her wrists so that she'd have the smell of him near her even when he wasn't there.

"Deena Scott, this is a terrible thing you're doing," she told herself as she pulled open his top drawer. Just socks and underwear. She saw he wore boxer shorts, which she approved of as being more classic than briefs.

The next drawer contained only shirts, shorts, and jeans. She checked the brands on the labels of his clothing. She approved of those, too.

The bottom drawer was the jackpot. Three different-colored folders sat one on top of the other. One was labeled "Manelli article." The second had "Expenses and receipts" written on it in Doyle's distinctive slanted hand, and the third had the abbreviation "Misc." written on it. "He's certainly organized," she said out loud. Organization was another quality Deena admired greatly.

"Here goes," she whispered, opening the folder marked "Misc." She looked for the wrinkled, berry-splotched paper she'd returned to him, but it wasn't there. There was no sign of the letter he'd been writing last night. Instead, another, different letter lay in the envelope. She knew it wasn't the same one, because this letter was written with a fine-point marker, and the other one had been in blue ballpoint.

"To my love," it opened. Not much help there, she thought as she read on, her heart racing at the passion of the romantic words. Finally at the end of the two-page letter she came to a sentence that said: "I will never forget my first sight of your raven-haired beauty."

Deena sat back on her heels, tears once again brimming in her eyes. So it was Kathy! Suspecting it had been bad enough, but now to know for certain that Doyle was in love with her cousin was even more awful.

A big tear splotched the ink on the letter Deena still held in her lap. She wiped it, smearing the ink even more. She put the letter back into the folder and picked up the one marked "Manelli Article."

She scanned the loose sheets of long, lined yellow paper that contained Doyle's notes for the article. It was all about the inn, and how warm and cozy it was, just the kind of place you'd imagine for the author of *Out at the Inn* to live. Her heart leapt when she caught sight of her name farther down the page. Skipping the paragraphs before it, she read: "And then there's Deena. What a peculiar, charming girl—so oddly old-maidish for one so young. It's as if she were one of the original Victorians who first ran the inn."

Deena felt as if someone had punched her in the chest. Returning the folders and closing the drawers, she ran out of Doyle's room and up to her own. She flung herself onto her bed.

What did Kathy have that guys always went for? Deena couldn't see it at all. She buried her head in her pillow and sobbed. "Old-maidish!" she cried. "Old-maidish!"

Chapter 6

"I t's pretty short notice, Doyle," Nancy objected. "Couldn't your photographer come tomorrow?"

"When I called in, my boss said she'd really like to do it today because the photographer is passing through on the way to his vacation spot, and if he sends the film back to her today with a courier service, she'll have it by Monday. Deadlines, you understand."

"Oh, I guess it doesn't matter," Nancy said, running her hand through her dark hair nervously. "I'm not going to get any better-looking by tomorrow."

"You look great," Doyle assured her. "He should be here at about four-thirty."

"Johnny," Nancy called to her son, who was reading comic books in the sitting room. "Find the girls and tell them to be ready to have their picture taken at four-thirty. You, too. I want you to take a bath and put on something clean."

Johnny looked down at the grass-stained white T-shirt he wore. "Do I have to?"

"Yes. Now go tell the girls."

"Tell us what?" Kathy asked, coming in through the front door.

"A guy from Doyle's magazine is coming to take pictures of us at four-thirty," Johnny explained.

"Cool. We're going to be in the magazine?"

"The article is about your mother's life," Doyle said, "and you're part of her life, aren't you?"

"She sure is," said Nancy. "I'm going upstairs to change. I don't think I want the New England literary community to see me in old jeans and a T-shirt."

"Am I hearing things?" said Lydia, who had walked into the reception area from the dining room. "There was a time when you wouldn't be seen dead in anything else."

Nancy playfully stuck her tongue out at her sister. "Times change, sister dear."

"I'm all for it," Lydia said. "We'll all spruce up for the photographer."

Kathy climbed the stairs to her room. At the second floor she saw Deena place a full trash basket outside of room four. Part of her wanted to just sneak past, but another part felt guilty about pushing Deena. She hadn't meant for her to go flying onto the ground like that.

"How come you're doing the rooms? What happened to Jennie?" she asked, standing in the doorway of room four.

Deena looked up from the covers she was tucking neatly under the mattress. Her eyes were swollen from crying. She narrowed them in a glare when she saw Kathy. How could Doyle possibly be in love with her? They had nothing in common. Deena went back to her bed-making, ignoring Kathy.

"I'm sorry I pushed you," Kathy forced herself to say. "Are you O.K.?"

"What do you care?" Deena snapped, plumping up the pillow with menacing punches.

"You're right, I don't care. I just stopped to tell you that you're supposed to look presentable this afternoon because we're all getting our pictures taken for Doyle's article." Kathy turned and left Deena standing there. Here's where Doyle's readers would get to see pictures of the "old maid," Deena thought glumly.

She sat down on the bed. If it had been this morning, she wouldn't have changed a thing about her appearance. She'd picked her clothes, set her hair, and put on make-up. But now her outfit seemed "old-maidish."

"I'll show them old-maidish," she said, getting up suddenly from the bed. She climbed the stairs to her bedroom and saw that Kathy had already thrown at least ten T-shirts on her bed in her search for the perfect one.

Deena had seen the ritual of Kathy dressing for a special occasion many times. Usually she didn't pay much attention to it. Now she sat, with arms folded, on her bed and watched everything Kathy did.

Kathy had selected a black T-shirt that had the words "Life stinks and then you die" written across it. She'd changed from the baggy denim shorts she wore into an especially tight and short pair of cutoffs.

Deena stifled the urge to object to Kathy's outfit. It seemed to her that it was wildly inappropriate. But what do I know? she thought with a sigh. She folded her arms tighter and forced herself to watch in silence.

"What are you staring at?" Kathy demanded.

"Nothing much," Deena replied flatly. She and Kathy

glared at each other for several seconds, and then Kathy returned to what she was doing. She slipped her favorite banana earrings into her pierced ears and tucked a layer of her long thick hair behind one ear to make the earring more visible. She stepped back and shook her head, admiring the effect of her earring against the dark hair.

Here comes the war paint, Deena told herself as Kathy picked up a pot of gel blush from the chaotic collection on her dresser. With deft hands Kathy applied her different make-ups. First the blush, then shimmering eye-shadows—pink, purple, and gold in different layers. She used black eyeliner and mascara unsparingly and finished off the look with a pink irridescent lipstick that was so pale and silver-flecked that it almost seemed white on her lips.

Kathy looked around the room, obviously in search of some finishing touch to her outfit that she couldn't locate. After digging through the floor of the closet and under various piles of clothing, she found her cherished orange high-top sneakers under her bed.

Deena unfolded her arms and rested her chin on the palm of her hand with her fingers covering her mouth. That's how much effort it took her not to say any one of the million remarks that were fighting to escape her lips. Words like: "You look awful. You'll embarrass your mother." Deena wasn't going to say a thing, however; great generals have always known that the best strategy in a war was to study your enemy silently.

Kathy looked at the clock. "It's only two; what are you going to do until the photographer gets here?" she asked.

"I have things to do," Deena said primly. "Please don't start worrying about me now."

"I won't," Kathy shot back. She didn't give Deena a second glance as she ran down the stairs.

Kathy spent the next hour sitting outside at the picnic table reading the latest issue of *Rolling Stone*. When she was done, she wandered back into the inn. In the front hall, she saw that the photographer had arrived ahead of schedule. He was busily setting up a shot of Doyle interviewing Nancy out on the front porch. Kathy watched from behind the screen door as the short, stocky man snapped shot after shot with his big camera. Her mother looked nervous but pretty in the flowered cotton sundress she'd put on for the pictures.

Johnny came up behind Kathy. "Do you think I look dumb?" he asked.

Kathy looked down at her brother. His curly brown hair had been wetted down with water so that it was plastered to his head in flat ripples. He wore a white shirt and a blue tie over his one pair of good blue pants.

"Kind of," she answered gently.

"He does not," Lydia said from the registration desk behind them. "He looks like a little gentleman." Kathy knew she should have realized her aunt was responsible for Johnny's appearance.

"You'd better get ready. He'll want to take pictures of us soon," said Lydia.

"I am ready. This is what I'm wearing," Kathy said, trying to sound casual.

"It most certainly is not," Lydia told her in that eerily calm voice she used when her temper was rising.

Kathy sighed deeply. "I think I look fine," she told her aunt, trying to keep a pleasant tone.

At that moment the photo session on the porch broke

63

up and Nancy approached the front door. She looked at her daughter and at Lydia and sized up the situation immediately. With a nod to her sister that said, "Let me handle this," Nancy put her arm around Kathy and led her away from the others over to the staircase. "I wish you'd put on something a little less tough-looking," she said unemotionally. "Something prettier."

"Mom," Kathy stamped her foot. "I don't want to look like some Goody Two-shoes twerp. Don't you want people to see the real me? Are you ashamed of me or something?"

"Don't be silly, Kathy," her mother whispered, beginning to sound angry. "Could you at least change the T-shirt to one with a more uplifting message and wear a pair of shorts that fit you better?"

"Terrific!" Kathy huffed. "Maybe you'd like me to wear one of Deena's stupid Literary Greats T-shirts."

"At least I can be sure Deena cares enough to look presentable for the photographers," Nancy whispered fiercely.

"Am I late?" Deena's voice came sailing down the stairs, pitched just a bit higher than usual. Nancy and Kathy looked up at her in stunned silence.

Deena stood on the stairs chewing a wad of gum. She wore Kathy's shiny metallic halter top and she'd cut the knees out of her own jeans. She'd pulled the front pieces of her hair up on top of her head and tied it with a rubber band so that it stood straight up in a ponytail. Deena had obviously dipped into her watercolors to paint a strand of her hair at the side with a bright red streak.

Deena had also dipped heavily into Kathy's make-up

supply. Her eyes were heavily lidded in blue and lined in black. Purple lipstick that Kathy had bought but never worn finished Deena's look.

"Deena," Lydia said quietly, too shocked to scold, "are you feeling all right?"

"Cool, Mom, never better," she answered, clomping down the stairs heavily in her wood-bottomed sandals. "When does the picture-taking begin? I'm rarin' to go."

"Deena, what's the matter with you?" Lydia asked.

"This is the new me, Mom. No more Little Miss Perfect Deena Scott. I'm spreading my wings, flinging free."

"Go upstairs and change immediately," Lydia ordered in a flustered voice.

Deena looked at her mother nervously and seemed ready to back down, but at that moment Doyle walked in the front door with the photographer. She had to show him her new image, show him he'd been wrong about her.

"Let me get a shot of these two together," the photographer said, putting his arm around Kathy's shoulder and ushering her over to where Deena stood at the landing. "This will be a great shot, really wild."

"I don't think—" Lydia started to object, but Nancy took her arm.

"Give it up, Lydia," she said. "Whatever the two of them have in mind, we'll never understand. Don't get your blood pressure going over it."

"But how is it going to look?"

"It'll look really wild," Nancy said with a laugh, winking at her sister.

The photographer was jumping all around Deena and

Kathy, taking pictures of them. "Hey, do we have to be together in every shot?" Kathy objected. "It's not like we're Siamese twins, you know."

"No, but you're Cranberry Cousins," Johnny piped up from his perch on the steps behind them.

"Quiet!" both Kathy and Deena told him at once.

All this time Doyle had been standing off in a corner, looking at Deena with a baffled expression. She caught sight of him staring at her and smiled, waving a wiggly fingered hi and shifting her hips flirtatiously.

The photographer had finished with them and was taking shots of Lydia and Nancy as they talked to some guests who had happened to walk in at that moment. "I want to get a series of shots of you doing what you do every day, Mrs. Manelli," the photographer told Nancy.

"Hey, Doyle, man," Deena called over to him. "Bet you never figured that when the weekend comes I cut loose, huh? I just keep the other image going for the sake of the guests. This is the real me."

"No, you sure had me fooled," he replied, looking at her skeptically.

"Have you flipped?" Kathy whispered to her.

"Bug off, cuzzy wuzzy," Deena told her. "I thought you'd like the new me."

That made Kathy stop and think. She was always complaining that Deena should loosen up. But now that she was acting differently, Kathy didn't like it. It was too bizarre, and it definitely was not Deena—everything she did looked kind of . . . off kilter.

"Is this like in that movie *Invasion of the Body Snatchers*, where alien life forms take over people's bodies and the people start acting really weird?" she asked.

"Do you think it's weird to act just like you do?" Deena asked her. She'd picked up Kathy's tape player from the front hall table and was now shaking to the beat of the ThunderMongers on the headphones.

"You were right about these ThunderMongers, Doyle," she said, snapping her fingers. "Really heavy lyrics. Totally mind-blowing, actually."

It was stuff like that, Kathy thought. Nobody said "mind-blowing" anymore, and she had to add that last "actually."

Deena plopped down on the sofa in the sitting room and kicked her feet up on the coffee table. She blew a big pink bubble and then sucked it back in. "Oh, baby, baby, I'm banging my head on a wall, why don't you call, call for me," she sang tunelessly at the top of her voice, along with the tape.

Doyle and Kathy exchanged bewildered looks. Kathy shrugged her shoulders at the baffled young reporter.

"Is Deena having a nervous breakdown?" Johnny asked his sister seriously.

"Could be," Kathy murmured. "Maybe when I pushed her today something got knocked loose."

Deena whipped the headphones down around her shoulders. "What are all you stuffed shirts looking at? Haven't you ever seen a gal who likes to have some fun?"

"Deena," Kathy said, pulling her cousin up off the sofa and over to the side of the stairs. "I don't know what's the matter with you, but you're making a total jerk of yourself."

"I don't care what you think, Kathy," Deena whispered in a low, angry voice. "If Doyle likes the way you are, then two can play at that game. I can be Miss Cool, too."

"You've gone totally berserk," Kathy said. "I don't know what you're talking about."

"Oh, don't you?" Deena sneered sarcastically.

"No, I don't."

"Fine," said Deena, "then tell me what you were looking at with such fascination this afternoon. Tell me what was so important for you to hide that you had to push me to the ground so that I wouldn't see it."

"That's none of your business," Kathy said, looking away from Deena uncomfortably.

"If that's how you want to be, then this is how I'm going to be," Deena said. "From now on this is the new Deena Scott."

Chapter 7

"Man, I'm tired," Kathy said, dragging herself up the stairs to bed.

"Yeah, man, me too," said Deena behind her.

Kathy shot her cousin a weary look. This new Deena was driving Kathy insane. She'd kept up her weird act all the way through dinner and into the evening. She'd even sponsored a New Wave dance contest among the guests—an event that, oddly enough, they had seemed to enjoy.

Deena topped the evening off by cornering Doyle, and some of the other guests he happened to be sitting with, in order to recite some rap poetry she'd composed quickly to go with her new image.

"I'm the big D, look at me, you will see that I feel free. That's free, fr-free-fr-free-free-free!" At that point Deena interjected a dance, standing ramrod straight and making robot movements that looked more like they belonged to R2-D2 than to a break dancer.

"There are certainly many facets to your personality,"

Doyle said, still wearing the quizzical expression he'd worn when he first saw Deena at the photo session.

Deena beamed at this. "Yes, a creative person must be open to all aspects of life," she replied.

Lydia had gone to bed early with a severe headache. It was only the fact that Nancy insisted they let Deena play out whatever she was going through that kept Lydia from physically dragging Deena up to the bathroom and throwing her into a cold shower to make her come to her senses.

It had been a long day for everyone. Now Kathy threw her clothes on the bedroom floor, slipped her big T-shirt over her head, and crawled into bed without even bothering to take off her make-up. Deena returned from the bathroom all scrubbed and combed out. The now pale red streak on her hair was the only remnant of the "new" Deena.

The new Deena was still there, though. She snapped on the stereo and boogied around the room a few times, just in case Kathy might have mistakenly thought her scrubbed face meant she was returning to her old ways.

In truth, though, Deena was exhausted herself. The emotional ups and downs of the morning, combined with the strain of trying to act like someone she wasn't, had left her feeling totally drained.

Kathy had already buried her head under the pillow when Deena flipped off the light on her side of the room. Deena lay in her bed and looked at the sleeping figure of her cousin, half-illuminated by the moonlight. She really was hiding her emotions well, Deena thought with just a touch of admiration. How could she have received a love letter like the one Doyle wrote her and not show any sign of feeling?

It occurred to Deena that maybe Kathy didn't care about Doyle, so his outpouring of affection meant nothing to her. But then why was she being so secretive about the letter?

Deena's mind wouldn't stop working overtime. Had Doyle been impressed with her new image? Maybe she could still win him over. Perhaps when he saw that Kathy wasn't interested in him and that Deena wasn't "old-maidish" after all, he'd change his mind and write Deena one of his wonderful love letters.

Deena tried to fall off to sleep. She settled into one position and then repositioned herself a minute later. Nothing felt comfortable.

She slipped out of bed and walked out into the hall. It was Friday night, the second night of the full moon, and the same silvery light flooded the hall. She walked over to the hall window and looked out into the yard.

There was Doyle, once again sitting at the picnic bench, writing feverishly. He looked up sharply and stared at the inn. It almost seemed that he was looking directly at Deena, so she stepped back from the window. When she returned, she saw that he was holding his head in his hands with the look of someone who was in deep emotional turmoil.

Deena hoped she'd at least confused him with the new Deena. Maybe he'd thought he loved Kathy, but now he wasn't sure.

Deena closed her eyes and tried to imagine what he was writing. . . . "I never saw this side of Deena before.

71

She's like a butterfly newly emerged from her cocoon, trying out her colorful wings."

As Deena climbed into bed, she realized she was suddenly exhausted. It had been a long day full of strange emotions. The thought that tomorrow she'd have to get up and start acting like Kathy all over again filled her with a tremendous weariness. Maybe it wouldn't be so difficult once she got the hang of it. At least she hoped not.

Deena shut her eyes and let her mind wander. She imagined that she and Doyle were married and living in a big city somewhere. She was wearing a tiger-print bustier top, a black leather mini, and fishnet stockings. She had on Kathy's banana earrings.

Doyle was in their apartment working on his computer, composing poetry. "How do you like this one, dear?" he asked her. "I call it 'Ode to a Dodo Bird.'"

"Don't ask me, Doyle, honey," Deena heard herself answer in the dream. "You know I don't have any opinions about poetry. I haven't had a thought in my head since the day I decided to be more like my cousin Kathy."

At that moment someone knocked on the door. Deena opened the door and saw Kathy standing there—only Kathy had changed drastically. Her long brown hair was tied back in a bun. She wore a pink angora sweater and a blue pleated skirt over knee-socks and loafers. She had a large dictionary under her arm.

"What's happened to you?" Deena asked.

"Since you've stolen my identity, I had to take yours," Kathy answered. "It's not so bad being you. I've come to like it quite a bit, actually."

"Kathy!" Doyle cried, leaping up from his computer. "You've come at last."

"Yes, Doyle!" Kathy cried, dropping her dictionary and running into his arms.

"Hey, wait a minute!" Deena cried. "I thought you didn't like her type."

"I love her type. I love her."

"But she's . . . she's old-maidish."

"I love old-maidish," Doyle told her. "I've been waiting for an old-maidish girl all my life."

"This has all been a big mistake!" Deena cried. "I'm the one who's old-maidish. She's really me. I mean, I'm really her. No, I mean I'm me and she's her, only we're not . . ."

Deena opened her eyes and blinked. She'd been somewhere between waking and sleeping. She turned and saw her cousin sleeping peacefully across the room from her, her banana earrings still in her earlobes. Deena checked Kathy's dressertop. It was still a mess. Deena's dresser was still neat. It wasn't too late. She wasn't too far gone to get her Deena-hood back.

She had to admit this was one of her dumber ideas, anyway. She couldn't compete with Kathy at doing what Kathy did best—being herself. She'd have to find another way to win Doyle.

With a wide yawn she told herself that she'd figure something out tomorrow. Relieved that at least she could go back to being Deena, she rolled over, stretched, and finally fell into a peaceful sleep.

Saturday morning started strangely for Deena. She awoke and saw that the digital clock radio read only six

73

in the morning, yet Kathy was already awake. Deena pinched herself to make sure she wasn't stuck back in the dream. No, she was awake all right.

Kathy was sitting, perched on the window. Her back was to Deena, but Deena could see that she had a white piece of paper out and was using her blue folder, which was open on her lap to lean on. From the way Kathy's right elbow was moving, Deena could tell that she was writing something on paper in the same binder she'd had yesterday. A secret love letter to Doyle, Deena assumed, all her hurt feelings from yesterday zooming back to the surface.

"Up early," Deena commented just a bit too loudly. Kathy jumped up, startled, and quickly flipped the folder shut.

"Yeah," she answered, rubbing her mascara-smudged eyes with the heel of her palm. "I guess I am."

Kathy grabbed a towel and headed into the bathroom, still holding her folder. Deena was consumed with jealousy and curiosity. She had to see what was in that folder. A few minutes later Kathy came out of the bathroom, freshly showered and without the folder.

"You left your folder in the bathroom," Deena said, trying to sound casual.

"What folder?" Kathy asked as she towel-dried her hair.

"The blue one you just took in there," Deena snapped.

"I don't know what you're talking about," Kathy replied, looking up at her with big innocent brown eyes.

"Yes, you do!" Deena cried, stomping her foot on the floor in frustration.

"Deena, dear, you haven't been yourself lately. I'm becoming very worried about your mental health," Kathy told her in a sweet voice that Deena knew was false. Kathy pulled on her shorts and an oversized cotton shirt with a tropical pattern while she shook her head sorrowfully.

"Well, I'm myself today, and I know when you're lying," Deena insisted.

"Poor Deena, once so brilliant, now so demented," Kathy said, patting Deena on the head patronizingly. "Such a shame," she muttered, walking out of the room.

"Aaaaaaaahhhhhhh!" Deena squealed in annoyance. "She is the most aggravating person on the face of the earth. I don't know how Doyle could be in love with her. I don't know how even her own mother could love her!"

Deena dressed and stomped downstairs. She caught sight of Doyle walking out the front door and went out to join him on the porch. "Hi, Deena," he said nervously when he saw her, glancing around as if he wanted to find a quick escape route.

"Oh, you don't have to run away," she said, smiling ruefully. "The old Deena is back."

"That's good. I liked her a lot better."

"You did!" Deena exclaimed, filled with new hope at his kind words. "Well, here I am. I wanted to tell you that I adored the poems you gave me yesterday. Do you have time today to discuss them in depth?"

"I have a pretty full day today," he told her with a tone in his voice that sounded a little guilty to Deena. "I'm getting close to my deadline for delivering the article, and I wanted to talk to Mrs. Manelli about a few more things. She's going to spend the day showing me some of her earlier plays and short stories."

"Sure, I understand. I have to finish up my sculpture for the art show anyway."

Just then Kathy came out onto the porch. "Deena, come on, I need help with breakfast."

Deena looked from Doyle to Kathy to see their expressions. "Hi, Kath," Doyle said pleasantly. "How's it going?"

Kath! Deena thought, outraged. That proved something was going on! She turned angrily on her heels and marched off the porch.

"Is she always so strange?" Doyle asked Kathy.

"Yup," Kathy answered, "but these days she's been a little loonier than usual. Don't ask me why."

That afternoon Deena sat sulkily on the porch and finished painting her sculpture for the art show. The library's deadline for entries was Monday, and she wanted to make sure hers was submitted in time. She used black paint to draw mountains and stars and planets at the base of the lumpy papier-mâché statue. The entire universe would be represented in this piece of art.

She had been working for half an hour when she looked up and noticed Kathy walking across the lawn, heading for the woods. What was going on? Kathy referred to the woods as "that place full of bugs and trees." It was odd that she would suddenly be out communing with nature.

"How's the project going?" Nancy asked, coming out onto the porch.

"O.K.," Deena said, putting down her brush. "I thought you were going to be working with Doyle on his interview."

"Later," Nancy told her as she sat down on the porch

76

floor and looked at the sculpture. "I told him I couldn't talk to him until this afternoon."

An alarm went off in Deena's head. "Where is Doyle now?" she asked.

"I'm not sure."

"Excuse me, Aunt Nancy, I have to go do something."

"Sure thing," Nancy answered. "And Deena, I just wanted to say that I'm glad you're back to your old self, and if you ever need to talk about anything, you know I'm here."

"Thanks," Deena said, realizing that yesterday's performance had everyone worried. "I'm really fine," she told her aunt. "I just have to see about something."

Deena went upstairs and knocked on Doyle's door. There was no answer. She listened at the bathroom doors and was embarrassed when an old man opened the door, dressed only in a towel and his slippers.

She checked the dining room, the sitting room, and the back yard. Doyle was nowhere to be found. Deena wandered into the kitchen, deep in thought.

"Have you seen Doyle anywhere?" she asked Johnny, who was feeding the kittens. She noticed how much they'd grown. They were almost cats.

"I saw him go out the back door," Johnny said absently.

Deena had a horrifying thought. Doyle had gone to meet Kathy in the woods.

Deena walked out the back door and peered into the woods. What a rat, she thought. It was wrong for a college graduate to use his superior intellect and maturity to lure a young girl to shameful behavior in the woods. No,

Deena was not going to allow this to go on right under her nose.

Clenching her fists and setting her jaw in an expression of stern determination, Deena marched into the woods at the spot where she'd seen Kathy enter. Brushing aside sticks and branches she ran down the narrow dirt trail.

She walked for almost ten minutes until she came to a place where the trail ended. There was no sign of anyone. Bent on finding them, she pressed on, following the dim sound of a brook she knew was at the bottom of a sloping hill.

After a few yards she caught sight of Kathy's tropical T-shirt. She was sitting by the brook. Deena looked around. She couldn't see Doyle. Crouching low, she approached her cousin, whose back was turned to her. Kathy was sitting, she saw now, with her bare feet in the brook.

She guessed that Doyle was probably off searching for a cozier spot. Deena thought of what she would say to Kathy.

Suddenly Kathy twisted around and looked her cousin in the eyes. A horrified expression came over her face. "Deena, there's a snake on you!" she screamed.

Chapter 8

"A aaaaahhhhhh! Get it off me! Get it off me!" Deena screamed as she ran frantically through the woods, waving her arms and kicking her feet. "Get it off me!"

In her frenzy Deena tripped on a rock and stumbled onto her hands and knees in the brook. She looked up to see Kathy convulsed with laughter before her.

"Is it gone? Is the snake gone?" Deena asked in a trembling voice.

"There was no . . . there was no snake," Kathy managed to say through her laughter. "You should have seen your face, though." She broke into another fit of laughter that sent tears rolling down her cheeks.

"Excuse me, but I fail to see the humor here," Deena said, getting up out of the brook. "Do you enjoy scaring me out of my wits?"

"Well, isn't that what you were trying to do to me, sneaking up behind me like that?"

"It most certainly was not. I don't indulge in such juvenile pranks."

"Then exactly what were you indulging in, skittering around out there in the woods?"

Deena checked around for signs of Doyle's approach. He was still nowhere to be seen. "I was saving you from yourself. What would Roy think of what you're doing?"

"I don't think he'd care much," Kathy replied.

"I think he certainly would care," Deena pressed on, wringing the water from her T-shirt. "And your mother, what would your mother say?"

"She'd probably freak—that's why I'm doing it in secret."

"So you admit it!" Deena cried triumphantly, her worst suspicions confirmed at last.

Kathy narrowed her eyes and studied her cousin. "Deena, I hate to say this, but I really think you've gone lunatic. What is it exactly that you think I'm admitting?"

"Oh, no," Deena scoffed, "don't get coy with me now that the cat is out of the bag. I don't know where he's hiding, but I know you're here in the woods to have a secret lover's meeting with Doyle." Deena spun around quickly. "Come out, come out, wherever you are, Doyle!" she called. "You can't hide from me much longer. I know what you're up to."

Kathy shook her head. "Cool out, Deena. I'm not meeting Doyle or anyone else here."

Deena spotted the blue folder Kathy had been writing in this morning sitting behind her. Four sharpened pencils lay on top of it. "I see, you've come out here to write love letters to him away from prying eyes."

"Yes, yes, you've caught me," Kathy said with a sigh,

80

raising her hand to her forehead dramatically. "I admit everything. Look for yourself."

Deena picked up the folder and opened it. Tucked into the front pockets were three pieces of paper. Each was a pencil sketch, expertly rendered. One was of a willow tree, the second was a fence with tiger lillies growing wild around it. The third was a sketch of Kathy at about age seven. Her eyes were large and sparkling with happiness in the drawing.

Deena looked at the papers in the back pocket. They were also sketches, not as professional but obviously done by someone with real talent. They were sketches of nature—a flower, the brook, the view from their bedroom window.

"What are these?" Deena asked.

"These are sketches my dad did," Kathy said, pointing to the drawings in the front of the folder. "He and I used to sketch together in the park all the time. He was a professional artist. I bet he would have been famous someday if he hadn't . . . hadn't, you know . . . died and all."

"Did you do these other sketches?" Deena asked.

"Yeah. They're not very good, though. I just like to do them, that's all—for the fun of it."

"They are good," Deena said, spreading the pictures out on the ground in front of her. "Why have you made this such a big secret?"

Kathy picked up a green leaf that had fallen to the ground and began folding it into a square on her knee. "Because I knew that if I showed you, you'd make a big deal out of it. You'd insist on showing everyone and force me to enter them in that library show."

"You're right, I would have. What's so bad about that?"

"The thing is, drawings like these would make my mother think of Dad. I know she misses him a lot and it isn't easy for her. I think she's been real lonely since he died, even though she has us and all. This is the happiest she's been in a long time; I don't want to ruin it for her."

"I knew you liked to draw, but I never thought you took it seriously. How come you started now?"

"I don't know. The other day when Johnny said that he liked to take walks in the woods, it reminded me of when I used to take walks with my father in the park. I remembered how much fun it was to sit and sketch, and since it's been sort of boring around here lately, I figured it would be something to do."

"I'm sorry," Deena said. "I thought you had love letters in this folder."

"I do in a way," Kathy said softly. "These sketches remind me of how much my father loved me. It's like he's here beside me again when I do nature sketches."

Deena saw that Kathy's eyes were glistening with tears. "Gosh, I've been acting like a jerk," Deena said, sitting next to her cousin and putting an arm around her shoulder.

"Yeah," Kathy said with a laugh in her voice as she quickly wiped away one mascara-black tear that rolled down her cheek, "that's nothing new."

Deena wrinkled her nose and stuck her tongue out at Kathy, but she kept her arm around her. Kathy was always so tough; she liked this softer side of her.

"Why *have* you been acting so bugged lately, anyway?" Kathy asked. "And why are you babbling about some secret love letters?"

"You'll think I'm a real ninny," Deena started, suddenly feeling like a fool. "But I thought you and Doyle were having a secret love affair and writing love letters to each other on the sly."

"Why would you ever think anything like that?" Kathy asked, pulling away from her cousin and scrutinizing her as if she was looking for signs of brain damage. "I only really talked to the guy that one time about the ThunderMongers."

"Yes, but you seemed to hit it off so well. And I know for a fact that Doyle is writing passionate love letters to someone at the inn."

"How do you know that?"

"I found part of one in the back yard." Deena looked away, trying to decide if she should confess the whole story. "And I went into his room and looked through his drawer and found another one," she confessed.

Kathy sat with her mouth open. "I can't believe it! Miss Perfect turns out to be a spy. Prying into the personal possessions of our guests—the welcome members of our Cranberry Inn family. For shame!"

"I am ashamed," Deena admitted with downcast eyes.

"You should be. That sounds like something I would do. So come on, tell me, what did you find?"

"Just what I said, a second love letter. He's really crazy over whomever it is he's writing to. He called her 'my beloved' and 'beautiful one.' It's definitely someone here because he keeps mentioning the inn."

"Maybe it's Jennie, the day maid," Kathy suggested.

"She's about his age and kind of cute. She also has a really great body."

"No, it's not her," Deena said. "Jennie has bright red hair, and in one line of the second letter he called the person his raven-haired beauty. That's why I thought it was you—that's also why I was trying to act like you."

"You're weird," Kathy said, laughing. "It's definitely not me. Who could it be?"

The girls sat and thought. Were there any guests with dark hair about Doyle's age staying at the inn? No. It was very mysterious.

Suddenly the girls looked at each other, struck with the exact same horrible thought. "You don't suppose..." Deena began.

"No, she's much too old for him."

"But they have been spending a lot of time together, and she does have dark hair," Deena pointed out.

"My mother! That's impossible. Totally impossible," Kathy insisted.

Deena wasn't so sure. "It makes a certain amount of sense if you think about it," she said. "Here's a guy, fresh out of college. He wants to be a writer, but he's just starting out. He meets a lonely widow who just happens to have a certain amount of literary fame—and who just happens to be the co-owner of an inn. I think it *is* your mother he's after."

"I guess it's really not that weird," Kathy said, regaining her composure. "I mean, look at Cher. She goes out with younger men and it's O.K. It's cool, even. What does age really matter if two people like each other? It's kind of out of date to get all bent over it, Deena."

84

"You haven't even thought about the worst part of it," Deena pointed out.

"What's that?"

"Doyle would be your stepfather."

"Uh-uh, no way," Kathy declared. "No way is that overgrown teen wolf going to be my stepfather."

"But what can we do about it?" Deena asked despairingly. In the course of a few minutes Doyle was no longer the man of her dreams. He wasn't even a romantic figure who was stealing off into the woods for a romantic interlude. He had suddenly been transformed into a craven opportunist threatening the good fortune of a hardworking but vulnerable widow.

"There's only one thing we can do," Kathy said matter-of-factly.

"What's that?"

"Kill him," Kathy said flatly.

"Kathy!"

"O.K., so maybe that's extreme, but we have to find a way to get rid of him before he hurts my mother," Kathy insisted seriously.

"You know, you just made a good point," Deena said. "We're forgetting something fairly crucial here."

"What's that?"

"Your mother! She's an intelligent woman. She's not going to be interested in some boy just out of college who writes her mushy letters. She is a businesswoman, a poet, a mother, for heaven's sake."

Kathy laughed. "You're right for once. We did get sort of carried away there. Mom's no dope; she'd see right through his scam. She probably laughed her head off when she got those goofy letters."

85

"Sure she did," Deena agreed, feeling giddy with relief.

Kathy got up and brushed the dirt from her shorts. "Let's go get some lunch," she suggested.

"I am hungry," Deena agreed.

Kathy picked up her folder and tucked the drawings back inside the folder pockets. "Me, too," she said as she headed up the sloping hill toward the inn.

"You really should mat one of your sketches and enter it in the library show on Monday," Deena suggested as she walked back up the dirt trail behind her cousin. "It would be a shame not to share your talent with others."

"This is exactly why I didn't want you to know about the sketches," Kathy said. "I knew you were going to make a whole production out of it."

Deena and Kathy continued to bicker pleasantly about the art show as they made their way through the woods. "O.K., hide your light under a bushel, see if I care," Deena stated as they emerged from the woods into the back yard.

"Hide my what under a what?"

"It's an expression that means you hide the light of your inner soul in a dark place so the world never gets to see it for the luminous thing it is."

"I don't want the whole world looking at my soul like a bunch of Peeping Toms."

"Oh, suit yourself," Deena gave in with a sigh. "But I still say they're excellent sketches."

"You know," Kathy said, wanting to change the subject and get Deena's mind off the sketches, "it kind of cracks me up that we thought my mother would go for a bunch of love letters from a guy who's just out of college."

"It is pretty funny, actually," Deena agreed as they headed for the front of the inn. "It's hilarious, in fact."

Kathy started laughing. "And to think," she said between giggles, "that we were worried about him turning out to be my stepfather."

"Can you imagine it?" Deena joined Kathy's laughter. "Picture this: 'Dad, have you been wearing my ThunderMongers sweat shirt again?'"

"Or how about this," Kathy gasped, holding her side with laughter. "'Dad and I will have a soda, please; we're not old enough to drink in this restaurant.'"

The girls staggered around the corner to the front of the inn, convulsed with laughter. "Stop it, stop it," Deena gasped, leaning against the porch. "I can't take anymore."

Deena turned back to her cousin and noticed that she had stopped laughing. In fact, her face was dead serious.

"What is it? What's the matter?" she asked.

"Look," Kathy replied, pointing to the porch. There, sitting on the porch swing, were Doyle and Nancy. Doyle was obviously telling her something that Nancy found hilariously funny. She was laughing almost as hard as Kathy and Deena had been just moments ago.

"Hi, girls," Nancy called to them as they came into sight. Deena had to admit that Doyle did look handsome in his heather-blue polo shirt and faded jeans. There was something different about him, too.

Deena and Kathy walked up the stairs, eyeing Doyle suspiciously. "Where were you?" Deena asked him.

"I went into town to mail something to my office. I figured I'd take advantage of the free time until Nancy could talk to me."

Kathy and Deena exchanged glances. Up until now he had always called her Ms. Manelli—but now it was "Nancy."

"I was just wondering," Deena answered coolly. "You told me you were going to be busy interviewing all morning, and it obviously wasn't true, that's all."

"Gee, sorry, Deena, it was just an unexpected change of plans."

"What happened to your glasses?" Kathy asked, noticing that he wasn't wearing them.

"I put my contacts in," Doyle answered.

"What is this, the Spanish Inquisition?" Nancy laughed. "Lighten up, you two. Doyle was just telling me the most hilarious story about the time he and his fraternity brothers put a stuffed armadillo on the dean's seat during an awards dinner. When the dean sat on it, he jumped up and started yelling, 'Help, help, I've been bitten by an armadillo!'"

She began laughing all over again, and Doyle chuckled at the memory. The girls were not amused, however.

"Don't you think that's a little childish?" Kathy wanted to know. "I mean, it was embarrassing for the poor guy."

"I believe they call that kind of humor sophomoric," Deena added. "To each his own, I suppose."

"Well, I happen to think the story is a riot, and I don't care what you two say," Nancy said, unconcerned by their lack of approval.

"The interview has been going real well," Doyle told them, gazing at Nancy. "Nancy is such a fascinating woman. I've never met anyone like her. She's done so many things, experienced so much. You don't know how lucky you are to live with such an unusual woman."

"Oh, we know how special Aunt Nancy is," Deena said pointedly. "That's why we want to make sure no one ever takes advantage of her good nature and trusting temperament. She's such a dear."

"You make me sound like an addled old lady, Deena," Nancy said. "I'm not senile yet."

"Yes, Mom, but you're not a teenager, either."

"Thank you for reminding me of that, Kathy," Nancy said, giving her daughter a bewildered look.

"I don't mean to embarrass you, Nancy," Doyle said. "It's just that I'm so impressed with all that you've done with your life."

"Yes, she has had a *long* life," Kathy chimed in.

"A *very* long one," Deena added.

"Stop it," Nancy said, laughing. "Anyway, I am having a ball doing this interview, Doyle. You are welcome to stay for as long as you like. We love having you here. Isn't that right, girls?"

Deena and Kathy looked at each other and then at Doyle. "Right," they droned at the same time.

"We're totally thrilled," Kathy added flatly.

Chapter 9

"We've got to come up with a plan," said Deena, pacing the floor of her bedroom. "There must be a way to defuse this time bomb of a romance."

"She did look like she liked him, didn't she?" Kathy agreed from her spot on her bed. "The way she was laughing at his dumb story yesterday! It wasn't even funny."

"I blame myself," Deena stated. "I was so dazzled by his surface charm that I blinded myself to the scheming, conniving cad that he really is. I should have seen through it. I was the one who first talked to him."

"No sense worrying about that now. Mom spent every free minute she had with him yesterday, and I'll bet she plans to do it again today if we don't do something."

"You're quite right," Deena replied. "The more time she spends with him, the more susceptible to his considerable charm she'll be. We can't let them be alone together for a second, that's the first thing."

"Good idea," said Kathy, swinging her legs around

and jumping up off the bed. "Between the two of us we should be able to keep them apart all day."

The girls dressed quickly. Since it was Sunday, the one day the inn served a full sit-down breakfast instead of a buffet, they were required to help out with the waitressing duties all through breakfast.

Kathy grabbed Deena's arm as they were about to enter the dining room. "It's worse than I thought," she whispered. "Look at her."

"What's the matter?" Deena asked, studying Nancy, who was going from table to table with a coffeepot in her hand offering fresh coffee to the smattering of guests who were already up for breakfast. "She looks fine to me."

"That's the point. That sundress she's wearing is new, she has make-up on, and look at her hair! It's set. She must have borrowed your mother's hot rollers. I don't think my mother ever set her hair in her life until this morning."

Deena looked back at Nancy. She did look especially feminine this morning, wearing a blue, Aztec-print sundress with wide straps and a fitted top that showed off her thin figure to its best advantage. Her hair was tied back. But Kathy had been right, the ends were curled, and she *was* wearing a coral shade of lipstick and possibly even mascara.

"You're right, things do look bad," Deena agreed. "We've got to stay close to her every second."

The girls spotted Doyle sitting alone at a table in the far corner of the dining room. He was eating breakfast and reading his copy of *Out at the Inn*. Nancy was heading toward him with her pot of coffee.

"Enemy sighted at oh-nine-hundred," Deena whispered. "He is about to make contact with subject. Prepare to attack immediately."

Kathy turned to her cousin and nodded. "Roger, message received."

Kathy and Deena made a beeline for Doyle's table. "Hi, Mom," Kathy called cheerily. "Let me take that coffeepot from you, you must be getting tired. You need rest at your age. You go sit down."

Nancy looked at her daughter quizzically, but handed her the pot. "Thanks, I could use a break."

"Join me for breakfast, please," Doyle said to Nancy, standing and pulling out the chair to his right.

"I'd love to," Nancy answered, taking the seat beside him. "Thanks to my sweet daughter, I can sit for a few minutes."

"I changed my mind," Kathy said quickly, handing the pot back to her mother.

"She means she forgot that we have to get into the kitchen and start helping out. It's past seven-thirty; we should be getting a rush soon."

"Deena, you know it doesn't get busy down here until almost nine-thirty."

"I just feel it in my bones. I think we're going to have an early breakfast rush this morning. Something just tells me we'd better get cracking."

"I think Deena's right," Kathy agreed. "Oh, and I think those people over there want coffee," she added, pointing to an elderly couple who were eating by the entrance.

"What makes you think that, Kathy?" Nancy asked, looking at the couple, who seemed wrapped up in their own conversation.

"Because they asked me on my way over," Kathy lied.

"Then please take this pot and go offer them coffee," said Nancy, beginning to sound exasperated.

"They specifically asked for you," Deena chimed in. "I heard them."

Nancy narrowed her eyes suspiciously at Deena, but pulled herself out of her chair. "Excuse me," she said to Doyle, "it seems duty calls, after all."

"No problem," Doyle replied. "We'll have all day to chat, I hope."

"Yes, we will," she answered, smiling at him in a way that made Deena and Kathy uneasy. "Lydia has agreed to take over some of my responsibilities for today so we can have some free time together."

"Great," said Doyle. "I'm looking forward to it."

"So am I," she said, turning to go give coffee to the couple who hadn't requested it.

"How are you two this morning?" he asked them pleasantly.

"We're just fine," Deena said huffily, turning her back to him.

"Yes, fine," Kathy repeated, following Deena to the kitchen door.

"We've got to do something quickly," Deena said. "This is getting to the crisis stage. If they spend the day together, we're sunk. Did you see the way she smiled at him?"

"I have an idea," said Kathy. "Doesn't your mother have an electric razor?"

"She has one, yes."

"Good, get it from her and here's what we'll do—"

"Girls," Lydia interrupted, coming out of the kitchen.

"Stop gabbing and get going. Didn't you notice that three tables of guests just walked in?"

"Sorry, Mom."

"Just get the razor, and I'll explain the rest after breakfast," Kathy said, heading toward the guests at the table. "I still have to figure out a few details of the plan, anyway."

"O.K." Deena spent the next two hours serving breakfast and feeling strangely happy. Even though they had a big problem on their hands, it was nice to be working with Kathy instead of fighting with her. It made her feel like they were almost . . . sisters.

After breakfast Deena went into her mother's bedroom and took Lydia's Lady Norelco off the dresser. Was Kathy planning to shave Doyle's head? No. Kathy would probably consider that an improvement.

Kathy was waiting for her at the front desk. "Timing is everything here," she explained to Deena, checking around guiltily to make sure no one was listening. "You find Doyle and tell him he's received a phone call at the front desk. I'll call from our private phone upstairs and pretend I'm somebody from where he works, and that he's needed at the office first thing Monday morning."

"You're a genius!" Deena whispered enthusiastically. "He told me he has a female boss, so it will work out perfectly—except I don't know her name."

"That's where the electric razor comes in," Kathy explained. "I saw a guy do it on TV a couple of nights ago. Every time he talked to his boss on the phone, he turned on the electric razor and pretended they had a bad connection. When his boss asked him something he couldn't answer, he brought the razor close to the phone and pre-

94

tended he didn't understand the question. The razor will disguise my voice, too."

"Brilliant," said Deena. "I'll never call you brainless again."

"This looks like a good time to do it, while you're mother is still in the kitchen and before Doyle and my mother go out somewhere."

"You get ready upstairs. I'll go find Doyle," Deena said. She stood near the phone until it rang. She picked it up quickly and said, "Hello, Cranberry Inn, can I help you?"

"Go get Doyle and stop fooling around," said Kathy on the other end of the phone.

"I wasn't fooling around," Deena whispered. "I want this to sound realistic in case anyone is listening."

"Just get him, please."

"I'm going, I'm going." Deena went to Doyle's room and knocked. He opened the door and smiled at her. "Phone call for you," she said.

"Thanks," he said, following her. "Deena, you've been acting strangely. Are we still friends?"

"Oh, absolutely, Doyle," she said sweetly. "Now hurry, the phone call sounded like it was long distance."

He bounded down the stairs two at a time and picked up the phone at the front desk. "Hello, hello." He held the phone away from his ear. Deena could hear the crackling of the electric razor even though she was several feet away.

"Hello, Doyle," Kathy said in a high-pitched voice on the other end, "this is your boss . . ."Here she brought the razor in close.

"I know you're my boss, Millie, why so formal?" he

answered. "Can you hear me? We have a terrible connection."

"I was just fooling with you, Doyle," Kathy replied, pulling the razor back from the phone. "Yes, this connection is dreadful, but what I have to say will only take a minute."

"Are you O.K.?" Doyle asked. "You sound really terrible. Are you sick?"

"Yes, a little cold," Kathy answered, lowering the register of her voice.

Deena was trying hard not to giggle. She smiled at Doyle and raced upstairs to join Kathy in their bedroom to hear what she was saying to him.

"We've had to push up the deadline for your story, so I need you to be in the office Monday to give it to me," Kathy croaked with the razor blade buzzing at her side. Deena stuck her face into a pillow in order to stifle the giggles that were now uncontrollable.

"Couldn't I put it in Monday's overnight mail?" he asked. "I need tonight to write it and that way you'd have it on Tuesday. I'm having such a great time here. Nancy Manelli is really a fascinating person."

"We didn't send you there to have fun," Kathy scolded. "I'm sure Mrs. Manelli has more important things to do than fool around with a youngster like you. Get back to the office and leave that poor *old* woman in peace."

At the last remark Deena's giggles turned to gales of laughter. She bit down hard on the pillow.

"You're the boss," Doyle conceded glumly. "Were you able to get in touch with that guy for the book review column, what was his name again?"

"Yes, you mean . . ." Kathy zoomed in close with the razor once again.

"What did you say?" Doyle shouted to be heard over the buzzing.

"I said his name was . . ." Bzzzzzzzzzzz, she made another pass with the razor.

By now Deena was breathless with laughter. She staggered around the room biting on the pillow.

"And another thing I've always wanted to tell you," Kathy went on, enjoying the role as Doyle's boss. "You'd better work harder at your writing. I've noticed some, um . . . mixed metaphors, and, um . . . dangling participles in your writing. Very sloppy, Doyle, very sloppy."

This convulsed Deena in another round of laughter so uproarious that she turned away from her cousin—and found herself staring at her mother, who was standing in their doorway with arms folded.

Kathy looked up at the same moment. "Bye, Doyle, gotta go," she said, slamming down the phone.

"What is going on here?" Lydia asked sternly. "I had a feeling something was up with all that whispering earlier."

"Just a little joke," Kathy said, laughing feebly.

"I'm going to tell you the truth, Mom," Deena spoke up. "We think Doyle likes Aunt Nancy."

"I think so, too. So what?" Lydia replied.

"No, Mom, I mean *likes* her, as in romance. That's why we were trying to get rid of him, before he breaks her heart and ruins all our lives."

Lydia shook her head. "I think you girls have very vivid imaginations," she said. "I want you to go down-

97

stairs and tell that young man the truth before he goes rushing back home."

"But, Mom, we have proof. We—"

"I want you to go right now!" Lydia insisted.

Lydia and the girls headed downstairs and almost crashed into Doyle, who was rushing up. "Mrs. Scott," he said to Lydia, "I'm afraid I'll have to check out this afternoon. I got a strange phone call, and it seems I'm needed back at the office."

"Deena has something to tell you," Lydia said, pushing her daughter gently forward.

"That wasn't your boss, it was Kathy," she said. "We were playing a little joke on you."

Doyle looked puzzled for a moment, then shrugged. "Oh, that's O.K.," he said. "In fact, that's good news. It means I can stay, and it also means that Millie isn't cracking up, which is what I thought."

"No, the only crazy ones around here are these two," Lydia assured him.

"It's really O.K.," he told her. "I used to do stuff like that when I was a kid. Excuse me, but I want to change. Nancy and I decided that it's such a nice day we'd go for a walking interview."

"Enjoy," Lydia said to him as he headed for his room. "You girls are free until supper; try to stay out of trouble, please."

"We will," Kathy said.

"Got any more plans?" Deena asked her, once her mother had left.

"Not yet, but I'm working on it," Kathy replied.

Chapter 10

"Well, this day has been a bust," Kathy said, throwing her clothes on the bedroom floor.

"You can't say we didn't try," said Deena glumly. "My feet ache from following them. They must have walked three miles."

"Three! It felt more like a hundred," Kathy said, rubbing her feet. "And I could have died when you popped up out of the bushes behind them and started screaming."

"You've obviously never been stung by a bee or you'd have more sympathy. It really hurts!"

"Yeah, and I'm sure they really believed it when you told them we were out taking a nature hike and just happened to be in the same spot at the same time."

"What was I supposed to say? We agreed that if he tried to kiss her or anything that we'd do something. We'd have had to make our presence known then."

"I was thinking that we could throw a rock at him

from a hiding place and run away, or something less obvious. Now my mother knows we're up to something."

"I don't think she does. She seems to be so focused on Doyle and this interview, she's not paying much attention to anything else."

"That's true," Kathy agreed. Her mother did seem to be preoccupied with something today. Was it . . . love?

"Anyway," Deena said brightly, "tomorrow is another day. I have to go to town to enter my sculpture in the art show. I'm going to ask you one more time: Why don't you enter your sketches in the show? We can make a mat for them tomorrow morning. I have some oaktag that will do the job well enough."

"No."

Deena picked up the blue folder from Kathy's dresser and opened it. She laid the sketches out on her bed. "I have some nice green oaktag that will be in keeping with the nature theme of these," she said, studying them.

"Deena, I said no! I don't want to upset my mother with old memories, and I'm not interested in some stupid art show. Now put those back."

"You're so pigheaded sometimes, Kathy!" Deena shouted. "Your mother wouldn't be upset."

"I wouldn't be upset about what?" The girls whirled around and saw Nancy standing in the doorway they'd left open.

Kathy glared a warning at Deena, but Deena had decided to seize the opportunity. "Aunt Nancy, you wouldn't mind if Kathy submitted these to the Cranford Library's Young People's Art Show, would you?" she asked, handing the sketches to Nancy.

Nancy looked the sketches over. For a moment the

100

girls saw the glistening of tears beginning in her eyes, but she blinked them back quickly. "You've really gotten good, Kath," she said at last. "You should enter these. Did you think it would upset me because Dad used to sketch with you?"

"Sort of, yeah," Kathy answered.

Nancy put her arm around Kathy and squeezed. "That was sweet of you, but you shouldn't have worried. I see something of your father in you and Johnny every day, and it makes me happy, not sad. It makes me feel that, in a very real way, he's still here with us."

"You miss him a lot, don't you?" Kathy said.

"I was really happy with your father. Not only do I miss him as a person, which I do, tremendously, but I miss sharing my life with a man in that way."

"Would you ever think of remarrying?" Deena asked.

"I never thought I would, but lately I've been remembering how much I liked being married. Who knows what the future holds?" she said. "Anyway, I'd like it if you entered those sketches. I think it would have pleased your father, and it would make me proud every time I went to the library."

"O.K., then I will," Kathy said. "I don't think this is exactly the kind of artwork people expect from Kathy Manelli, though. You don't think they're too twerpy?"

"You could never be twerpy, Kathy," her mother said with a laugh. "Good night, girls."

" 'Night," said Deena, feeling all warm and happy inside. She loved these kinds of personal, family talks.

"Now look what you did, you twit!" Kathy snapped as soon as her mother left the room.

"What?"

"You got her thinking about remarrying! Why don't you just gift wrap her and put her on his doorstep?"

Deena's hand flew up to her mouth. "You're right, that was dumb of me. Sorry."

At that moment Nancy knocked and stuck her head in the door. "I almost forgot why I came up here before. I want to ask you two what's going on between you and Doyle. It almost seems as if you're out to get him. Is there something you want to tell me about him?"

Kathy and Deena exchanged darting glances. Neither one of them had the heart or courage to explain their fears about Doyle to Nancy. Besides, she might tell them to mind their own business and that would make getting rid of him twice as hard.

"We're just fooling around, Aunt Nancy," Deena spoke up. "No harm intended."

"Yeah, just having some fun. It's been pretty boring around here lately, so we're amusing ourselves," Kathy added.

Nancy eyed them both skeptically. "O.K., but you guys have been acting very weird," she said. "Lay off him tomorrow, O.K.? It's important that this article go well for him, and he doesn't need strange vibes floating around distracting him."

"Sure," Kathy answered, "no problem."

"Thanks, good night again," Nancy said, closing the door.

" 'None are so blind as those who will not see,' " Deena quoted the Bible sorrowfully. "Her love has blinded her to the perilous fox in her henhouse."

"What are you babbling about?" Kathy snapped irritably.

102

"I'm merely saying that her concern about Doyle isn't a good sign."

"That's for sure," Kathy agreed. "Well, there's nothing we can do about it tonight—so good night."

The girls were so tired that they were asleep in a few minutes. Kathy's sleep wasn't peaceful, though. She fell into a series of dreams in which she was being chased by a man she couldn't see. At one point she was running through a park trying to escape the man when she saw her mother standing on a small island in the middle of a lake. She looked again and saw her father standing next to her mother. She jumped in the lake and swam to them, but when she got to the island, her mother and father were both gone.

The next morning Kathy awakened to find that Deena was out of bed already. She dressed quickly and found her cousin on the front porch surrounded by scraps of green paper. Tape, scissors, pencils, and a ruler were scattered around her.

"Ta-da! As promised," she said proudly to Kathy. "A Kathy Manelli original." She flipped the green paper over, and Kathy saw that she'd mounted three sketches together in one long mat with three squares cut out. "I remembered that you're only allowed to enter one piece and I couldn't decide which sketch was the best so I mounted them this way. I think it was pretty clever, if I do say so myself."

"They do look nice, Deena. Thanks," Kathy said, impressed with how good the matted sketches looked.

"What's that sound?" Deena asked, cocking her ear to hear a low buzzing off in the distance.

Kathy recognized it immediately. "He's home early!" she shouted happily, running down the front steps. Just as she'd predicted, Roy came zooming up the dirt road and into the front yard on his motorcycle.

"Hi, babe!" he cried, jumping off his bike. Kathy threw herself up at him, wrapping her legs around his waist and hugging him hard. "Hey, hey, I guess you did miss me, after all," he said happily. "Uncle Malcolm's stuff was in order and it was hot as a blast furnace down there, so we came right back after the memorial. I got home late last night. I couldn't wait to see you, so I rushed right over first thing."

"I'm glad you did," she said, taking his hand and leading him up to the porch. "Deena and I have a big problem on our hands and maybe you can figure out a way to help us."

Roy and Kathy joined Deena on the porch. "Hey, Kath, when did you do these?" he asked, picking up the sketches.

"Isn't she talented!" Deena said. "She just needed someone with a little drive to get her going. I feel like van Gogh's brother, Theo, who helped the artist fulfull his artistic potential."

Kathy and Roy both looked at Deena with the blank stares she'd gotten used to seeing whenever she discussed art. Oh, well, they'd appreciate her someday.

"We don't have time to discuss art," Kathy said. "We have a problem." Kathy and Deena filled Roy in on every detail of the Doyle situation.

"Maybe he really likes your mom," Roy suggested. "She's a pretty neat lady."

"Come on, Roy," Kathy protested. "I'm sure Mom

was good-looking in her day, but face it, she's old. We're closer to his age than she is."

"He wants the easy life here at the inn, and he wants to use Aunt Nancy's fame to further his own career. You should see the blatant, shameless letters he's been writing to her."

"Yeah?" Roy laughed. "Are they hot stuff?"

"Don't joke, Roy, this is serious. Mom really seems to like him. She's falling for it all."

"O.K., O.K., if you guys say he's bad news, I believe you. You're going to have to stay on his tail at all times."

"We know that, Roy," Kathy said with a moan. "We've been trying, but it hasn't been that easy. I think Mom is actively trying to ditch us at this point."

"Set up for breakfast, girls," Nancy called at the screen door. "Hello, Roy. Did you have a nice trip?"

"Fine, Mrs. M. I'd like to say you're looking especially lovely this morning," he said, surprised to see that she was wearing a dress and make-up.

"Thank you, Roy," she answered. "I got tired of looking like a workhorse. For some reason I felt like sprucing up a bit."

"Mom," Kathy said, "can you drive us into town after breakfast? We want to submit this stuff to the library show. It's due today."

"Sure," her mother answered. "Now come on, set up."

"Good thinking," Deena said. "That will get her away from him for the morning, anyway. Maybe we can find a way to stall her once we're in town."

"I'll meet you at the library at noon," Roy said. "Maybe I'll have thought of something by then."

105

The girls spotted Doyle talking to Nancy and Johnny when they entered the dining room. "Mom, would you show me how to use the new coffee maker?" Kathy asked.

"I showed you last week."

"Well, I forgot."

With one thing and another, Deena and Kathy managed to keep Nancy away from Doyle throughout breakfast. After the breakfast buffet had been cleared, and all the other morning chores finished, they stood on the front porch, art in hand, ready to go into town.

"Where's Mom?" Johnny asked, walking into the hall, slapping a baseball into his mitt.

"Getting the van," Kathy told him.

"Want to come to town, Johnny?" Deena asked, knowing that Johnny always had a way of delaying his mother in the local sports store.

"Naw, my friend Ralphie's coming over, and we're going to play ball."

"Good try," Kathy said, following her cousin's line of thought. Nancy pulled the old red van around to the front of the house and the girls piled in. "Well, what are we waiting for?" Kathy asked her mother. "Let's get going."

"I'm waiting for Doyle," she said. "I promised to show him some spots in town that are mentioned in my poems."

"Lovely day, ladies," said Doyle brightly as he climbed into the van. "I'm looking forward to seeing Cranford through the eyes of its premier poet." Nancy blushed and smiled happily at his remark.

The ride into town was pure torture for Kathy. Doyle

and her mother complimented each other constantly and seemed generally thrilled by everything the other had to say. Kathy had never seen her mother acting like this—and she didn't like it.

Nancy dropped the girls off at the Cranford Library. "I'll pick you up here at about two," she told them.

The librarian fussed over Kathy's sketches and said she'd been looking for something good enough to hang in the front entrance. She eyed Deena's sculpture for a moment or two. "I know just the place to put this, as well," she said, patting the sculpture on the head as if it was a sick child.

Roy was waiting for them outside the library on his motorcycle when they came out. "I hate to tell you this," he said, "but on my way over here I saw your van parked in front of the Castaways."

"That cute little restaurant by the water?" Deena asked.

"Yep, the one with the porch overlooking the water where you can eat. My buddy Hank is working there as a bus boy."

"We'd better get over there right away. It sounds much too romantic to me," said Kathy.

Roy drove Deena over to the Castaways, which was less than ten minutes away, and then came back and got Kathy. "We saw them sitting in the outdoor part. They were looking pretty cozy. Your mom was reading something and then she reached out and squeezed the guy's hand," Roy informed her.

"It was probably another one of those sappy love letters. We'd better get there fast."

When they got there Kathy and Roy joined Deena,

who was crouched down peering through the cracks in the wooden fence that surrounded the deck, leaving only the part facing the ocean exposed. "They've ordered lunch. Your mother keeps reading something and touching his hand and all. It looks pretty serious," Deena updated them in a dramatic whisper.

They watched a few minutes longer. Nancy was now holding Doyle's hand and talking to him very sweetly and sincerely. "We've got to do something," moaned Kathy.

"There's Hank," said Roy, indicating a boy with a short crew cut, who wore the white jacket of a bus boy and held a tray of dirty dishes. "I have an idea," Roy added.

When Hank came close to the fence, Roy caught his attention with a series of low *psssssst* sounds. "Hey, Roy, what's up?" Hank asked, setting his tray down on a table.

"Meet me outside. I need a favor. It'll just take two seconds," Roy requested.

Hank came out front and Roy went to meet him. The girls saw Hank shake his head no, but Roy produced some money and that seemed to change his mind. Then they watched Roy go to the public phone in front of the restaurant and make a phone call.

"I wonder what he has in mind," Kathy mumbled. "That's one of the things I love about Roy, you can always count on him to come up with a plan."

Deena looked back at Nancy and Doyle. A waitress came and said something to Nancy. Deena figured that Roy must be calling Nancy on the phone, since Nancy got up and left the table.

Less than a minute later Hank walked near the table with a tray full of dirty glasses containing the dregs of old drinks—beer, piña coladas, sodas.

Kathy's hand flew to her mouth in surprise when she saw what happened next. Deena covered her eyes and turned away. Pretending to have slipped, Hank sent the entire tray of dirty glasses sliding onto Doyle's lap.

Doyle jumped up, completely covered with sticky drinks. "I guess that put an end to his romantic afternoon," Roy chuckled, rejoining them at the fence.

"I can't believe you did that!" whispered Deena. "Don't you think that was a little extreme?"

"I thought you wanted that guy cooled out?" Roy replied, looking bewildered.

"We did," admitted Kathy, surpressing her laughter, "but we didn't think you were going to totally demolish him."

"Well, I couldn't think of anything else to do," Roy said defensively.

"It was a good plan in a mean sort of way," said Kathy. "Kind of brilliant, really."

"Thanks, I thought so, too," Roy replied. "We were lucky. Hank wouldn't have done it except that his boss is out sick today, and he needed some extra dough."

By then Nancy had returned to the table and was helping Doyle wipe his clothes clean with some napkins. Doyle was laughing and making light of the situation, but the intimate mood had clearly been broken.

"We'd better get out of here before my mother comes out and catches us," Kathy suggested. "It looks like they're going to leave."

"No, let's stay put until they go. We won't have time to leave," said Roy.

Deena, Kathy, and Roy flattened themselves against the fence and waited until the coast was clear.

"Uh-oh," the three of them moaned at once. Charging toward them—her eyes sparkling with anger—was Nancy.

"Hi, Mom," said Kathy nervously. "We saw what happened in there. What a shame."

Hands trembling with rage, Nancy pointed back at the van. "March," she commanded through clenched teeth. "Now!"

Chapter 11

"I wonder if we're still confined to our rooms or if the punishment is over at dawn," said Kathy on Tuesday morning.

"We have to help out with breakfast, so I guess we should just go down and act as if everything was O.K.," Deena replied uncertainly from her bed. "Your mother sure was angry."

"She looked like she was cooling down until you said that we suspected Doyle of being an enemy agent and that's why we had Hank dump the tray on him!"

"What was I supposed to say? I had to think of something. Anyway, the real problem is what do we do now?" Deena got up and started laying out her clothes. "Maybe we should just sit down and tell your mother why we're doing what we're doing."

"What! And tell her that we think she's so over-the-hill that Doyle couldn't possibly really be in love with her? That would make her feel terrific."

"We wouldn't have to put it that way," said Deena,

yanking a yellow T-shirt over head. "We could simply say that Doyle is a . . . a vicious, self-serving user who is preying on her vulnerability and fear of a lonely old age."

"Brilliant, Deena. That would make her feel like a million bucks, I'm sure," said Kathy sarcastically.

"Perhaps that isn't exactly the right phrasing," Deena conceded, "but I still think the time has come for the truth."

"I have to think about it some more," said Kathy, running a brush through her hair. "Just don't open your yap until you talk to me first, O.K.?"

"Have it your way," Deena said with a sigh. "But I say the truth will set us free."

The girls went downstairs to help out with breakfast. It was Kathy's day to serve the guests in their rooms, which left Deena alone to watch helplessly as Nancy sat at the table and spoke with Doyle all through breakfast. She couldn't imagine how she'd ever thought he was handsome. Now it seemed to her that he had a weak chin, thin hair, and his eyes were set too closely together. But after yesterday's events, she didn't dare interrupt them in any way.

"Johnny," she said, grabbing her cousin by the shoulder on his way to the kitchen. "Why don't you go over and see what Doyle and your mom are doing?"

"Because I don't care," he answered, looking at her suspiciously.

"Never mind," she muttered. It looked to Deena as if she and Kathy had failed. Nancy was clearly enthralled with Doyle, and there was nothing they could do about it. Deena still thought they should put the cards on the table with Aunt Nancy.

"Deena, stop daydreaming and get the coffee moving," Lydia called from the kitchen.

"O.K.," she said. But her own mother said they were imagining things when they tried to tell her. Deena let out a long sigh.

Kathy and Deena got together in the sitting room after the morning chores had been completed. "She's acting like I'm not even alive," moaned Kathy. "That's worse than being stuck up in our room."

"She hasn't paid any attention to me, either," Deena said glumly. "One good thing has come out of all this, though," she added. "We've hardly fought at all in the last two days. I like that."

Kathy turned to her cousin and couldn't help smiling. "I like it, too," she admitted.

Just then the familiar sound of Roy's motorcycle filled the room. Three minutes later he walked into the front hall.

"Over here, Roy," Kathy whispered, waving him into the sitting room.

Roy joined them, looking around nervously. "Is the coast clear? Is your mother going to throw me out on my head if she sees me here?"

"None of us is too popular with her right now," Kathy told him.

"I had to come over, because I wanted to tell you something," Roy said. "I was picking my little sister up at the library, and a bunch of people were walking around judging the art show, and just as I was leaving I saw them put the first place prize on your sketches, Kath."

"Ooooooohhhhhhhhhhhh!" Deena squealed, throwing her arms around her stunned cousin, nearly knocking Kathy off the couch.

"Wow, fifty bucks just for a little sketching," Kathy said in a shocked but happy voice.

"You didn't happen to notice if my sculpture won an honorable mention or something, did you?" Deena asked.

"Sorry, Deena, it was kind of stuck back in a corner. It was hard to see, but I didn't notice anything on it."

"Don't feel bad," Kathy said. "I'd be glad to split the award. I mean, if it wasn't for you, I wouldn't even have been in the contest."

"That's really nice of you, Kathy," Deena said, genuinely touched by Kathy's generosity. "I couldn't take your prize money. Besides, if you think about it, great artists are never recognized in their own lifetimes."

Deena might have rambled on about the sufferings of great artists, except that just then Nancy walked by the sitting room, arm in arm with Doyle. Nancy turned and looked at the three of them with a disapproving glance, but she kept walking.

"Did you see that!" whispered Deena frantically. "They were arm in arm. She doesn't even care who knows anymore."

Deena, Kathy, and Roy got up quietly and looked out the window to the porch. Nancy and Doyle were standing very close, facing each other. Nancy leaned in toward Doyle and kissed him lightly on the lips.

"That's it!" shouted Deena. "This has gone too far."

"Deena, don't do anything." Kathy tried to stop her, but it was no use. Deena was already out the door and onto the front porch in seconds.

114

"I'm sorry, Aunt Nancy, but I am compelled to speak my mind here," she stated. Nancy and Doyle stepped back and looked at Deena as if she'd lost her mind. "I must expose this predator as the literary social climber that he is," Deena pressed on.

"What are you talking about?" Nancy asked.

"It's very clear that he wants to ride the gravy train of your success to launch his own feeble career. Don't let him do it, Aunt Nancy! You've worked too hard to let this . . . this cad take advantage of you."

"Just a minute, here, Deena," Doyle stepped forward. "I think you have the wrong impress—"

"Don't try to fool me, you . . . you wolf in poet's clothing. I've been on to your shifty little scheme right from the start," Deena yelled furiously. "And as one who sincerely loves this tender, talented woman, I insist that you leave the premises this very minute!"

The words were barely out of Deena's mouth when an old gray Falcon from CranFords car service came rumbling up the road. It was then that Deena spied Doyle's suitcase tucked away behind a wicker chair. Doyle reached for it and waved to the cab driver to wait a minute.

"You can't have asked for faster action than that," Kathy whispered to Roy as they stood hidden behind the curtain, observing the scene.

"That Deena sure gets things accomplished, you have to give her that," Roy chuckled.

Deena just stood on the porch with her mouth open in surprise. "If you'll excuse us, Deena," said Nancy, "I'd like to say good-bye to Doyle alone. Perhaps you'd like to apologize to him before he leaves."

"There's no need," Doyle said, shaking his head good-naturedly. "Deena wouldn't be Deena if she didn't feel passionately about things." He took her hand and squeezed it. "I just hope you know I would never do anything to hurt your aunt. I have too much regard for her."

Nancy smiled at Doyle and walked down to the waiting car with him. Deena, Kathy, and Roy watched as the car drove away. Nancy waved after it and then turned back toward the inn with a serious expression on her face.

"I think this is my cue to leave," Roy said, heading for the front door.

"Yeah, call you later," Kathy agreed. "There may be some fireworks around here."

Nancy had already grabbed Deena by the arm when she came storming in the front door. " 'Bye, Mrs. M.," Roy said quickly as he slipped out the front door.

"Yeah, 'bye, Mrs. M.," Kathy repeated, heading for the stairs.

"Oh, no, you don't," Nancy said, grabbing her daughter by the arm with her free hand. "We are sitting down and talking about this, and I don't want to hear any nonsense about enemy agents this time, is that clear?"

"Aunt Nancy, it's really my fault," Deena began. "I figured out that he was sending you love letters, and I told Kathy. We just didn't want to see you get hurt."

"Why did you presume I was going to get hurt?" Nancy asked, sitting down on the couch and pulling the two girls down with her. "I think I'm old enough to take care of myself."

"That's just the point, Mom," Kathy said. "Don't you think he was a little young for you?"

Nancy let go of their arms and studied Deena and Kathy with an amused expression. "I can't believe how unhip you girls are," she said. "Don't you read? It's very stylish for older women and younger men to go out."

Kathy and Deena looked at each other. "Then how come he left?" Kathy asked. "He's not coming back, is he?"

"No," Nancy said a bit sadly. "I was very flattered. It's not every day that an attractive young man pays so much attention to me. I was enjoying having a summer romance, but yesterday he finally worked up the nerve to show me the letters he'd been writing."

"What happened then?" Deena asked.

"I was reading one when I was called away by a mysterious phone call," Nancy said pointedly. "And then Doyle had a tray unceremoniously dumped in his lap, so we couldn't discuss things any further. But last night I knew what I had to do, and I asked him to leave."

"Because you knew he was trying to take advantage of you, right?" Kathy said.

"No," Nancy told her, annoyed. "Because I suddenly realized how serious he was, and I couldn't take advantage of a young, romantic boy who was sincere in his feelings—not when I was just enjoying a flattering flirtation. It wouldn't have been right. Why is it so difficult for you two to believe that he really fell in love with me? Do you think of me as being so decrepit that no man would ever look twice at me?"

"It's not that, Aunt Nancy. It's that he was *so* young and you're so much more..."

"Worldly and sophisticated," Kathy finished.

Nancy sighed. "You'll be surprised at how young the

117

two of you will feel when you're thirty-eight," she said. "I suppose it must seem like a thousand years old to you now."

"Sorry, Mom," Kathy said.

"It's just a little hard to accept your apology right now," Nancy said, looking suddenly very sad. "I guess I'm still too angry. I have to help Lydia in the kitchen, excuse me."

"I really goofed this time," said Deena after Nancy left.

"We both did," Kathy agreed.

Nancy was busy in the kitchen for several hours. Then she drove off in the van without saying anything to Kathy or Deena.

"Where did Mom go?" Kathy asked Lydia.

"Into town. She said she needed some time to herself."

Nancy returned home in time to help with dinner. She was polite with everyone, even Deena and Kathy, but something in her eyes seemed very far away.

After dinner Kathy found her mother sitting on the porch by herself. She stood at the door, nervous about approaching, and watched her mother slowly turn the pages of an old photo album.

Sensing her daughter's presence, Nancy looked up. "Hi," she said with a gentle smile that told Kathy it was safe to join her. Kathy pulled a wicker chair up next to her mother's.

She looked at the pictures silently. The album was an old one. In it were pictures of her mom and dad from when they were in college. They looked so strange to Kathy. Her father's hair was down past his shoulders, and he wore bell-bottom jeans and a colorful T-shirt. Nancy wore a long peasant-style dress. Her hair was waist long and hung in two braids. They looked into the camera seriously.

There were pictures of their wedding, in a beautiful garden. Then came pictures of Kathy as a baby, then Johnny. Suddenly Nancy looked up and held her fingers over her lips. Kathy saw there were tears in her eyes.

Kathy put her hand on her mother's arm comfortingly. Nancy smiled at her and wiped the tears away quickly. "I miss your father so much," she said softly.

"Me, too," said Kathy.

"No one has ever cared more for my happiness than he did," Nancy said gently. "And no one will ever replace him."

"I know that," said Kathy.

"Kath, we have to talk about what happened with Doyle. We're both going to have to accept the idea that your father is gone. Up until now I don't think I really have accepted it. But this thing with Doyle made me come to terms with it. It made me realize I'm lonely. I'd like to find someone I can share my life with."

"You have us," Kathy protested.

"You know it's not the same thing. Doyle wasn't right for me, but someday someone will be. You're going to have to realize that and not resent it."

Kathy looked down at her hands. "I didn't resent it, really. It was just that as long as nobody took Dad's place, then it was almost like he wasn't really dead. It was more like he'd gone on a long trip and someday he was coming back."

Nancy covered her daughter's hands with her own. "I can see how it would seem that way, but we both have to move on."

"I know," said Kathy in a choked voice. Nancy reached over and hugged her daughter. Kathy hugged back, letting the tears fall freely. "I love you, Mom," she said.

"And I love you," Nancy answered, brushing the tears from Kathy's eyes.

Kathy sat with her mother for another ten minutes. The two of them watched the sun set. Except for the crickets, it seemed extremely quiet and peaceful.

"Excuse me," Deena called hesitantly from the door. "Can I join you?"

"Sure," Nancy answered. "Pull up a chair. We're just enjoying the sunset."

Deena joined them and sat quietly for a few minutes. "Are you still mad at me, Aunt Nancy?" she asked. "I'm really sorry."

"No, I'm not mad anymore," Nancy said. "In a way it's nice to know you'd go to such lengths for me."

"I'd do anything for you, Aunt Nancy," Deena said sincerely.

"I know you would," Nancy replied, smiling at her niece.

The phone rang at the front desk, and shortly thereafter Lydia stuck her head out the door. "Phone for you, Nan." Nancy rose and left Deena and Kathy sitting on the porch.

"I for one have learned some valuable lessons," Deena said.

"Me, too," Kathy agreed. "For one thing, I'll never

butt into Mom's business again. She's entitled to date whomever she chooses. And for another, I'm not letting you suck me into any more of your crazy ideas."

Deena let Kathy's remark pass. "I've learned that each person has to work out his or her own destiny without interference or comment from others—no matter how well-intentioned."

Nancy came back onto the porch wearing a bright smile. "That was John Blackman from *The New England Journal*. He's coming up here tomorrow afternoon."

"You mean that grouchy old guy with the wrinkled sports jacket who was here on Thursday?" Kathy asked.

"Did he forget to ask you something?" Deena wanted to know.

"No, he's asked me out to the movies, and I said yes. I have a feeling he might be more my type."

"Not that guy!" shouted Kathy.

"Aunt Nancy, he's much too old for you!" Deena wailed.

Suddenly Deena and Kathy looked at each other guiltily and clapped their hands over their mouths.

Nancy just looked at Deena and Kathy . . . and laughed.